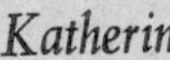

That night I lay awak
was trying to tell my Once
before I had given away my heart and had experienced the joy of loving and being loved, the happiness of feeling safe, comforted and cherished . . . and I had known the agony of losing it all.

Gradually the pain had become bearable and my spine had stiffened; I found I could stand on my own feet. I was independent now and I intended to remain independent, barricaded in my stronghold. Alec was a dear; I wanted him as a friend—just a friend and nothing more . . .

Available in Fontana by the same author

Katherine's Marriage
Gerald and Elizabeth
The House of the Deer
The Young Clementina
Celia's House
Winter and Rough Weather
Amberwell
Summerhills
Still Glides the Stream
The Musgraves
Bel Lamington

D. E. STEVENSON

Katherine Wentworth

Collins

FONTANA BOOKS

First published 1964
First issued in Fontana Books 1967
Second Impression February 1970
Third Impression August 1973

Printed in Great Britain
Collins Clear-Type Press
London and Glasgow

All characters in this novel are entirely fictitious and no reference is intended to any actual person, whether living or dead

PART ONE

CHAPTER 1

There are some days in Edinburgh when rain falls sullenly from leaden skies and the city looks black and grim and unutterably dreary; there are days when the wind blows like a knife, careering down the side streets, whisking up clouds of dust, tipping off hats and sending them bowling across the road . . . but when Edinburgh smiles her citizens forget her vagaries and remember only her beauty.

On this particular day in March the weather was kind – it was a day borrowed from April – and the citizens were enjoying the sunshine. Some of them were strolling in Princes Street Gardens where already the trees were beginning to bud. I watched them, standing at the railings and looking down. Most of my life had been spent in Edinburgh so I knew the city in all her moods – grim, and mischeivous and genial – I had seen her blanketed in snow, with icicles dripping from every gable; I had seen her in festive garb, to welcome royalty; with hundreds of flags fluttering gaily in the breeze.

To-day was different – I couldn't have told you why – the beauty of it caught my heart and I stared up at the Castle, stared at the huge black rock with its crown of buildings – old and grey and steeped in history – as if I were a visitor from a foreign land and had never seen it before. Above the jagged outline the sky was a tender blue and across it moved three large white clouds, slowly as a procession of dignified dowagers at an Assembly Room ball.

Behind me was the rush and noise of the traffic in Princes Street but I heard it only as the background to my tapestry of dreams.

This was the first day in the year that there was real warmth in the sun. I had opened my sheepskin coat and now a sudden impulse prompted me to take off my knitted cap and put it in my pocket. I shook my hair free . . . it was lovely to feel the sun, and the gentle breeze blowing through my hair.

'Goodness, it's Kit Loudon!' exclaimed a voice at my elbow.

The speaker was a woman in a mink coat and a smart green hat with a feather in it; her face was pale and fine-drawn; her hair, which lay in smooth waves beneath the green hat, was yellow. I had a vague sort of feeling I had seen her before, but when and where . . .

'You haven't changed a scrap,' she declared, smiling and holding out her hand. 'Besides, you used to do that at school – take off your hat and shake your head like a dog coming out of the water – and you used to say "I hate hats" and cram it into your pocket.'

I smiled and said, 'I've always hated hats.'

'What fun to meet you like this! You're just the same old Kit – I'd have known you anywhere.'

Unfortunately I couldn't return the compliment, it had taken me several puzzled moments to identify the woman, but she had mentioned school, and I saw now that her eyes were a curiously light brown – almost yellow – and she had a trick of opening them suddenly and very widely.

'Zilla!' I exclaimed.

'Yes, of course. Look here, Kit, let's go and have tea together. Do say you will. I want to hear all about you,' she added eagerly.

I was a little surprised. Zilla and I had never been great friends at school – for one thing she was two years my senior, which in those far-off days had been an immense gulf. It was only because we were both keen on games that there had been any contact between us. However, as it happened, I was free this afternoon so there was no reason why I should not accept her invitation.

As we crossed the street together from island to island I tried to remember all I could about Zilla Maclaren and my mind went back to the green playing-fields of Dinwell School. Zilla had been captain of the first eleven when I was a very humble bowler – the sort of bowler who is summoned in despair when the other bowlers are exhausted. I remembered Zilla at the wicket: a tall lithe figure clad in a white flannel skirt with pads on her legs. Her hair was the colour of barley sugar – queer, spiky sort of hair which stood on end when she was excited. It was all coming back now. I remembered that Zilla always had the best of everything: the best bat that money could buy, the best tennis rackets – and lovely clothes! As I followed the mink coat across the street it was obvious to me that Zilla still had the best of everything.

Her parents had been fat and uninteresting, rather over-dressed when they had appeared at school functions (I remembered that quite clearly). They had taken her out to lunch on Sundays, driving up to the entrance in an enormous car; and she had had an older brother who had turned up at a cricket match and was obviously bored to death at the spectacle.

'But of course he's a Cambridge Blue,' somebody had said. This was held to excuse him – as no doubt it did.

As we went into the restaurant together I caught sight of our reflection in a large mirror opposite the door. We were an incongruous couple: Zilla in mink, with her perky hat and high-heeled shoes; I, bareheaded, in a shabby sheepskin coat and faded tartan skirt. However it was Zilla who had suggested having tea together so presumably she did not mind.

We went upstairs and found a table in the window . . . and there before us stood the Castle, dreaming of past greatness in the afternoon sun.

'Isn't it splendid!' I exclaimed involuntarily.

'What?' said Zilla. 'Oh, the Castle. Yes, it's looking rather fine to-day. Of course I've lived here all my life so I'm a little bored with the Castle. You can't escape from it – I mean it's always in the picture – but that's heresy, isn't it?"

I smiled vaguely but did not reply.

'You're married!' exclaimed Zilla, glancing at my ring.

'Yes. At least I was. He died four years ago.'

'Have you any children?'

'Two – and a stepson.'

Zilla looked at me in surprise. 'You don't seem old enough, Kit.'

'Nonsense! You know how old I am.'

'Twenty-seven, I suppose, but you certainly don't look as much. You could pass for twenty-two – or less.'

'With my back to the light,' I suggested, smiling at her. Once again I couldn't return the compliment for Zilla looked a good deal more than her twenty-nine years.

She drew off her gloves and smoothed them thoughtfully. 'What a lot you've done,' she said. 'I've done nothing.'

'Nothing?' I echoed in surprise.

'Oh, I've travelled a lot of course. Do you remember Jean Playfair at school? She and I travelled about all over the world and went to all sorts of interesting places. I simply love travelling. Then Jean married a London stockbroker – a frightfully dull man – and I couldn't find anybody else congenial. I still go abroad when I can but it isn't easy nowadays. Since my parents died I've been keeping house for Alec; you remember Alec, don't you?'

'Your brother, who was at Cambridge?'

Zilla nodded. 'He bought a house at Barnton, overlooking the golf course. Alec is fond of golf and can play there or practise in the evenings when he comes home from the office. He used to play every evening in the summer but now he seems to prefer pottering about in the garden . . . But tell me about you. What did you do when you left school?'

'I managed to get a job in Oxford, working in a library. It was very interesting and I liked it. That's where I met Gerald.'

'You mentioned a stepson.'

'Yes, Gerald had been married before and had a little boy of seven years old.'

'That must have been difficult for you.'

'Goodness, no! It was lovely to have Simon. There was nothing difficult about it. Gerald was doing historical research and some coaching in the evenings so we managed to find a little flat in a beautiful old house not far from the river. We were there for four years. . . ."

I stopped suddenly, partly because the waitress had brought our tea but more because I had been swept back into the past and I didn't want to talk about it, especially to a woman who was to all intents and purposes a stranger. We had been so happy in that little flat – Gerald and Simon and I – it had been quite perfect. Then the twins had arrived, long before they were expected, causing a good deal of surprise and alarm. Their hold on life had been so tenuous that Gerald had christened them himself the night they were born. He explained to me afterwards that he had done it carefully, according to the directions in his prayer-book, so he was sure it was all right. He had done it, not because he believed for a moment that an unchristened infant was in danger of hell, but because he thought it would be nicer for the babies to have names . . . and remembering Paris, where we had spent our honeymoon, he called them Denis and Marguerite.

We had a few weeks of anxiety about the babies, but soon they began to flourish and we were able to bring them home from hospital.

I had been afraid that Simon might be a little jealous of the twins, for naturally they needed a great deal of care and attention, but Simon adopted them as his own and nothing pleased him better than to help me to look after them. He would sit on a low chair near the fire to watch them have their bath, and he loved giving Daisy her bottle.

Gerald pretended that the twins were a joke. I remembered him saying teasingly, 'This is a nice thing to do to an old grey-haired man like me.' He was only thirty-five but his life had not been easy and there was grey in the thick dark hair above his ears. 'An old done man,' said Gerald and hobbled about my room and made me laugh. In reality he was proud of the twins; I had discovered this curious fact one evening when Professor Dudgeon dropped in for a chat. The babies were asleep in bed . . . and suddenly, without a word, Gerald had risen and gone out of the room, returning a few moments later with a baby in each arm.

'Allow me to present Denis and Marguerite, sir,' he said – and with that he sat down and displayed their charms with a proprietary air which amused me considerably.

'Dear me, how very small!' remarked the professor.

'They're putting on half a pound a week.'

'That seems – er – very satisfactory. Did you say they were twins, Wentworth? They do not resemble each other in the least.'

'They aren't identical twins; that goes without saying.'

'Ah,' nodded Professor Dudgeon. 'Not identical. You say "that goes without saying"? I am not a geneticist, so I'm afraid . . .'

Gerald was not a geneticist either, but he explained that a male and a female child are never identical twins.

'Dear me, how interesting,' commented Professor Dudgeon. 'One wonders why that should be the case.'

Perhaps Gerald did not feel competent to enlighten the

professor or perhaps it was because Simon was sitting on the window-seat, listening with both his ears. Whatever the reason, Gerald changed the subject by displaying the babies' hands. 'Look, sir, aren't they amusing?' he said.

Thus adjured the professor put on his spectacles and did as he was told. 'How very curious! Just like – er – real hands!"

'They *are* real hands!' exclaimed Simon indignantly.

But I knew exactly what Professor Dudgeon meant; the babies' hands were pink and soft, and small as rose-petals, but just like real hands.

The babies lay and stared; they were perfectly contented –as they always were with Gerald – and presently their eyes closed and they went to sleep in his arms.

By this time the two men were in earnest discussion about a promising young student who had unaccountably 'gone stale' so I was able to remove the babies and carry them back to bed.

Simon followed me and helped to tuck them in. 'Daddy shouldn't have wakened them, it was naughty of him, wasn't it?' said Simon.

'Daddy can do whatever he likes,' I replied.

Simon nodded thoughtfully. 'You promised to obey him. I heard you say it – quite loud.'

It was strange that I should remember this incident so clearly – as clearly as if it had happened yesterday instead of seven years ago – it was only one of the many delightful and amusing incidents that had happened during the four short years of my life with Gerald at Oxford. I thought of this as I watched Zilla pouring out the tea.

'Oxford,' said Zilla thoughtfully. 'It's a beautiful city – so alive and interesting. Why did you come back to Edinburgh?'

'Principally because of Aunt Liz. It didn't seem to matter what I did or where I went, and she wanted me, so —'

'I remember your aunt!' Zilla exclaimed. 'She was tall and thin and wore glasses. She used to come to school concerts and things, didn't she?'

'Yes, my parents died when I was a small child and Aunt Liz looked after me. She's my father's sister – the only relation I've got – so it seemed natural to come back to Edinburgh and be near her. I don't live with her of course; it wouldn't work.'

'Where do you live?'

'In India Street,' I said.

'Down there!' exclaimed Zilla. 'I wouldn't like that!' Obviously this was true (mink coats are not very common in India Street) but all the same it was a comfortable little flat and I had been lucky to get it. The rooms were well-shaped – I had been able to fit in all the furniture that Gerald and I had collected – and the sitting-room window had a lovely view over the Forth to the hills of Fife.

'Do you ever hear from Lina Hardwicke?' asked Zilla.

'Yes, of course. She's a great friend of mine.'

'I know. That's why I asked. Lina was clever, wasn't she? One of Miss Humble's bright girls.'

This had been a great joke at Dinwell School. Miss Humble was fond of saying, 'Be bright, girls.' If we had done particularly well, it was in our reports: 'A bright girl, I am satisfied with her progress.' It was the highest praise, seldom bestowed.

The remembered joke brought us in closer touch and we smiled at each other.

'Lina was quite bright,' I said. 'When I was at Oxford we saw quite a lot of each other. She read Law and took an Honours degree.'

'How amazing! What is she doing now?'

'She's married,' I said – and smiled. It really was rather funny, for Lina had talked about a Career (with a capital C), but she had fallen for a large young man with curly hair – admittedly very attractive and had married him without delay. They lived in Birmingham and had four children and were very badly off.

'What a waste,' said Zilla as she thoughtfully stirred her tea.

'I suppose it is – in a way,' I agreed. 'Lina could have married and had children without bothering about Law – a course of Domestic Science would have been more useful – but they're blissfully happy and that's the main thing. I haven't seen Lina for ages but she writes to me when she has time.'

Zilla had kept up with quite a number of school friends – far more than I had. Some were married, some had jobs of one kind or another.

'This is fun,' declared Zilla. 'I'm glad I found you; and I don't mean to lose you again, Kit. You'll come and see me, won't you? Alec is away all day so it's rather lonely. I haven't enough to do.'

I looked at her in amazement. It was incredible. Zilla was actually complaining because she hadn't enough to do!

'You'll come and see me, won't you?' she repeated.

'Yes, I should love to,' I said. 'I'm afraid I must go now, Zilla. It's been fun meeting you again.'

'You needn't go yet.'

'I must, really. The twins are at a party and I've got to fetch them at six.'

'But there are all sorts of things I want to talk to you about.'

'Thank you for my nice tea,' I said and rose to go.

'Kit!' she cried. 'Wait a minute. You must tell me your phone number – and I don't even know your name! Give me your card.'

It seemed ridiculous that she didn't know my name – I couldn't help laughing – and of course I had no card, I had never possessed visiting-cards in my life, but fortunately I had a used envelope in my bag so I scribbled the number on it and gave it to her.

'Wentworth!' she exclaimed. 'Is that your name? I know some people called Wentworth, they live near Wandlebury.'

'I expect they're Gerald's relations,' I told her.

There were more questions coming, I could see, and as I had no time nor any inclination to discuss Gerald's relations I said good-bye and hurried away. It had been amusing to meet Zilla like that but I didn't expect an invitation to Barnton. She would lose the envelope and forget all about me.

CHAPTER 2

It was after six when I arrived at the Fishers' house where the birthday party was taking place but, as I stood on the steps waiting for the door to be opened, I heard the sounds of revelry, so obviously it was still in full swing.

Isabel Fisher opened the door herself, looking hot and dishevelled. 'Oh, have you come to fetch them?' she asked. 'Nobody has gone yet. Do come in, Kit. We're playing

Blind Man's Buff. At least it started like that, but it seems to have degenerated into a free-for-all,' she added as she showed me into the drawing-room.

I was inured to children's parties so, although deafened, I was undismayed by the pandemonium.

'Isn't it frightful?' yelled Isabel in my ear. 'You're lucky, Kit.'

'Why?'

'You can get by with one a year, can't you? I'm obliged to have three – all different days. See what I mean?'

I saw. 'It will be better when they're older,' I shouted.

'That's what I used to think but Laura's is the worst of the lot – and she's going to be twelve. If you really want your two —'

'I do,' I told her. 'Thank you awfully for having them; I'm sure they've enjoyed themselves immensely.'

'They have. No doubt about that – but don't make them say it. Children hate saying it and it's quite unnecessary. Your two have been angels. I wish I could say it about some of the others! If you really want to take them away just wade in and get them. I must fly!'

There was no difficulty in getting Den. He was watching me from across the room and came at once when I beckoned. His face was white and there were blue shadows beneath his eyes, so I knew he was tired. But Daisy adored parties and was never tired; I saw her in the thickest cluster of children; her cheeks pink, her blue eyes shining and her two golden pigtails flying as she whirled round and round with a boy slightly bigger than herself. As Isabel had said, the only thing to do was to wade in and get her.

'Oh, Mums!' cried Daisy as I seized her hand. 'Oh, Mums – no! It isn't nearly time – I'm enjoying myself!'

Obviously she was, and I might have relented and let her stay a little longer if it had not been for Den.

Den had always been a worry; he was small for his age and thin and pale. Some weeks ago I had taken him to see a children's specialist who had examined him thoroughly and said that there was nothing radically wrong. He just needed care and plenty of milk. 'Is he a book-worm?' Dr. Ferguson had inquired. He was, of course, and enjoyed books which I thought quite unsuitable for a child of seven years old. 'Less reading and more outdoor exercise,' said Dr. Ferguson. This was not as easy as it sounded for if I prevented him from reading he mooned about like a miserable little ghost and was cross and naughty.

When I saw Den with those marks like bruises under his eyes my heart missed a beat – it felt like that, anyhow – all I wanted was to get him home and into bed, so I dragged my daughter out of the room. I found her shoes and stood over her while she changed.

'Nobody has gone yet,' protested Daisy. 'It's a lovely, lovely party; it'll go on for hours. Why can't we stay to the end?'

'You were asked from three to six and it's long after six.'

'Nobody else has gone – and we haven't said good-bye to Mrs. Fisher. We ought to say, good-bye-and-thank-you-very-much-for-a-lovely-party.'

'You needn't,' I said. 'Mrs. Fisher has let you off; but that doesn't mean you don't have to say it to other people. Hurry up and put on your coat.'

Den was ready and waiting so we let ourselves out of the front door and walked down the street: Den silent, Daisy chattering.

'It was the nicest party I've ever been to. James had a gorgeous cake with cherries in it – and eight candles. We had paper hats and crackers with charms in them. James wanted to play Kiss in the Ring, but Mrs. Fisher said Nuts in May was nicer . . . so we played Nuts in May and then we played "I sent a letter to my love" and then we played Musical Bumps. Oh, and I got a bangle in the Lucky Dip – look, Mums, isn't it nice and jingly? – and Den got a book. Where's your book, Den?'

'I left it in the hall.'

'What?' squeaked Daisy.

'You heard,' said Den wearily. 'It was a silly book about dressed-up rabbits. I didn't want it.'

By the time I had got the children to bed it was nearly nine o'clock and I was too tired to bother about supper. I ate some bread and butter and drank a cup of milk. Then I sat down for a few minutes to glance through the morning paper which was still lying upon the hall table in its pristine folds. But I had not sat there long when I found my head beginning to nod and I knew that if I sat there any longer I should fall asleep.

This had happened before on several occasions and I had wakened in the middle of the night, cold and stiff and miserable. It had been an unpleasant experience – rather a frightening experience – and I had made up my mind not to allow it to happen again. I folded up the paper, put the guard on the fire and went to bed.

2

The day following the birthday party was Saturday so I kept Den in bed for breakfast, a treat which he enjoyed. He sat up and ate an egg and read *Greenmantle* which, although an excellent story, was not what I should have chosen for him.

'But I like it,' declared Den, hugging it to his bosom in case it should be snatched away. 'Why should I have to read silly books if I don't want to?'

'You can't possibly understand it.'

'I do!' he cried, hugging it tighter. 'I don't know *all* the words of course but that makes it more interesting.'

It was no good saying any more.

Saturday was an easy day for me. There was no rush in the morning and I didn't have to cook the children's dinner; they always went to lunch with Aunt Liz on Saturdays. Sometimes I went too, but more often I sent them alone and had a quiet time by myself. I loved my children dearly but it was pleasant to get them off my hands and do exactly as I felt inclined. To-day however was a special occasion, Aunt Liz was sixty, and although she pretended to be too old for birthdays she liked them to be remembered and celebrated in the traditional fashion.

Aunt Liz had a flat in Heriot Row so we had not far to go, we arrived at half past twelve; the door was opened as usual by Bella, who had been with Aunt Liz since I was a child.

'Goodness!' exclaimed Bella when she saw us. 'Goodness gracious me! I'd clean forgotten you were coming! It's not Saturday, is it? What'll I do about your dinner? There's nothing but a couple of chops in the house.'

The children roared with laughter, for this was Bella's joke, perpetrated every Saturday, but still as funny as ever.

'I smell roast chicken and sausages,' shouted Daisy, leaping about the hall like a maniac. 'And I bet you've made meringues, Bella. Have you made meringues?'

'Why should I make meringues when I didn't know you were coming?' inquired Bella, keeping up the farce.

Disturbed by the noise, Aunt Liz emerged from the sitting-room and asked what it was all about.

Aunt Liz was an Edinburgh lady to the backbone. She was tall and straight and lean, with well-marked features and thick grey hair. When her face was in repose she looked severe, but her eyes had a twinkle in them and her infrequent smile was friendly. Her usual garb was a tweed coat and skirt (exceedingly well-cut, the skirt a trifle longer than was fashionable) and sensible lacing shoes, the colour of chestnuts, polished and shining.

'Come in, come in!' said Aunt Liz. 'Daisy, stop prancing like that, you demented creature. What's the matter with you?'

'It's your birthday,' declared Daisy, embracing Aunt Liz and thrusting the parcel into her hand.

'Many happy returns of the day,' said Den, advancing ceremoniously to tender his offering.

'Fancy you remembering!' exclaimed Aunt Liz, smiling sweetly.

We moved into the sitting-room; Aunt Liz opened her parcels and expressed her pleasure at their contents.

'Just what I wanted,' she declared. 'I need a shoe-horn badly and a handkerchief is always useful. Kit, there was no need for you to spend your money on a pair of gloves. Oh, I like them, of course, they're the kind I always wear.'

Naturally they were the kind she always wore. If they had been in any way different she would not have worn them.

As usual there was a fine array of birthday cards on the chimney-piece.

'What a lot you've got!' I said admiringly.

'There are a lot of silly people in the world,' she replied, looking at the cards with pleasure. 'It's just a waste of money. They'd be better to give their shillings to feed the hungry instead of sending birthday cards to an old woman like me. Did I tell you I'd taken on the job of secretary to the Hunger Campaign, Kit?'

'Not another?' I exclaimed. Already Aunt Liz was a

member of various committees with various charitable aims, including the relief of orphans, unmarried mothers and the aged and indigent sick . . . and being an exceedingly energetic and capable woman she usually got stuck with most of the work.

'Well, it's important,' said Aunt Liz apologetically. 'And to tell the truth I can't enjoy my own food unless I feel I'm doing my best to help people that are starving. When are you expecting Simon?'

The sudden change of subject was typical. Aunt Liz had a horror of sentimentality and her reason for assuming her new commitment had been on the verge. . . .

'Tuesday week!' cried Daisy before I could answer. 'Oh, goody, goody, goody! Darling Simon's coming on Tuesday week. How many days is that?"

'Ten days,' said Den without a moment's hesitation.

'Then he'll be here for his lunch the following Saturday, I suppose,' said Aunt Liz in her usual downright way.

Lunch was ready now so we went into the dining-room and sat down to an excellent meal. Needless to say, Daisy had been correct in her assumption that there would be roast chicken and sausages and meringues. To-day, because it was her birthday, Aunt Liz produced a half-bottle of hock in which to drink her health, and Den and Daisy at their earnest request were each given about a teaspoonful, measured out carefully into delicate glasses. They enjoyed the grown-upness of it, but not the taste.

'Just like medicine,' whispered Den to Daisy as he put down his glass.

Fortunately Aunt Liz was slightly deaf.

We talked of one thing and another: I told Aunt Liz about my meeting with Zilla and her complaint that she hadn't enough to do.

'Perhaps you've met her,' I said. 'Couldn't you rope her into one of your committees?'

'Zilla Maclaren?' asked Aunt Liz. 'No, I don't know her personally but Sheila Brown was talking about her the other day. They had her on the Orphan Committee for a bit and she was just a pest so they were very glad when she faded out. The woman was not dependable.'

There was no more to be said. 'Not dependable' was the absolute end.

As usual on Saturdays we played Happy Families after

lunch. Aunt Liz had an ancient pack of cards, somewhat dirty and dog-eared, but very much more amusing than the modern version of the game. Aunt Liz belonged to a bridge club and was one of the leading lights, but she did not despise the childish game; on the contrary she played it with zest. It always amused me to see her sitting up very straight in her chair, with her pince-nez perched upon her aquiline nose, listening carefully to every question and answer and when it came to her turn pouncing unerringly upon the holder of the cards she wanted.

'Kit,' she would say, 'is Mr. Bones the Butcher at home? Thank you . . . and Miss Bones? Yes, I thought so. Daisy, is Master Bones at home? Good, that's the family complete,' and her eyes would sparkle with pleasure and satisfaction.

The game nearly always became a duel to the death between Aunt Liz and Daisy; for Daisy had a wonderful memory and was on the tips of her toes from beginning to end. Den and I were also-rans, perhaps because we weren't so vitally interested, so keen on winning as the other two. To-day, for the first time, it struck me that Daisy resembled her great-aunt; not in appearance but in her zest for life. Neither of them was clever – in a scholastic sense – but both had a natural shrewdness of intellect which on occasions almost amounted to ruthlessness. 'I've no use for her,' Aunt Liz would say of some woman who didn't measure up to her standard.

All this was very interesting but it prevented me from concentrating on the game and I was aroused from my thoughts by Aunt Liz demanding three members of the Bun family one after the other. Unfortunately all three were 'at home.'

'You were dreaming, Kit.' she declared as she gathered them up. 'It's no good dreaming when you're playing Happy Families. If you'd been listening you'd have realised that I'd got Mr. Bun. I couldn't have asked Den for Mrs. Bun if I hadn't got one of the family.'

It was now discovered that Aunt Liz and Daisy had an equal number of families in their possession.

'Another game!' cried Daisy, bouncing up and down with excitement. 'We must have another game – please, please, please!'

'I'm afraid we can't,' said Aunt Liz with genuine regret. 'I've got a meeting at half past three, but we'll have another next Saturday and I'll beat you!"

As we walked home together I noticed Den had a book under his arm.

'What's that?' I asked.

'It's *The Thirty-Nine Steps*,' he replied. 'I found it in the bookcase and Aunt Liz said I could have it to read if I was careful. It's by the same man that wrote *Greenmantle*. Aunt Liz used to know him. Isn't that wonderful? She said he was a Great Scotsman as well as a great writer of stories. Aunt Liz knowing him makes it a hundred times more interesting.'

CHAPTER 3

Almost a week had passed since my meeting with Zilla; I had ceased to think about her when she rang up one morning and asked me to tea.

'It's quite easy,' she said. 'There's a bus which stops at the end of the road. Our house is called The Cedars; you'll have no difficulty in finding it. I shall be in all the afternoon so come as early as you can.'

I thanked her and said I would go. Aunt Liz was coming to tea and she enjoyed having the children to herself.

The day was fine and sunny. My spirits rose as I caught the bus and set off on my adventure; it was not a very Big Adventure but my life was somewhat circumscribed by children and household duties, so the mere fact of setting out alone for an unknown destination was quite exciting.

Zilla had said I should have no difficulty in finding The Cedars, but I wandered about and was obliged to ask several people before I discovered it at the end of a *cul de sac*. It was my own fault, really, for I had imagined Zilla's house would be one of the modern houses, built quite recently, whereas it was a Victorian mansion, standing alone, withdrawn from its upstart neighbours and surrounded by a high stone wall. There were two large cedars, one on each side of the entrance. The house was solid and unpretentious, built of grey stone with a slate roof.

Zilla had been waiting for me and welcomed me warmly.

I noticed she looked better to-day, more like the girl I remembered.

'Perhaps you'd like to see the house,' she said. 'It was frightful when we bought it, but we've made a lot of improvements. Are you interested in houses?'

I said I was very interested indeed so she took me round and showed me everything. It was a beautiful house with a wide staircase and well-shaped rooms; the Maclarens had put in fixed basins and extra bathrooms; they had built a veranda outside the drawing-room windows; they had put in central heating and enlarged some of the windows. The furniture was exquisite: lovely old chests and gate-legged tables, fitted carpets, Persian rugs and wide luxurious sofas. The kitchen premises were the last word in perfection; there was an Aga Stove, a deep-freeze cabinet, a dish-washer, and several large, glass-fronted cupboards – in fact there was everything that has been devised to delight the heart of a cook.

'It must be a joy to cook here!' I exclaimed.

'Oh, I don't cook,' replied Zilla. 'I've got a woman who does all that. She has gone to the village to get some things I wanted but she'll be back to make our tea.'

'It's a lovely house, Zilla. Simply perfect.'

'Do you think so?' she said. 'It's better than it was, of course, but you can't do a great deal with a plain oblong house like this. You should see the Carews' house. That really is perfect. There's a tower, so one end of the drawing-room is rounded which makes it very attractive. I'd rather have a really old house – like the Carews' – or else a modern house. This one is neither the one nor the other.'

We went out through the veranda and sat on a long swing seat which was shaded by a green-and-white-striped awning. The garden was delightful, with a smooth green velvety lawn and masses of flowering shrubs. They were not yet in bloom but beneath them there was a carpet of crocuses, yellow and white and blue.

'Now we can talk,' said Zilla. 'There wasn't time to talk properly on Friday and you rushed away before I could ask you about the Wentworths. The people I mean have a beautiful old place called Limbourne.'

'That's Gerald's father,' I said.

'Do you mean your husband was a son of Sir Mortimer Wentworth?'

'Yes.'

'How interesting!' exclaimed Zilla. 'Limbourne is a beautiful place, isn't it?'

'I've never been to Limbourne. There was a quarrel.'

'A quarrel? Oh, Kit, what a pity! Why did you quarrel with them? Sir Mortimer is very well off; he could have done a lot to help you.'

It seemed queer that Zilla should take such an interest in my affairs. The Wentworths had treated Gerald shamefully and I didn't want to talk about them . . . but here I was, sitting on a seat in Zilla's garden, and there was no escape. Without being positively rude I couldn't refuse to answer her questions. Zilla was sitting sideways with one leg tucked beneath her and her strange yellow eyes were fixed upon me with an inquiring gaze.

'Why did you quarrel with them?' she repeated.

'They quarrelled with Gerald,' I replied. 'It all happened long before I met him.' I said it in a final sort of way, hoping she would take the hint and abandon the subject.

'Didn't your husband tell you what happened?' she asked.

That made me angry – perhaps she intended it should. 'Of course he told me!' I exclaimed. 'It would have been very funny if he hadn't; Gerald and I shared everything. His parents wanted him to stay at home and look after the estate (it's a big estate with several farms so it would have been a whole-time job) but Gerald wasn't interested in farming. He was interested in languages and archaeology and had taken an Honours degree at Oxford. He went to Rome and while he was there he met an Italian girl and married her.'

'That was the quarrel?'

'Yes, his parents were furious with him – but it wasn't fair, was it? It's very wrong to try and arrange other people's lives.'

'But surely if he was Sir Mortimer's heir —'

'He wasn't!' I cried. 'That was just the point. Gerald's elder brother, Henry, is Sir Mortimer's heir. If anybody had to stay at home and look after the property it should have been Henry, because of course when Sir Mortimer dies it will belong to him.'

'He's a barrister,' said Zilla.

'Do you mean you know him?' I asked in surprise.

She nodded. 'He's a friend of my friends, the Carews. I met him several years ago when I was staying with the Carews at their flat in London. He seemed a pleasant person and he's supposed to be very clever. I wonder what he'll do when his father dies.'

'What do you mean, Zilla?'

'I mean he wouldn't want to give up his practice as a rising barrister and bury himself at Limbourne. Has he got a son?'

'Yes, his son is called Mortimer. It's a family name.'

'Tell me more about them.'

I didn't want to talk about the Wentworths but I saw I should get no peace until I had told Zilla all I knew – which was not very much, really. The break between Gerald and his family had been complete so any information about his relations had come to us in bits and pieces from outside sources.

'Gerald's father is a widower,' I said. 'Lady Wentworth died years ago – before I met Gerald. The family consists of Henry and Florence and Peter. Henry and Florence are a good deal older than Gerald. Peter is younger. I believe Peter Wentworth is in the army – but I'm not sure.'

'Is Florence married?'

'I don't know.'

'You don't seem very interested in them, Kit. Why don't you make up the quarrel? They're nice people and they could be very useful to you.'

'How could I make it up? They were horrid to Gerald – they were most unfair. Surely you see that.'

'Unfair?'

'Yes, I've told you. They wanted Gerald to look after the estate, but it wouldn't have been a career. When Sir Mortimer died Gerald would have had to hand over the whole thing to Henry – and what would he have done then? Gerald wanted a career of his own, for which he was qualified. He didn't want to keep the place warm for Henry and then find himself high and dry.'

Zilla nodded thoughtfully. 'I see what you mean. It was rather unfair – but all the same I'm not surprised that the Wentworths were angry with their son for marrying an Italian girl without their consent. The Wentworths are an old family and very proud of their lineage. Couldn't Gerald have explained it to them and smoothed it over?'

'He tried to – they returned his letters unopened.'

'Goodness!' exclaimed Zilla, opening her eyes very wide. 'That was pretty steep.'

'They simply cast him off. They were all against him. They made it perfectly clear that they didn't want to have anything more to do with him.'

'Was he upset about it?'

'I think he was, at first, but afterwards he just accepted it and didn't bother any more about them. Gerald lived in Rome for a time and then came back to Oxford with his little son.'

'What was *she* like?' asked Zilla.

I looked at her in surprise. 'Do you mean Violetta? I never saw her; she died when Simon was born . . . but she was very young and very, very beautiful. Gerald had a painting of her. I'll show it to you some day if you're interested.'

'It must have been rather uncomfortable for you, wasn't it?' asked Zilla with a curious sidelong glance.

'Oh, I wasn't a bit jealous – if that's what you mean,' I replied.

It was true that I had never felt jealous of Violetta.

Perhaps I might have suffered a few qualms if it had not been for Antony Finch who was Gerald's best friend. Shortly after Gerald and I had become engaged (I was still living in lodgings in Oxford and working in the library) Antony came in to see me one evening – and of course we talked about Gerald. I told Antony how happy I was and added that I wondered what Gerald had seen in me. Why had he chosen *me*? (It was the sort of thing any girl might say when she had just become engaged to the man she adored.)

'What do you mean, Katherine?' asked Antony.

'I'm not beautiful – like Violetta.'

'Violetta was the most beautiful creature I've ever seen,' declared Antony. 'It was a joy to look at her – but she had a six-year-old brain.'

I looked at him in astonishment.

'Yes, really, Katherine. She was like a child – and Gerald treated her as a dearly-loved child. Violetta adored him; they seemed happy together, but I was worried about the future. You see I know Gerald so well. He needs a wife who can be a companion to him; someone to share things with him – joys and sorrows and jokes and all the worries of everyday life. Violetta was a young man's dream.'

I asked Antony to tell me more, not because I was inquisitive but because I felt that if I knew the whole story I should be able to understand Gerald better. I was so much younger than Gerald that sometimes I felt inadequate. When Antony saw that I was being quite sensible about it he told me of Gerald's first meeting with Violetta.

At that time Antony had a junior lectureship at Oxford and during the summer vacation he went to stay with Gerald in Rome. He found Gerald unhappy and unsettled. He was enjoying Rome and had managed to get a very interesting post as secretary to an archaeologist, who was in charge of some excavations, but his family wanted him to return to Limbourne. His father had written several times to tell him that it was his duty to come home and help to manage the estate. Gerald wanted his friend's advice – but Antony was doubtful what to say.

One Sunday the two went off together for one of their long expeditions into the country. They took a bus and then got out and walked for miles. Presently they came to a place amongst the hills where there were terraces of vines. They were walking fast and talking – as they always did – then suddenly Gerald stopped dead. He was gazing entranced, like a man who sees a vision.

There was a girl standing at a gate with a basket of grapes held by one hand against her hip. She was like a young goddess, beautiful and serene. Antony would have been content to look at her and take the picture away with him in his mind, but Gerald went forward and spoke to her. He spoke to her for some time and then she smiled and gave him a bunch of grapes from her basket and ran up the steep path as lightly and gracefully as a fawn.

Gerald said very little on the way home – except that her name was Violetta and her father was the owner of the small vineyard – and, as Antony was obliged to return to Oxford the following day, he heard no more about it. He was too busy to think about it much for there was always a lot of work at the beginning of the term, so he was astonished and dismayed when he received a letter from Gerald to say that he was going to marry Violetta. He had been to see her several times and had found she was as good as she was beautiful – who could say more?

He had spoken to her father, they were to be married at once. It was a crazy letter, the letter of a young man who had been completely bowled over by his first dream of love.

Antony told me a good deal more and I was grateful to him for opening my eyes. Now that I understood what had happened I found that I could understand Gerald better and, as time went on, there was much to substantiate Antony's story. Gerald often spoke of Violetta, and in a perfectly natural way; spoke of her beauty and sweetness and her pretty ways exactly as if she had been a child. He told me that he used to make little parcels – a cheap little brooch or a string of beads or perhaps a coloured handkerchief – and hide them in the flat. He smiled and added, 'It was so amusing to see her delight when she found them.' The best proof of all was Gerald's astonishment when I asked him about his work and he discovered that I was able to take an intelligent interest in all he was doing. Very soon we became real companions, sharing joys and sorrows and jokes and the worries of everyday life – just as Antony had said.

In love like ours there was no room for jealousy.

Zilla had been silent for a few moments but now she said, 'How funny that you weren't jealous, Kit! Especially if she was so beautiful. Several of my friends have married widowers and there's usually a sort of feeling —'

'There wasn't in our case. I was grateful to Violetta because she gave me Simon. I still feel grateful. He was a serious little boy, too old for his age and rather delicate, but he soon became stronger. We had fun together, Simon and I.'

2

By this time it was nearly five o'clock and I was longing for tea. I had been talking too much about my own affairs and I was wondering how to change the subject when the door of the veranda opened and a woman came down the steps carrying a large tray. She was a comfortable-looking woman, short and fat with neatly braided hair.

'Did you get my stamps, Ellen?' asked Zilla.

'Yes, Miss Maclaren, I put them on your desk, and I

got some tomatoes for the salad and some cooking apples. They didn't have cheese biscuits.'

'They never have anything I want,' said Zilla crossly, 'I particularly wanted the biscuits because Mr. and Mrs. Carew are coming for drinks.'

'Does that mean dinner will be late, Miss Maclaren?'

'Probably,' replied Zilla in a casual tone of voice. 'You can't serve dinner until they've gone, can you?'

'Well, I better not make the soufflé then,' murmured Ellen under her breath.

While they were talking Ellen had arranged the tea on a round wooden table and was now returning to the house. Her wide hips waggled as she walked.

'Look at her!' exclaimed Zilla. 'Isn't she a sight? I got her a very nice grey dress but she won't wear it – just those flowered overalls which make her look like a tub. I don't know what my mother would have said if she had seen Ellen!'

'I think she looks comfortable. You're lucky to have her. You must be very happy here, Zilla.'

'Happy!' she exclaimed. 'What's happiness? It isn't just having a roof over your head and enough to eat.'

'It would be to thousands and thousands of people.'

'Well, it isn't to me. This place is a backwater; I'm stagnating here. There's nothing to do and nobody interesting to talk to. I want Alec to sell this house.'

'But, Zilla, I thought you said he worked in an office in Edinburgh.'

'He doesn't need to work at all. We have quite enough money to buy a flat in London. He could retire quite easily and we could enjoy ourselves; we could travel about and see the world; we could go to New Zealand and stay with our cousins there . . . but Alec won't hear of it. Men are frightfully selfish, aren't they? When I think of what a good time we could have if only Alec would listen to me and be sensible it makes me boil with rage. I feel tempted to spread my wings and live my own life but Alec won't hear of it. He needs me to look after him.'

'Perhaps he will marry,' I suggested. 'Then you would be free to do as you liked, wouldn't you?'

Zilla laughed. 'You don't know Alec; he's thirty-six and he hasn't *looked* at a girl in all his life. I've trotted out several suitable damsels but there was nothing doing.

He isn't particularly attractive, but if I were not here some designing woman might get hold of him and marry him for his money. Men are so helpless, aren't they?'

I was silent because I did not agree and because I was upset at the way she had spoken of her brother.

Fortunately she seemed to take my agreement for granted. 'This place gets me down,' she continued. 'I'm never well in Edinburgh; I feel quite different when I get away. It's so bad for me to have nothing to do.'

'But there are lots of things you could do!'

'You mean social work? I tried various things but I got bored – and the other women didn't understand me at all. You can't tie yourself down, can you? I mean if you're asked out to lunch or to a party you can't refuse because you're expected to turn up at a dreary meeting. There were days when I just felt I couldn't bear it. My nerves are so sensitive that I get upset very easily. Sometimes I feel I could stand on a chair and scream. I don't suppose you've ever felt like that.'

I had felt like that quite often. I had felt like that when a fall of soot came down the chimney and the whole room (including the chair-covers which had just come back from the cleaners) was smeared with a layer of oily soot. I had felt like that when the twins had measles and Den's temperature soared to 105 degrees, and the woman, who had come to help me, dropped a tray and broke three plates, and the electric cooker went wrong and a patch of damp appeared on the ceiling of my bedroom. It had all happened on the same day and it was just too much . . . But I had never felt like that because I hadn't enough to do.

'No, I can see you've never felt like that. How lucky you are!' said Zilla with a heavy sigh.

There was silence for a few moments while we drank our tea and ate delicious scones made by the unappreciated Ellen.

'Well, that's quite enough about my problems,' said Zilla. 'Tell me about yours.'

My problems wouldn't have interested Zilla, nor anybody else for that matter. They were extremely dull. For instance I had just discovered to my dismay that Daisy had grown so enormously since last year that her summer frocks were far too small and no amount of letting out and letting down would make them wearable.

'Haven't you any problems, Kit?' asked Zilla.

'Lots of small ones,' I told her. 'For one thing I'm worried about the summer holidays. We usually go to lodgings in North Berwick for a fortnight in August, but this year the woman can't have us. I've had a letter to say she's ill. It's a pity because the children enjoy the sands – but it can't be helped. I shall just have to try and find somewhere else.'

'You wouldn't like a cottage in the Highlands, I suppose?'

'I thought of that, but I'm afraid it would be too expensive.'

'This one wouldn't.'

'Zilla! Do you mean you know one that I could get at a reasonable rent?'

'It's mine,' she said smiling. 'It's a primitive sort of place at the back of beyond; there's nothing to do and nobody to talk to, but —'

'Zilla, do you mean it?'

'Of course I mean it. The cottage will be empty so you can have it for the whole of August if it's any use to you.'

'You could let it. I mean you could get quite a high rent for a cottage in the —'

'Too much bother,' said Zilla languidly. 'I let it once to some friends of the Carews who wanted it for the shooting; the dogs slept on the beds and chairs and the sofa in the sitting-room – shooting dogs, Kit! The whole place smelt of animals. You haven't got animals, have you?'

'No,' I said, laughing. 'Only three children; they're quite enough for one woman to look after.'

'Well, there you are, Kit. If you want a primitive cottage at the back of beyond you can have Craig-an-Ron for August. You'll find it dull and the midges will be frightful.'

Neither dullness nor midges mattered to me if I could get a cottage for the holidays, a quiet country cottage where the children would have freedom to run about and enjoy themselves. It seemed too wonderful to be true. 'Oh, Zilla, how kind of you!' I exclaimed.

'Well, don't blame me if you're bored to death,' said Zilla.

'Where is it, exactly? I mean how can we get there?'

'It's about six hours' run in the car.'

'Is there a train?'

'There's a train to Inverquill; that's the nearest town. If you went by train you'd have to hire a car to take you to Loch Ron – the cottage is on the shore of the loch. I shouldn't advise you to go by train.' She smiled and added, 'Now tell me about Sylvia. Have you kept in touch with her?'

I wanted to hear more about the cottage, but I didn't like to press her for any further information. It was so kind of her to offer it to me that I felt obliged to do as she wanted. I banished the cottage from my mind and talked about Sylvia who had been at Dinwell with us but, alas, was not very bright.

3

It seemed strange that Zilla should be so anxious to talk about school – and school-friends. Our school-days had been so long ago that I scarcely ever thought about them. I had far too much to do and to think about in my present life to dwell upon the past.

Obviously Zilla was different. She was still talking about school and reminding me of things that had happened when a tall broad-shouldered man with dark hair came through the french window of the veranda and walked towards us across the lawn.

'Here's Alec,' said Zilla. 'What a nuisance! I shall have to make fresh tea. You know Alec, don't you?' She raised her voice and added, 'Alec, you remember Kit.'

'Yes. At least . . .' he began, looking at me doubtfully.

'Of course you don't remember me,' I said as I rose to shake hands with him. 'It's a hundred years ago – and even then you didn't really see me. I saw you, of course, but that's different.'

'It sounds very mysterious,' said Mr. Maclaren.

'It isn't,' I told him. 'I was one of the crowd, that's all.'

'It was at Dinwell,' put in Zilla. 'You came with Father and Mother to watch a cricket match and you were very high-hat about the whole thing – strolled about with your nose in the air. Didn't he, Kit?'

'Oh well, it was natural,' I said uncomfortably. 'You

couldn't expect him to take any interest in a girls' cricket match. We all understood that.'

Mr. Maclaren had sat down by this time. He said, 'I seem to have behaved very badly. Will you forgive me and let bygones be bygones, Miss – er – er. Zilla, why on earth didn't you introduce us properly?'

'Oh, I thought you knew,' said Zilla. 'She used to be Kit Loudon, but she's married now, of course. I shall have to make fresh tea for you, Alec. This won't be worth drinking.'

'Don't bother,' he said quickly. 'Please don't bother, Zilla. I don't really want any tea.'

Zilla took no notice; she rose and went away.

There was a slightly uncomfortable silence after she had gone. The introduction – if you could call it that – had been made ungraciously and was incomplete. I was wondering if I should tell him my name when the silence was broken.

'Do you still play cricket?' asked Mr. Maclaren politely.

I laughed involuntarily. 'Goodness, no! At least I hadn't played cricket – or thought of it – until last year. Then I had to, because of Simon. He wanted some coaching in the Easter holidays, but I couldn't afford proper lessons so I had to do something about it myself. I found I could still bowl quite reasonably enough to give him a little practice and he got into his house eleven, which was what he wanted.'

'Excellent! Simon is your young brother, I suppose?'

'No, my stepson. This year he's hoping to get into the first eleven, but I'm afraid it's doubtful. My bowling won't be much good to him now.'

'Why not?'

I smiled and replied, 'Because he's too big and clever. It's the same with chess. I taught him to play but now he can beat me hollow.'

Mr. Maclaren smiled too. 'Oh, I see,' he said. 'It's slightly galling when that happens, but of course one can always bolster up one's self-esteem by the reflection that one has been a very good instructor.'

This idea was new to me. 'I hadn't thought of it like that. I'm just *pleased*, that's all. You see, Simon's father died, so I've had to try . . .' I stopped suddenly. It was quite ridiculous to talk like this to a complete stranger.

'I see,' said Mr. Maclaren thoughtfully.

There was another short silence.

'This is a lovely garden,' I said at last.

'I'm fond of it,' he admitted, almost apologetically. 'It was a dull sort of garden when I bought the place, with beds of flowers cutting up the lawn, and a shrubbery – mostly laurels. What I wanted was a big expanse of lawn and flowering shrubs and herbaceous borders – lots of colour! And I made a big rockery over there in the corner. It was a big job and it took several years. Gardeners have to be patient, especially in this part of the world.'

'You mean things don't grow very well?'

'They grow quite well, but they take their time about it.'

'It's beautiful,' I told him. 'It's so peaceful.'

He nodded. 'Yes, I like pottering round in the evenings after a day in the office. It's a rest and a refreshment. I have a man twice a week to keep it tidy but I do all the planning. Would you like to walk round and have a look at it, Mrs. – er —'

'Wentworth,' I said smiling at him. 'Yes, I've been longing to walk round your garden but I'm afraid I haven't time. My bus goes at six.'

'I could easily run you home later.'

'Oh no, why should you bother?' I rose as I spoke and added, 'I'm afraid I shall have to go now, Mr. Maclaren. I don't want to miss the bus.'

'Won't you let me take you home in the car?'

'No, really —'

'It wouldn't take ten minutes —'

We were standing there, arguing about it, when Zilla returned with the tea.

'Zilla!' exclaimed Mr. Maclaren. 'Do persuade Mrs. Wentworth to stay. I've been telling her that I can take her home later.'

'You can't,' said Zilla firmly. 'The Carews are coming for drinks. Kit can easily go home in the bus. We arranged that.'

'Blow the Carews!' said Alec Maclaren *sotto voce*.

'Here's your tea, Alec,' added Zilla. 'You had better sit down and drink it while it's hot.'

Zilla walked to the gate with me to see me off. 'He's so selfish,' she complained. 'He didn't even thank me for making fresh tea . . . and the Carews are my friends.

If they were his friends it would be a very different story. You heard what he said about them, didn't you?'

'He didn't mean it, Zilla.'

'He did,' she declared. 'He doesn't like them coming to the house because they're my friends – not his. Last time they came he was annoyed because he said they stayed too long and we had dinner a little later than usual. The Carews are so gay and friendly. You'd like them, Kit. I must arrange for you to meet them. . . .'

'Zilla,' I said desperately, 'did you really mean it – about the cottage?'

'Of course I meant it,' replied Zilla, laughing. 'What an old goose you are!'

As I went home in the bus I thought a lot about Zilla. It seemed sad that she couldn't settle down and be happy in that lovely house. I felt puzzled about her; she was such a queer mixture. I didn't like the way she treated her brother, and I had been annoyed with her for her curiosity in my affairs, but it was extremely kind and generous to offer me the cottage. I wondered if it were big enough – whether we could all fit in – and just how 'primitive' it was. Perhaps there was no bathroom! Could I bear it if there were no bathroom? I decided not to mention the cottage to the children until it was settled.

It was not until I got home that I found I had lost my scarf. This was a major disaster for it was a very pretty one and quite new. I tried to remember where I had left it, but I couldn't be sure. If it was at Zilla's she would keep it for me, but if I had left it in the bus it was unlikely that I should ever see it again.

CHAPTER 4

The next morning was dull and rainy. I got the children off to school as usual and then decided to clean the kitchen cupboard (the task had been on my mind for weeks). Clad in a faded overall with my hair tied up in a duster I set to work without delay. The glass and china dishes had been taken out and washed, the shelves scrubbed; it only remained to put back the dishes – and I was thinking longingly of a cup of coffee – when the door-bell rang.

It was sure to be Aunt Liz; she often dropped in at eleven for a cup of coffee . . . but it was not Aunt Liz, it was Mr. Maclaren.

'I've brought your scarf,' he said, handing me a little parcel. 'Zilla thought you might want it.'

'How kind of you! I was afraid I'd lost it. Won't you come in?'

'Well, just for a minute – if it wouldn't be a bother,' he replied.

It was a bother, of course. I was dirty and untidy and I wanted to finish the cupboard, but it was my own fault for asking him. To tell the truth I had been certain he would refuse. It just showed that you should never offer an invitation unless you really meant it!

'Yes, do come in,' I said as warmly as I could. 'I was just going to make coffee. You'd like a cup, wouldn't you?'

'That's very kind of you, Mrs. Wentworth.'

Fortunately the sitting-room was tidy so I left him there and went to get the coffee, wash my hands and take the duster off my head. When I returned with the tray he was standing at the window, looking out.

'You've got a beautiful view,' he said.

'Yes, I love it – and it always looks different. I like it best when there's a slight haze and the Fife hills are a misty blue. You can't see them at all to-day.'

'I can imagine them, which is almost as good. Shall I move the table for you?'

'Yes, and pull in that chair.'

We sat down together and chatted. I asked him about his work and he seemed pleased to talk about it; he told me he was a W.S., a junior partner in a well-known Edinburgh firm of lawyers.

'Zilla wants me to retire,' he said. 'But what on earth would I do with myself? Besides I enjoy the work, it's interesting and rewarding, and I want to get on and make good. Do you think it wrong to be ambitious?'

'No, indeed I don't! People aren't much good unless they're ambitious. Zilla would be annoyed with me for saying so, but honestly I think it would be a great mistake to retire. Time enough to think of that when you're twice your present age.'

He smiled and said, 'Yes, Zilla would be annoyed. She doesn't like Edinburgh, you see. Do you like living here?'

I said I did – and explained that I had lived here most of my life. I found myself telling him about Oxford. He seemed interested.

Presently he said rather diffidently, 'I expect you're wondering why I've come, Mrs. Wentworth.'

'To bring my scarf,' I suggested.

'Yes, of course – but I could have sent the office-boy with your scarf. Zilla said I was to send the boy.' He paused and then continued. 'The fact is I wanted to see you and talk to you about Simon.'

'About Simon?' I echoed in surprise.

'Yes. Perhaps I could give him some coaching in the Easter holidays. I don't play cricket now – I haven't time – but I still belong to the club so I could take him down there in the evenings and we could have a bit of practice at the nets.'

'How kind of you to think of it! But wouldn't it be a most awful bother?'

He smiled and said, 'No, it would amuse me to do it – if you think it would be any good.'

'Any good! It would be splendid. You see, he's really keen and I've been wondering what I could do about it.'

'Well, we'll consider it fixed – if Simon approves.'

There was not much doubt about that. 'Simon will be thrilled,' I declared emphatically. 'He'll think you're simply wonderful.'

'That will be a pleasant change,' said Mr. Maclaren rather sadly. 'All the same I'd rather you didn't mention it to him. I'll sound him carefully myself. Boys of sixteen are sometimes a bit touchy, so —'

'Simon isn't,' I said laughing. 'But of course I won't tell him if you'd rather not.'

Now that the matter was settled I expected Mr. Maclaren to go, but he seemed in no hurry.

He began to talk about Zilla. 'She's so pleased to have met you again. She's lonely, you know.'

'But she has lots of friends, hasn't she?'

'They aren't the right kind. For instance those Carews; they came to drinks last night after you had gone.'

'Zilla likes them.'

He nodded. 'I can't understand it,' he said. 'There's something – something bogus about them. Oh, I suppose they're quite amusing in their way – if you like that kind of thing. Jack Carew laughs all the time and makes silly jokes. He calls me Old Sobersides. Madeline never ceases talking for a moment – mostly about people one has never heard of, so it's difficult to look interested and intelligent.'

'Why does Zilla like them?'

'She says they're "good company".' He sighed and added, 'She's making plans to go abroad with them in August and I wondered if you could persuade her not to go.'

'I couldn't possibly!'

'Couldn't you try, Mrs. Wentworth? You see, Zilla isn't at all strong. I'm afraid it will be too tiring for her, tearing about the Continent with two such exhausting companions.'

'I couldn't,' I repeated. 'In any case she wouldn't listen to me.'

'Perhaps not,' he said gloomily. Then he added, 'But you'll go and see her as often as you can, won't you? She enjoys talking to you.'

'I'm rather a busy person, Mr. Maclaren.'

'Do try to go. She gets so bored and miserable.'

'It seems strange when she has so much to make her happy.'

'I don't think Zilla could be happy anywhere; it's a matter of temperament,' he said seriously. 'It doesn't make any difference whether you've got a lot or very little. If you feel miserable you can't help it. You can't *make* yourself happy and contented.'

'That isn't true!' I cried.

He looked at me in surprise – as well he might, poor man!

'Oh, I'm sorry,' I said hastily. 'I don't mean that I disbelieve you, of course. I just mean that people needn't give in to being miserable and discontented. They can get the better of it if they try hard enough.'

'It sounds as if you were speaking from experience.'

'Yes,' I said.

'Could you tell me about it?' he asked.

I was silent for a moment or two. 'It would be – difficult,' I said at last.

Could my experience help Zilla? I didn't see how it could be of any value at all but he was looking at me so appealingly that I couldn't refuse. I said, 'Well, I told you about Gerald, didn't I? It happened quite suddenly. One day I was as happy as a king and the next day my life was in ruins. I was down and out, nothing mattered any more. It seemed – unfair. Why should this terrible thing happen to me? I was wicked about it. I was even wicked enough to – to blame God . . . terribly, terribly wicked and miserable. For weeks I floundered about like Christian in the Slough of Despond.'

'And then?'

'Then I saw it was affecting the children – they were Gerald's children and I was making them unhappy – so I climbed out of the bog.'

I had never before told anybody about that dreadful time – but he had asked, so I had told him. I wondered what he would say. He said nothing for quite a long time, leaning forward and gazing at the floor.

At last I could bear the silence no longer so I said, 'The first thing I did was to go and buy a new frock – a coloured one – I had been wearing black, you see. It sounds silly, doesn't it?'

'No,' he replied. 'It sounds brave. Thank you for telling me.'

'So you see people can climb out of the bog if they try.'

'If they're brave enough – and have other people to think of.'

I felt inclined to say, 'Zilla might think of you,' but I didn't. As a matter of fact I felt rather dazed; it had been an effort to speak of that time. I hadn't told him half of it, of course – the whole wretched experience had been condensed into a few short words – but remembering it had upset me rather badly.

Mr. Maclaren rose to go. 'Thank you,' he said. 'Thank you – for everything. I'm afraid I've taken up a lot of your time this morning. Are you going out? Can I take you anywhere in the car?'

'I'm too busy to go out.'

'Busy?' he said. 'What do you do, Mrs. Wentworth?'

'Come and see,' I said and led the way to the kitchen.

It was a muddle, of course, but everything was nice and clean: the empty cupboard and the glass and china, stacked in shining array on the table and the chairs.

'Good lord!' he exclaimed. 'Isn't there a woman to do that?'

'Just this woman,' I replied, laughing at his dismay. 'Cupboards have to be cleaned occasionally and this seemed a good day to tackle the job. It's nearly done now. Everything is cleaned; I've just got to put the things back. Then there's the dinner to cook. The children come home from school at half past twelve. I told you I was a busy person, didn't I?'

'Yes,' he said. 'But I didn't understand —'

'Well, you understand now, don't you? And please don't be sorry for me because I'm perfectly happy.'

'Yes, I can see you are,' said Mr. Maclaren. He thanked me again and went away.

2

'Don't blame me if you hate the place,' said Zilla.

We had met at Brown's for morning coffee and to settle details about the cottage. I had made a list of everything I wanted to know, but so far I had not managed to obtain from Zilla any very useful information. She had repeated several times that it was 'frightfully primitive' and 'horribly isolated' but that did not get me much further.

'There's a road, I suppose?' I asked in dubious tones.

'Oh yes, and a very good garage. We had to build it for Alec's car. My little car doesn't matter, it can stand out in the yard, but Alec is terribly particular about his Rolls.'

The garage did not interest me because I had no car. I reminded Zilla of this fact which, if she had thought for a moment, she must have known already.

'Then it's hopeless,' she said. 'Unless you could hire, of course.'

'The children have bicycles,' I told her.

'Oh, bicycles! Well, I suppose you could get about on bicycles. Loch Ron village is two miles away, but it's no great shakes. Just a butcher and a grocer and a few other shops. You would be better to take the car and get what you need in Inverquill – it's only twelve miles.'

Should I remind her again that I had no car? I decided not to.

'What about linen?' I asked.

‘Use mine,’ said Zilla. ‘It’s all there – and plenty of dishes and silver and cutlery — you needn’t take anything like that. The cottage is ready to walk into.’

‘That’s awfully kind of you, Zilla. It sounds marvellous.’

‘It isn’t marvellous. It’s a wretched place, an absolute hovel.’

‘How many bedrooms are there?’

‘Two.’

‘Two!’ I echoed in dismay.

‘Two decent bedrooms. There are two others in the attic – very monkish, if you know what I mean.’

‘But there are beds in them, I suppose.’

‘Of course there are beds.’

‘Is there a bathroom, Zilla?”

‘My dear girl, you don’t suppose I could *exist* in a place without a bathroom? I put it in myself and piped the water from the burn. It’s peaty, of course, especially when the burn is in spate. Oh, did I tell you that there’s no electricity? I thought of having it put in but it would have cost the earth.’

‘There are lamps, I suppose?’

‘Yes, lamps. Isn’t it frightful? You can’t have television or a fridge or a radiator, you can’t even have an electric blanket. I told you it was primitive, didn’t I? There’s no telephone either.’

The waitress came with our coffee and Zilla continued to talk.

‘I don’t know why I bought the place,’ she said. ‘At least I do – really. I thought it would be amusing to go up there for an occasional week-end – just pigging it, you know. I had a craze for fishing at the time. Fishing is quite fun if you catch lots of fish, but so often the conditions are wrong; it’s too bright or too calm or too windy or something. Alec doesn’t mind; he can fish for hours quite happily when there isn’t a fish within miles.’

‘Zilla,’ I said, ‘what do you cook on?’

Zilla laughed. ‘My dear, there was an old-fashioned kitchen range made of iron! I wish you could have seen it. Really it was fit for a museum and nothing else. It must have been a hundred years old and it used tons of coal, which had to be carted for miles. I tore it out, of course. I don’t know how people existed in the old days, do you?’

'I expect there's an oil-stove to cook on,' I said. I simply had to know. Cooking is terribly important when you have three hungry children to feed.

'There's Calor gas or something,' Zilla replied. 'It's a funny sort of contraption but Mrs. MacRam seems to manage it all right. She's the woman who comes in daily.'

'Would she come to me, do you think? It would be such a help to have someone in the holidays so that I could go out with the —'

'Of course she'll go to you. I thought you understood that. The woman is there. I employ her. She's the wife of the shepherd and they live in a little cottage on the hill. She looks after the place in the winter and keeps it aired. When we're there she comes in and "does for us" as the saying is. You needn't have Mrs. MacRam if you don't want her, but she'll be frightfully offended.'

'I shall be delighted to have her – and pay her, of course.'

'You needn't pay her. I employ her and pay her quite enough. You can give her a present if you like.'

'Zilla, this is all terribly kind! Are you sure —'

'I've told you at least three times that if you don't go the cottage will be empty all August. I don't want it to be empty because the Mitchells are sure to ask for it and I must have a watertight excuse because they're friends of Madeline Carew. I told you about the Mitchells before, didn't I?'

'Dogs?'

'Yes, three – lying on the beds and the chairs. If you're there I can say they can't have it.'

The matter was now perfectly clear to me. I wished that Zilla were a little more gracious in bestowing her benefits (her manner irritated me intensely), but beggars can't be choosers so I thanked her again as warmly as I could.

Soothed by an excellent cup of coffee and a cigarette, Zilla became more agreeable. She told me that she was going to France in August with the Carews.

'I'm looking forward to it immensely,' she declared. 'They've got a flat in London – just the sort of flat I want – and they've asked us to go and stay there for a few days before we set off. I haven't mentioned it to Alec yet. I expect he'll be difficult about it.'

'Is he going abroad with you?'

'No, of course not – he'd be a frightful nuisance – but he really must come with me to London; it's such a bore travelling alone. I must go now,' she added. 'I've got some shopping to do before lunch.'

I, also, had shopping to do and the children's dinner to prepare so I called the waitress and paid for our coffee (it was at my invitation that Zilla had come) and we went our ways.

CHAPTER 5

Tuesday – the day when Simon was due to arrive home for the Easter holidays – came at last. The children had got their holidays so they were under my feet all day, full of excited questions. Where was Simon now – at this moment? Did I think he would lose his luggage, as he had done before? Last, but not least, could they stay up and see him when he arrived? Already I had said no five times. I said it again quite firmly but promised that if they were awake when he came he would go in and see them in bed.

Simon arrived about nine o'clock – his train was late. I should have liked to meet him at the station (for to be honest I was quite as excited as the twins at the prospect of seeing him again) but as I could not leave the children alone in the flat I was obliged to wait as patiently as I could. By this time the children were asleep, worn out with excitement. I wasn't sorry.

As usual, when he returned from school, Simon looked enormous, but I had come to the conclusion that this was not because he had grown like a beanstalk but because I was used to the size of the seven-year-old twins.

Simon had had dinner in the train so he did not want much supper and when he had finished we settled down for a chat.

'I've got a lot to tell you,' he said. 'I've been making plans about my future.'

'You're going to Cambridge when you leave Barstow.'

'Can't afford it.'

'Simon, I told you! Aunt Liz will help. She's quite willing to —'

'But I'm not willing, Mums.'

'I thought that was what you wanted.'

'Yes, but I hadn't considered it properly. Listen,' said Simon earnestly. 'It's like this, you see. If I could get a scholarship it would be all right, but I haven't got the brains. I work reasonably hard but I haven't a dog's hope of a scholarship.'

'Aunt Liz said she would pay for you to —'

'I know, but I can't accept it from her. You see, she doesn't like me.'

'Whatever makes you think she dislikes you?' I cried in horrified tones.

Simon smiled. 'You've got it wrong. I didn't say she disliked me, I just said she doesn't like me. You can like a person or not like them or dislike them. It's three different things – three totally different feelings.'

'Yes, I suppose it is.'

'Aunt Liz doesn't like me,' declared Simon. 'She adores you and the twins but her feeling for me is – sort of tepid. For one thing she thinks you spoil me. Perhaps it's true.'

'It isn't true! Daddy was terribly against spoiling and I've brought you up exactly as he would have wanted. I've made you behave properly and smacked you when you were naughty. You know that perfectly well.'

Simon was chuckling. 'Oh yes, you used to smack me quite hard but I didn't mind – even when it hurt – because you loved me all the time. You loved me best of all.'

'I didn't!'

'Next to Dad,' said Simon, nodding. 'You still do. That's another reason why Aunt Liz doesn't like me. She's jealous.'

'What nonsense! She's a sensible woman.'

'Very sensible,' agreed Simon. 'And of course she doesn't know she's jealous – she would be horrified at the mere idea – but deep down inside she's jealous. You ought to love the twins best because they're your own, and you ought to love her next because she's your aunt. Instead of which —'

'Simon, that's enough,' I said firmly.

He was silent at once but I saw that he was smiling.

As a matter of fact I had never thought about it before but, now that Simon had forced me to think about it, I realised that it was true. I loved Simon best. It was partly because he was so like Gerald and partly because he was my very own. The twins belonged to each other in a mysterious sort of way – or perhaps it was not really mysterious for they had shared a cot and a pram in babyhood and had never been parted for a single day. As they grew older they shared toys and games; they indulged in private jokes – quite incomprehensible to their elders – and although they quarrelled quite often they presented a united front to the world. If you touched Den you touched Daisy – and vice versa. We were a complete family devoted to each other, but the family, inside itself, was divided into pairs. Simon and I were one pair, the twins were the other. However, I was not going to admit that.

'What do you propose to do if you don't go to Cambridge?' I asked rather coldly.

'Earn money,' replied Simon promptly. 'It's high time I started to earn my own living instead of costing you the earth. I shall go into business when I leave school; and you needn't smile like that because it's all arranged.'

'What!'

'It's all arranged – subject to your approval. You know Mark Butterfield, don't you? I mean you've heard me talk of him. We've been friends ever since we went to Barstow. Well, Mark's uncle is the boss of a big firm in the City – export-and-import merchants. Mark has been destined for Butterfield's since he was a kid and Mr. Butterfield says he'll take me too. We'll start at the bottom – Mark and I together – working in the warehouses and learning the job thoroughly.'

'You can't dash into it like that! We shall have to think about it and —'

'Yes, of course,' agreed Simon. 'But it's a fine opportunity – really it is. Mr. Butterfield is awfully decent. He took us out to lunch last Sunday and gave us a slap-up meal . . . and he talked to me a lot and asked all sorts of questions. Then, when we got back to Barstow, he saw Mr. Talbot and asked him about me. Mark told me that. When Mr. Butterfield was going away he said to Mark, "You can tell your friend if he's in the same mind when he leaves school, I'll take him."'

'Simon, we shall have to find out —' I began in alarm. 'I mean we don't know anything about him – or the firm. We don't know —'

'He's got a Bentley,' declared Simon. 'It's a terrific machine – absolutely super. That shows you!'

The Bentley certainly was impressive, though perhaps I was not quite so impressed as Simon had expected.

'Well, not to worry,' said Simon in soothing tones. 'I've got another two years at Barstow and we needn't decide definitely until then. That's what Mr. Butterfield said. By that time you'll have got used to the idea of your stepson working in a warehouse.'

'It isn't that, Simon. I'm not a snob. It's just that I *do* want you to go to Cambridge.'

'You'll have to wait for Den,' said Simon, rising and stretching himself. 'Den is the brainy one of the family. He'll get a scholarship to Cambridge as easy as pie. Look at the time, Mums. We'd better go to bed.'

CHAPTER 6

Mr. Maclaren had made me promise not to tell Simon about his offer. It was ridiculous, of course, because any boy who was keen on cricket would have been thrilled at the idea of being coached by a man who had been chosen to bat for Cambridge and had acquitted himself with distinction . . . but Alec Maclaren was modest about his cricket and also about himself. His manner was shy and diffident; I had noticed that. Perhaps Zilla was to blame; she lost no opportunity of putting him in the wrong. I remembered that when I had said, 'Simon will think you're simply wonderful,' he had replied a trifle ruefully, 'That will be a pleasant change.'

During the next three days Simon talked a great deal about cricket and about his chances of being chosen to play in the first eleven. Daisy and Den, knowing nothing whatever about it, were certain that he would be included in the side.

'There's just a chance,' said Simon. 'It all depends on my batting. I wish I could have some coaching – but of course I can't. Don't worry, Mums, it won't be the end of the world if they leave me out.'

I discovered that Mark had gone to stay with his uncle at Wimbledon and was being coached by a professional cricketer who had played for his county some years ago.

'It costs a lot,' explained Simon, 'but Mr. Butterfield has bags of money so he doesn't mind.'

It was difficult to remain dumb.

On the fourth day we had just finished breakfast when the door-bell rang. Simon went to answer it and I heard the sound of conversation in the hall; then Simon opened the door of the sitting-room and ushered in our visitor.

'It's Mr. Maclaren, Mums. He says he knows you. He says he's going to play golf at Muirfield and can I go with him and have lunch. I said I was sure it would be all right,' said Simon eagerly.

'How kind of you, Mr. Maclaren! Do you really want him?'

'Of course I want him,' Mr. Maclaren replied. 'If I hadn't wanted him I wouldn't have asked him. The point is whether Simon would enjoy it. I'm playing in a match, so —'

'I could caddie for you,' put in Simon. 'Have you got one of those bags on wheels?'

Mr. Maclaren laughed and said he had. 'But I didn't intend you to caddie for me. I just thought you might like to walk round and then have lunch at the club. I'm going now.'

'I'll be ready in two ticks,' cried Simon, dashing out of the room.

I followed to see what he meant to wear and to warn him not to be a nuisance to the players, not to speak unless spoken to and to do exactly as he was told.

'Goodness, how old do you think I am!' he exclaimed, tugging at the laces of his shoes.

'Oh, I know,' I said hastily. 'But when people are playing golf they don't like talking – that's all.'

Simon chuckled. 'Don't worry, I won't talk. I'll take a squib in my pocket and let it off behind Mr. Maclaren just as he's going to putt . . . or perhaps it would be better to borrow Den's trumpet; that would shake him!'

'You can't go in that shirt!'

'Oh, Mums, it's quite *clean*!'

'The collar is frayed.'

'But I've brushed my hair!'

'You can brush it again after you've changed.'

'But he's waiting!'

'It will be much quicker if you don't argue.'

Simon realised that this was true so he bowed to the inevitable. He was not ready in 'two ticks' but he was ready in exactly seven minutes, clean and tidy in his grey flannel suit, blue shirt and school tie. I thought he looked very nice indeed and I hoped Mr. Maclaren would think so too.

As they went off together down the stairs Mr. Maclaren looked up and said, 'When do you want him back?'

'Mums doesn't mind,' said Simon quickly.

I laughed. 'I'll expect him when I see him,' I said.

The twins were hanging out of the window gazing down into the street.

'What a great big lovely car!' cried Daisy admiringly.

'It's a Rolls,' said Den. He sighed and added, 'Simon is a lucky dog.'

The car drove away and the excitement died down. I began to clear the breakfast dishes which still littered the table.

'To-day's Saturday,' said Den suddenly. 'Had you forgotten it was Saturday, Mums?'

'Aunt Liz is expecting Simon – she said so,' added Daisy.

Needless to say I had forgotten it was Saturday. However, Aunt Liz was a sensible woman so I did not think she would mind. The only thing to do was to ring up and explain what had happened.

Unfortunately Aunt Liz did not seem quite as sensible as usual; she was a trifle astringent. 'It doesn't matter in the least,' she said crisply. 'There is no need whatever for all those excuses, Kit. Naturally the boy preferred to go off for the day with a total stranger than to come to lunch with me. I suppose I shall see him some time.'

'Yes, of course. When would you like —'

'I'll fetch the twins at twelve. Are you coming, Kit?'

'Well, not to-day. I'm going to turn out the sitting-room, but I'll call for them in the afternoon.'

'I'm taking them to the cinema in the afternoon. If they're home about six I suppose it will do.'

'Yes, that will be splendid,' I said.

2

It was a pity that Aunt Liz was annoyed, but she would soon recover – and anyhow it couldn't be helped. I realised that Mr. Maclaren had arranged the expedition to Muirfield so that he could make friends with Simon before broaching the subject of cricket. Perhaps it would have been a good plan if Simon had been a prickly sort of boy but, Simon being Simon, it was quite unnecessary.

It was a lovely day. I had fully intended to turn out the sitting-room, for with the children off my hands it was a splendid opportunity to get down to the job . . . but it really was a perfectly lovely day: the sun was shining, the sky was blue and there was a westerly breeze. After a few moments' hesitation I decided that the sitting-room could wait. I made some sandwiches, put them in my pocket and set off by myself.

There was no difficulty in deciding what to do with my stolen day. I took the bus to Cramond, and from there I walked along the shore and smelt the sea and watched the birds and enjoyed the peace of being alone. If I had been a poet I might have written an ode to solitude. It would have been a good poem, for I felt convinced that nobody who has not been cooped up in a small flat with children can appreciate the bliss of being alone.

There was quite a strong breeze on the shore, and it was not warm, but I found shelter behind a rock and sat down to eat my lunch. The sea was unusually blue to-day and the wind was blowing white horses down the firth, the gulls were wheeling and diving, uttering their eerie cries. How lovely to be a seagull, to soar high up into the sky and float gently down the wind with wings outspread! How lovely to be clothed with warm white feathers! How lovely to dive into the sea and catch a fish for one's dinner!

A seagull has no worries about clothes and butchers' bills; a seagull does not have to catch a bus. I glanced at my watch and discovered that unless I hurried I should lose the bus back to Edinburgh, so I rose and went home.

Supper that evening was a very cheerful meal; we had all enjoyed our day and had plenty to say about what we had done. Daisy gave a full account of the film they had seen and Den reported that Aunt Liz was in good form and had asked us all to tea to-morrow. Simon had had a 'smashing' time and was tremendously excited at the prospect of batting practice. Mr. Maclaren was calling for him at five o'clock on Monday – it was all arranged.

CHAPTER 7

Simon came home from his first batting lesson literally steaming with excitement. Alec was marvellous, there was nobody like him. Alec had said this and Alec had said that; Alec had made him loosen his shoulders and alter his stance; Alec had shown him a cut to leg . . . it had all been simply smashing.

'Who said you could call him Alec?' I inquired.

'He did,' replied Simon, chuckling. 'And it was quite easy because he wasn't a bit sidey – or anything – he was just like another chap.'

'Did he bowl?' I asked.

'No, he got the man to bowl to me while he stood and watched. He didn't say a word for ages. Then he began to tell me things. Gosh, Mums, he knows what's what! You should have seen him when he got his bat and had a go himself! He said he was rusty but the man said there wasn't much rust about *him*. (The man's name is Nottingham – he's English – an awfully good chap.) Well, Nottingham kept on saying he ought to come back and play for the club, but Alec said he had no time for cricket nowadays; he could get a game of golf whenever he liked – at short notice.'

'Were you the only people there?'

'No, there were several other fellows – much older than me, of course. Alec introduced me to them: he said, "This is a young friend of mine, Simon Wentworth." I was proud, I can tell you! Two of them hung about and watched for a bit, but it made me nervous so Alec sent them away. He said he'd take me again on Wednesday at the same time. You see he doesn't get away from his office until five. That'll be all right, won't it? Oh, and Mums, listen! Alec said I was to tell you not to mention it to Zilla in case it upset her. Who's Zilla and why should it upset her?'

'Zilla is his sister.'

'Well, why should it upset her to know he's coaching me?'

I hadn't the slightest idea but I had to say something. 'She's rather highly-strung.'

'She sounds batty,' declared Simon. 'But anyhow I've given you the message. You won't let on, will you?'

'No, of course not.'

'Gosh, I'm tired,' said Simon, sitting down suddenly. 'And hungry,' he added.

Fortunately I had some cold meat to give him and there was plenty of bread and butter. He devoured the meal ravenously, still talking of all that had happened. When he had finished he insisted on fetching his bat and, having moved the table out of the way, demonstrated the famous leg cut.

By this time it was ten o'clock so I persuaded him to have his bath and go to bed. I, too, went to bed feeling happy for Simon but slightly worried about the message.

2

Tuesday afternoon was wet and gloomy so I suggested that Simon should take the children to the pictures. They wanted me to go with them but the sitting-room was still waiting to be turned out so I sent them off by themselves.

The tiresome job was just finished when the door-bell rang and I found Mr. Maclaren standing on the mat.

'Goodness, I thought it was to-morrow!' I exclaimed in dismay.

'It is to-morrow,' he replied.

We both burst out laughing.

'Well, you know what I mean,' he said. 'To-morrow is the day I arranged to take Simon to the club. I've called in on my way home from the office because I wanted to see you.'

'Come in and have tea,' I suggested.

'Better not; Zilla is expecting me. Did Simon give you the message? Perhaps you thought it a bit strange but –

but I think it might upset her if she knew I was coaching Simon, so if you don't mind —'

'No, of course not,' I said. 'It's most awfully kind of you; Simon is absolutely thrilled.'

He smiled. 'I'm "thrilled" too. Simon is good and he's going to be very good indeed. He just wants some practice and a few hints. Nottingham agrees that he's outstanding. I thought you'd be pleased.'

'Pleased isn't the word! How good of you to bother, Mr. Maclaren!'

'Simon calls me Alec.'

I laughed. 'Yes, I noticed that: Alec is marvellous – there's nobody like him; Alec knows what's what; I ought to have seen Alec when he got out his bat and had a go himself – and so on and so forth.'

'And I shall call you Katherine,' said Alec, smiling. 'Simon says that's your proper name.'

'Simon seems to have given you quite a lot of information.'

'Yes, quite a lot.'

'Are you sure you won't stay for a cup of tea? I'm just going to make some.'

Alec hesitated and glanced at his watch. 'No, I'd better go,' he said reluctantly. 'Zilla is expecting me. You understand, don't you?'

3

The days passed very quickly. Simon had half a dozen batting lessons and was reported to be doing well. 'He's a bit erratic,' Alec said, 'but that's natural. When he settles down and gains confidence Simon will be a very fine bat.'

We went to lunch with Aunt Liz and we made several expeditions, taking sandwiches and having a substantial meal when we got home.

It was Gerald's idea that when you went for expeditions into the country each person should carry his own food (Gerald would have nothing to do with picnic-baskets) and I was determined that Gerald's family should follow in his footsteps. I got four small knapsacks, so we each had one; the children took it for granted that this was the right thing.

One day we went to Fairmilehead in the bus and walked up a path which led over the Pentland Hills. We sat in a sheltered hollow and enjoyed our light lunch. I looked at the three, lounging comfortably on the sheep-bitten grass – smooth and green as velvet – and wondered what Gerald would think of them. Would he be pleased with his children? Would he think I was bringing them up on the right lines? Quite honestly I thought he would be satisfied; they were frank and fearless, they were sufficiently disciplined to be obedient when obedience was necessary, but within limits they were free to follow their own sweet will. Freedom had been so important to Gerald that he had given up his family and his home to obtain it.

When we had finished lunch the children folded up their sandwich-papers and put them in their knapsacks with the banana skins. They did this quite naturally without thinking.

'I'll tell you something,' said Daisy, who often prefaced her remarks with this promise – or threat! 'When I went a picnic with the Fishers they had a big basket full of food and cups and plates: it took two people to carry it – there was an awful fuss about who was to do it – and when we had finished lunch they left a lot of rubbish on the grass.'

Simon chuckled. 'I bet you told them off properly.'

'Of course,' said Daisy. She rose and ran off to explore a pile of rocks. Den followed.

'She's a scream,' said Simon. 'It makes me feel very old to think I used to give Daisy her bottle.'

'Poor old man!'

Simon moved nearer to me. 'What were you thinking about when we were having lunch, Mums?'

I looked at him sitting beside me on the grass. He had always been like Gerald and, now that the soft contours of childhood had disappeared and the bones of his face were more visible, he had become even more like Gerald . . . and Gerald used to smile like that, suddenly, with a wide mischievous grin which showed his beautiful white teeth and crinkled the corners of his eyes. It might almost have been Gerald sitting beside me; the thin face, the clear grey eyes, the dark eyebrows and the unruly lock of dark hair which strayed on to his forehead.

'Come on, Mums. What were you thinking about?' he repeated.

'I was wondering what Dad would think of you; whether he would be satisfied with his family. Then I thought about freedom. Dad valued freedom so highly that he broke away from his family and his home. He gave up comfort and wealth. He had to work hard to make a living . . . but you know that, Simon.'

'Freedom,' said Simon. 'Yes, it must have been terribly important to Dad; or do you think he didn't love his family very much?'

I didn't want to answer this. I said, 'Freedom is important but it can be misused. If you want freedom you must discipline yourself. Remember that.'

'It's like cricket,' said Simon thoughtfully. 'You see a ball coming and you feel like having a good old slosh, so you step out and slosh for all you're worth . . . and the next thing is you see it soaring straight for somebody's hands. So that's the end of *you* and you find yourself walking back to the pavilion (and, gosh, what a long walk it is!) trying to look as if you didn't give a damn.'

'You've missed the point —' I began.

'No, I haven't,' said Simon with his sudden wide grin. 'No, I haven't missed the point. The point is that if you haven't got freedom there's no scope for you to discipline yourself.'

Simon had put it the other way round but the two ways made one truth.

He rose and stretched himself. 'That hill wants to be climbed,' he said and set off with long strides to climb it.

I was about to call out and remind him that he must be back in time to catch the bus, but Simon knew as well as I did that the bus left at five o'clock. He would discipline himself and be back in plenty of time.

The thought amused me.

4

The holidays were nearly over now and for weeks I had seen nothing of Zilla. She had rung up once or twice and asked me to tea but I had explained that it was difficult for me to get away while the children were at home. It was difficult, of course, but if I had really wanted to go I could have managed it. The fact was I shrank from the thought of having tea with Zilla; I was afraid that in the course of conversation I might let out the secret. We were seeing quite a lot of Alec (he came to fetch Simon two or three times a week and sometimes had tea with us before they went off to the cricket club). Zilla was clever, she would pounce upon me at once: When had I seen Alec? Where had I seen Alec? Why had I begun to call him Alec? Then I should have to tell lies about it. I didn't like lies and I could see no reason for secrecy. I could not believe that Zilla would mind her brother coaching Simon. Why should she mind? But Alec did not want her to know, so the secret must be kept. When Simon went back to Barstow and Alec ceased to call at the flat it would be easier.

Simon's train left at ten o'clock and we all went to see him off. When we came out of the station Daisy was in tears and Den was as grumpy as a bear. I felt bereft; the three months of term stretched before me like a desert – three whole months before I should see him again!

We were walking along Princes Street when we ran straight into Zilla. If I could have avoided her I would have done so; I was in no mood for a friendly chat.

'Hallo!' exclaimed Zilla. 'You look a bit down in the mouth.'

'Simon's gone!' wailed Daisy. 'We shan't see darling Simon for months and months and months!'

'Shut up, you silly ass!' growled Den.

'What on earth's the matter with them?' asked Zilla.

'Nothing,' I replied brightly. 'We've just been seeing Simon off to school.'

'Oh, is that all? I thought something must have happened. When are you coming to see me, Kit? What about lunch on Saturday?'

I was about to accept the invitation when I remembered that Aunt Liz had arranged to lunch with some friends on Saturday so I should have the children on my hands. I explained this.

'You had better bring them,' Zilla said. 'Alec is going to Muirfield so we can have a good chat.'

'Couldn't we arrange another day? I mean the children will —'

'No, Saturday,' said Zilla firmly. 'I hate being by myself all day. One o'clock – or sooner. You'll come in the bus, of course.' She turned as she spoke and the next minute she was lost in the crowd.

CHAPTER 8

The idea of taking the children to lunch at The Cedars did not fill me with enthusiasm; on Saturday morning I woke with the feeling that something horrible was going to happen to-day . . . yes, of course, lunch with Zilla! I was so reluctant to go that I almost wished one of the children would develop a cold – a slight one, of course – to provide me with an excuse, but they both seemed in the best of health though not in the best of spirits. They missed Simon; I was glad that they would be starting school on Monday.

The bus went at twelve. I was busy getting the children ready and telling them about The Cedars:

'Miss Maclaren isn't used to children, so you must be very good. You must behave like grown-up people. Don't forget to shake hands – your right hand, remember. You'll be able to play in the garden but you mustn't pick the flowers.'

'We can pick the daisies, can't we?' said Daisy.

'There won't be any daisies.'

'Funny garden with no daisies!'

'Daises are weeds,' said Den.

'They aren't!'

'They are. People poison them.'

'Well, anyway, I'm really a marguerite. They aren't weeds.'

'You're a daisy and you're a weed,' said Den mulishly.

'I'm not!'

'You are.'

'Don't argue,' I said.

There was a thundery sort of silence.

'Do be good,' I said earnestly. 'I want Miss Maclaren to see how nicely you can behave. Surely you can be good and nice just while we're there.'

'How long have we got to be there?' inquired Den.

It was at this moment that the door-bell rang. I left them and went to answer it and discovered Alec, waiting outside.

'Are you ready?' he asked. 'I thought I'd pick you up. The bus is always crowded on a Saturday.'

Den and Daisy had followed me into the hall and welcomed Alec with delight. They were even more delighted when they heard of the treat in store. There were no more arguments and we were all ready to go in ten minutes. As he climbed into the back seat and settled down beside Daisy, Den heaved a sigh of sheer bliss and remarked that he had never been in a Rolls before.

It was only half past eleven – too early for lunch – so Alec took us for a spin to Queensferry. The children clamoured to 'go fast.'

'Not here,' replied Alec. 'Wait till we've passed the limit.'

I glanced at him and saw that he was smiling so I kept a careful look-out for the sign and was not surprised when the car suddenly bounded forward like a greyhound released from the slips. Den and Daisy had been looking at two gipsy caravans so they were unprepared and were flung backwards in a tangle of arms and legs. There were shrieks of laughter and delight at this gorgeous joke.

'Too fast for you?' asked Alec, slowing down a little.

'Faster, faster!' cried Daisy, like the Red Queen.

'Pass that car in front, Mr. Maclaren,' cried Den. 'You can – easily.'

We did – easily – with Daisy leaning out of the window and waving frantically at the somewhat astonished occupants.

Alec was silent, intent upon driving, but there was a good deal of chat in the back seat; Den and Daisy always had a lot to say to each other.

Presently Daisy leant forward and said, 'What's her name?'

'Whose name?' asked Alec.

'Your car, of course. Den says cars are always girls, so I wondered what she was called.'

'Oh – er – Clara,' said Alec solemnly.

The name seemed to give satisfaction and the subdued chatter in the back seat continued until we arrived at Queensferry, where we got out to walk about and stretch our legs.

I had been here often, of course, but every time I came the railway bridge astonished me by its immense size. We watched a line of cars driving on to the ferry which was about to cross the Forth. The children were very anxious to go in 'the boat' but there was not time, so Alec promised to bring them some other day instead.

2

It was about twenty minutes to one when we got back and turned in at the big gates of The Cedars. Ellen had been on the look-out for us and was waiting on the doorstep.

'Here's Ellen!' said Alec. 'She'll look after you. I'll just take the car round to the garage.'

The children jumped out and shook hands with Ellen in their best 'party' manner. It was a slight error in etiquette, but Ellen was delighted; she whispered to me that they were 'dear wee things – such nice manners, too.' Then she took our coats and hung them on pegs in the hall cupboard.

I had liked Ellen before, but to-day I liked her even better; she was comfortable and kind. I chatted to her for a few moments and admired a large bowl of beautifully arranged flowers in the hall.

'Yes, they're nice,' she agreed. 'I do all the flowers for Miss Maclaren. There's such lovely flowers in the garden and Mr. Maclaren lets me pick whatever I like – so it's quite easy.'

'Why, Ellen, you're an artist!' I exclaimed. It really was surprising to discover that this plain, square, matter-of-fact woman had such a flair for arranging flowers.

There was no time to say more; the drawing-room door opened and Zilla appeared.

'Hallo, here you are!' she said. 'I thought I heard talking. How nice to see you, Kit! I've been looking forward to a nice long chat. Come into the drawing-room.'

We followed her into the drawing-room and again the children shook hands very politely indeed. I was just congratulating myself upon their good behaviour when Daisy spoilt the effect.

'Were you *really* at school with Mums?' she inquired, fixing Zilla with wide-open eyes. 'Mums said you were – but you look much too old.'

Zilla was displeased and showed it; she was not inured to home-truths delivered by the young and innocent.

There was an uncomfortable silence; I could not think what to say – it would be useless to disagree with Daisy for I knew she was quite capable of sticking to her point and arguing, which would make things ten times worse.

At last I gave Daisy a little push. 'You and Den can go out into the garden. It would be fun to explore, wouldn't it?' I said.

'But, Mums, I don't want —'

'You heard,' muttered Den. 'We've got to be good.'

They went out together through the french windows and disappeared.

'What delightful children!' said Zilla insincerely. 'You must be proud of them, Kit.'

I smiled vaguely and said nothing.

'They aren't a bit alike, are they?' said Zilla. 'The boy looks very delicate. You should give him malt.'

'Den is rather small for his age,' I admitted.

'And so pale! Really, Kit, you ought to do something about it. Why don't you take him to a doctor and have him overhauled. My doctor is quite marvellous, I'm sure he would discover what was the matter with the child.'

This enraged me – goodness knows why. 'Oh, Den's all right,' I said casually.

Zilla was peering out of the window. 'I hope they won't do any damage, Kit. They won't pick the flowers, will they?'

I was pretty certain they wouldn't pick the flowers, but I took a chair near the window so that I could keep an eye on them while I listened to Zilla talking. Presently I saw Alec coming from the direction of the garage; he joined the children and they went away together and disappeared from view. Obviously there was no need to bother about them any more.

Zilla was telling me about the arrangements for her holiday with the Carews; they were going in August, taking their car and making an extensive tour of the Loire valley. She had a book about the châteaux and showed me the pictures.

'I like to know about the places I'm going to visit before I go. It makes it more interesting,' she explained.

I agreed with this wholeheartedly – and looked at the pictures – and did my best to banish my envious feelings. Envy is wicked, I told myself firmly. Besides, you aren't really envious of Zilla. You'll be perfectly happy at the cottage with the children. You wouldn't change places with Zilla, would you? I had just made up my mind that nothing on earth would induce me to change places with Zilla when the gong rang loudly. Immediately afterwards Daisy appeared, walking across the lawn with her hands full of sweet-peas; she was followed by Den and Alec in earnest conversation.

Zilla was intent upon her pictures so she did not see the little party until they were coming up the veranda steps. Then she saw Daisy.

'Who said you could pick sweet-peas!' she exclaimed angrily.

'We didn't,' said Daisy. 'Mums said we weren't to, so Mr. Maclaren picked them for us. He said they belonged to him.'

'Alec!' cried Zilla. 'Alec, what are you doing here? I thought you had gone to Muirfield.'

'I decided not to go.'

'I'd no idea you intended to be home for lunch!'

'I'm sorry, Zilla. I didn't think you would mind.'

'Oh well, it doesn't matter. There's plenty of food.'

'He brought us in his car!' said Daisy. 'It was lovely. We went like lightning; we passed all the other cars on the road.'

Zilla turned to me. 'I told you to come in the bus.'

'Yes,' I said. 'We intended to, of course, but your brother very kindly gave us a lift in his car.'

'It was ever so much nicer,' put in Den.

Zilla's eyes flashed. 'Alec!' she exclaimed furiously. 'How did you know they were coming?'

'It's all right,' said Alec in soothing tones.

'It isn't all right. You've no business to upset my arrangements. How did you know they were coming?' she repeated.

'Ellen happened to mention it,' replied Alec uncomfortably.

'Ellen? It wasn't her business to —'

'Don't worry, Zilla. It happened quite naturally. I was just leaving the house this morning and Ellen was there seeing me off, as she always does. She said you were expecting visitors to lunch – Mrs. Wentworth and the children – and asked if there were any strawberries in the garden. There aren't, of course, it's too early for strawberries. I advised her to make meringues.'

'Good for you!' cried Daisy ecstatically.

'That's how it happened,' said Alec.

'It was most inconsiderate of you,' declared Zilla. 'You know perfectly well that it upsets me to have all my arrangements altered at the last minute. I told Kit to come in the bus. She has come in the bus before – it's quite easy. What induced you to bring her?'

'I was there, so I thought —'

'You told me you were going to play golf.'

'I changed my mind, that's all,' said Alec. 'Let's go and have lunch, shall we?'

'I must put my sweet-peas in water,' said Daisy. 'Where can I do it, please?'

'I'll show you,' said Alec. He took her hand and they went away together. I followed with Den for his hands were dirty, and I wanted him to wash. Near the front door there was a little flower-room with a sink which suited our purposes.

Alec said in a low voice, 'I'm terribly sorry, Katherine. It's all my fault, of course – I should have phoned – but I never thought for a moment she would be upset.'

'Don't worry, it doesn't matter.'

'I expect it's because she wanted to have you to herself. I'll disappear after lunch . . . but I'll run you home whenever you like. Just say the word.'

'We'll go home in the bus.'

'No, I can easily —'

'It will be better,' I said firmly.

By this time the children had washed their hands and Daisy had put her flowers in a bowl of water, so we went into the dining-room where Zilla was waiting for us. I saw that she was still cross so I talked feverishly about Dinwell and reminded her of a match we had played against St. Leonard's. We had been beaten of course – that was inevitable – but Zilla had made a very creditable fifty and carried her bat.

The treatment was successful. She actually smiled.

After that everything went quite smoothly: Alec began to look less miserable and the children behaved well.

There was no time to think about the curious little scene until late that night when the children were in bed (Alec had disappeared after lunch, murmuring that he had some letters to write; I had chatted to Zilla while the children played in the garden and we had returned home in the bus), but late that night as I sat by the window making a summer frock for Daisy, I thought it over seriously. Why had Zilla been so furiously angry? Alec had been of the opinion that it was because he had come home unexpectedly to lunch, but my opinion was different. Zilla had been angry because he had picked us up and brought us to The Cedars in his car. I don't know why I was sure of this; but I was sure.

3

Some days later Alec called at the flat. It was eleven o'clock and I was getting ready to go out, but I asked him in and we had coffee together. He had had a letter from Simon and had brought it to show me.

'Wasn't it good of him to write?' said Alec. 'It's a delightful letter; I was sure you would like to see it.'

There was nothing in the letter that I didn't know already – Simon was a good correspondent – but I was pleased that he had written to thank Alec for all the trouble he had taken during the holidays.

'You see he's in his house eleven,' said Alec. 'They haven't chosen the first eleven yet. They'll be fools if they don't choose Simon.'

Alec looked so worried that I almost laughed. 'We must hope for the best,' I said. 'After all he's only sixteen; it's a bit young, isn't it? He's sure to be in it next year.'

'I want him to be in it this year,' said Alec.

There was a short silence while I poured out the coffee.

'I was wondering if you were doing anything special on Saturday,' said Alec as he took his cup. 'I thought you might like to come for a spin in the car. We could go to Moffat and have lunch; it's a beautiful road up the Tweed valley. I just thought . . . perhaps . . . you might like it.'

'It sounds lovely,' I said. 'The only thing is —'

'Simon said you were usually free on Saturdays.'

'Yes, usually,' I told him. 'But next Saturday I promised Aunt Liz to go to lunch with her. I have to go occasionally: I can't always dump the children on her and get away.'

'Well, what about the following Saturday? Would that be all right?'

'I thought you always played golf on Saturdays.'

'Yes, but I'd rather take you for a run. Do come, Katherine. I'm sure you would enjoy it.'

I hesitated.

'What's the matter?' asked Alec.

'It's Zilla. I don't think she would like you to take me.'

'She needn't know anything about it.'

'That seems – rather queer.'

'Oh, I know it sounds queer, but I can't tell Zilla everything. I must have some sort of life of my own. I simply must,' said Alec earnestly. 'You see Zilla doesn't like me to go anywhere without her – except to Muirfield which bores her stiff – she doesn't like me to have friends of my own; she doesn't like it when I go about and meet people or do anything different from my usual routine. For instance the other night one of my partners, Andrew Forth, asked me to dinner – he's a very good fellow with a charming wife. When I told Zilla I was going she was terribly upset because they hadn't included her in the invitation. But it wasn't a party or anything. Andrew had asked me because he wanted to discuss some business matters. I explained that to Zilla but she wouldn't listen, she wanted me to ring up and say I couldn't go . . . but I wanted to go, so I went. When I got home Zilla was very ill.'

'Very ill!' I echoed.

'Yes. She was lying in bed. She looked dreadful. She was in a sort of coma. Her eyes were wide open and staring but she didn't seem to recognise me at all. I was so alarmed that I wanted to ring up the doctor . . . but she wouldn't let me.'

I could not help wondering how she had prevented Alec from ringing up the doctor when she was in a coma. 'Wasn't Ellen there?' I asked.

'Yes, but Ellen hasn't much sympathy with Zilla.'

I hadn't much sympathy either.

'You understand, don't you—' said Alec anxiously. 'If I were to give in to Zilla, and do everything she wants, life wouldn't be worth living. If I take my own way it upsets her and makes her ill, so it's better not to tell her things, isn't it?'

Alec's problem required serious consideration. I said slowly, 'Of course it would be ridiculous to give in to her and let her rule your life – why should you? – but if I were you I should take a strong line. Say what you're going to do, and do it.'

'How can I!' he exclaimed. 'If you had seen her lying there, in a sort of coma! And it has happened before, several times. She gets upset so easily – you saw that the other day at lunch – and her nerves go all to pieces. The doctor told her she might die some day; that's what frightens me.'

I felt inclined to say that we shall all die some day. 'Did the doctor tell you that?' I asked.

'He told Zilla. I haven't seen him. Why do you ask?'

'Because it's a funny thing for a doctor to tell a nervous patient – that's all. Alec, why don't you let her take a flat in London? That's what she wants, isn't it?'

He gazed at me in absolute astonishment. 'Let her?' he said. 'I've done my best to persuade her to do it. I went the length of asking a friend of mine to find a suitable flat. It isn't easy, of course, but he's in the business and he managed to find two. Zilla wouldn't even look at them. She had a frightful attack of nerves and said I wanted to get rid of her. She was in bed for three days.'

There were various things I could have said – and wanted to say – but what was the use of saying them? Instead, I gave him another cup of coffee and promised to go to Moffat with him on Saturday week . . . if possible.

'Good!' exclaimed Alec, smiling happily. 'Splendid! Let's hope it will be a lovely day.'

'If possible,' I repeated warningly.

'What does that mean, Katherine?'

'It means I'm a mother, that's all.'

CHAPTER 9

When you are busy the days pass and quickly lengthen into weeks. It was the end of June now and Edinburgh was looking lovely, with lilac and laburnum and hawthorn flowering in all the gardens. I had promised to go to Moffat with Alec if possible but there seemed to be a sort of fate militating against the expedition. One Saturday Den was in bed with a cold, another Saturday Aunt Liz was obliged to go to Glasgow to attend a conference inaugurated by one of her charitable societies; yet another Saturday was quite impossible because Daisy's dancing class was having a display and Daisy was taking part in a Parasol Dance.

During this time I saw Alec quite often, he called in to see me about one thing or another, principally to ask for news of Simon.

One afternoon I was out shopping; I did not hurry back as I knew Aunt Liz was coming to tea at the flat and would look after the children. They were having tea together when I came in; Aunt Liz, her back as straight as a ramrod and her glasses perched upon her nose in their usual precarious fashion, the twins lounging with their elbows on the table. They were laughing so uproariously that they did not hear me come in. I stood and looked at them in amusement . . . Aunt Liz would never have allowed me to behave like that when I was a child!

Aunt Liz saw me first. 'Oh, Kit, there you are!' she exclaimed, raising her voice to be heard above the noise. 'There was a telegram for you.'

'A telegram? What was it about?'

'We don't know what it was about,' said Den.

'It was silly nonsense,' cried Daisy.

'Be quiet, children,' said Aunt Liz. 'I can't hear myself think. Kit, listen, I took the telegram and wrote it on the pad. I don't know what it means but I asked the girl three times so it must be right.'

'"What I tell you three times is true,"' said Den solemnly.

I took the pad and looked at it. The telegram had been despatched from Newcastle. There was only one word in the message – 'BLACKBIRD.'

‘Goodness, what can have happened!’ I exclaimed.

‘Don’t you understand it?’ asked Aunt Liz anxiously.

‘No. I mean why is he coming?’

‘Who is coming?’

‘Simon, of course. Something must have happened. Why is he coming home in the middle of the term? And what on earth is he doing at Newcastle?’

‘How do you know he’s coming?’

‘Oh, it’s from an old song called “Bye-bye Blackbird.” Simon used to sing it in his bath. I’ve forgotten how it goes, but it means he’s coming home to-night.’

‘Why on earth couldn’t he send a sensible message?’ demanded Aunt Liz.

‘Perhaps he hadn’t enough money,’ I said.

2

It was very late when he arrived. When I had kissed him and had merged breathless from his bear’s hug he stood back and looked at me

‘I had to see you,’ he said.

‘Simon, why? What’s the matter?’

‘I had to see you,’ he repeated. ‘I’m sorry I’m so frightfully late but I couldn’t help it. I started at six o’clock this morning —’

‘Simon! Did something happen to the train?’

‘I didn’t come by train. I walked as far as the main road and got a lift in a long-distance lorry. We didn’t come straight to Edinburgh – he had to pick up loads at different places – that’s why I’m so late. I hadn’t enough money to come by train, besides —’

‘Simon!’ I cried in dismay. ‘You didn’t just —’

‘I didn’t do a bunk – I’m not as crazy as all that. I went to Mr. Talbot and said I had to see you. At first he was a bit sticky about it so I showed him the letter and explained. Then he took me to the Head and I had to explain all over again – and he said I could go. He’s awfully human, you know, and I think he saw I was pretty desperate. I *was* desperate,’ said Simon frankly. ‘I’d made up my mind to come whether Mr. Desborough gave me permission or not.’

I gazed at him in amazement.

'Could I have some food?' he asked. 'I mean if it isn't too late. I've had nothing all day except a cup of coffee and a bun when we stopped at Newcastle. You see, I hadn't much money. Mark lent me what he could, but I wanted to tip the lorry driver, he was an awfully decent fellow, so —'

'It's all ready,' I said. 'But you'd better wash first.'

He held out his hands. 'Yes, they are a bit dirty. That lorry —'

'And your face too,' I called as he went out.

His hands seemed much larger. They were almost a man's hands, I thought, as I hurried to heat up the soup . . . and his wrists were quite thick and bony. Funny how quickly they grow! It did not seem long since his wrists had been thinner than mine, and much more delicate. Simon was almost a man, but he had gone to wash when I told him as if he had been seven years old. My first anxiety – that he had run away from school – had been put at rest but it had been replaced by another anxiety. There must be something seriously wrong if Mr. Desborough had allowed him to come.

'Look!' said Simon, holding out his hands. 'I gave them a good scrubbing – and my face too. Glory, what a feast!'

'Sit down and eat it,' I said. 'Here's some hot soup to begin with.'

He sat down and started on the 'feast.'

Now that he had washed and had brushed his hair I saw that he was very pale and there were blue shadows beneath his eyes.

'You're not ill?' I asked anxiously.

'Goodness no, just a bit tired, that's all. I've been on that rackety lorry all day – and I haven't been sleeping well.'

'Not sleeping well?'

'Thinking,' he explained.

Obviously he was hungry – quite ravenous in fact – so I waited with what patience I could until he had demolished a large plateful of cold tongue and potato salad and several slices of brown bread and butter. After that the pace slowed down and he was ready to talk. I poured out his coffee with plenty of milk and sugar in it and said, 'Well, what's it all about?'

'I had to see you,' he repeated for the third time. 'I

couldn't tell you in a letter – it's too important. We've got to discuss it. Grandfather wrote to me.'

'Your grandfather?'

'Yes. It's quite a decent letter. I'll show it to you – but I want to explain to you first that whatever you say I'm not going to Limbourne, unless —'

'Do you mean he's asked you?'

Simon nodded. 'But I'm not going, unless —'

'Why has he asked you?' I cried. 'Why ignore you all these years and then suddenly —'

'He has ignored us all,' Simon pointed out. 'It's only now – because his son is dead – that he's written to me. He says, "No doubt you will have seen the notice of your Uncle Henry's death in the papers." Well, of course I hadn't. I mean I take *The Times* at school but I don't read the births and deaths and things. I don't suppose you've seen it either; it wouldn't be in the *Scotsman*. We don't get jam like this at Barstow,' he added. 'School jam is just sweet mush. I like whole strawberries in my jam.'

'Simon, I don't understand. Why should he write to you because your uncle died? You've never even seen him, have you?'

'Well, that's the amazing thing. It really is amazing – quite fantastic,' declared Simon with his wide grin. 'Believe it or not, Mums, it means I'm the heir. The estate is entailed so, even if he wanted to leave it to somebody else, he couldn't.'

'Limbourne!'

'Yes, Limbourne. Isn't it queer?'

'But I thought,' I began doubtfully, 'I thought Henry Wentworth had a son, and if so —'

'You must be wrong about that. I mean if he had a son the estate would go to him, wouldn't it? He'd be the baronet and everything.'

'Baronet?'

'Yes, when the old man dies I'll be a baronet.'

I was absolutely speechless. As a matter of fact I knew so little about Gerald's relations that I had been under the impression that Sir Mortimer was a knight. Perhaps it would be more true to say that I had never thought about it at all.

'Comic, isn't it?' said Simon, helping himself to another large spoonful of home-made jam. 'Mark laughed like a drain when I told him.'

'That's why he wants you to go to Limbourne?'

'Yes, that's why. At first I decided not to go; why should I do what he wants? I mean, after the way he treated my father and my mother it just wasn't good enough. It wasn't *me* he wanted, it was the heir to his blue-pencil baronetcy. He wanted to make sure that the heir didn't eat peas with his knife —'

'But you ought to go, Simon!'

'Yes, I came round to that. I ought to go because of Dad. It would have been Dad, you know. It should have been him.'

I nodded.

'So then,' said Simon gravely, 'then I tried to think what Dad would have done if it had been him. The answer was easy. Dad would have gone – on his own terms.'

'On his own terms,' I repeated in bewilderment. 'What do you mean?'

'So I shall go – on my own terms. I'm in a strong position. A general in a strong position can make his own terms. See what I mean?'

Suddenly it dawned on me. Simon was in a strong position because whatever he did – or did not do – his grandfather was obliged to accept him. 'Yes, I'm beginning to see. Go on, Simon. What are your terms?'

He leaned forward and put his elbows on the table. 'I'll tell you,' he said. 'I shall do exactly as Dad would have done. Dad wouldn't have gone to Limbourne without you. Neither shall I.'

'Simon! I don't want to go!'

'I'm not surprised.'

'It's a crazy idea!' I cried. 'He doesn't want me – it's you he wants. What am I to him?'

'You're his daughter-in-law; Den and Daisy are his grandchildren – just as much as I am. You and I and the twins are a whole family. I shall make that perfectly clear.'

'Simon, listen. You must go, but —'

'I shan't go without you. Dad wouldn't have gone without you, would he?'

'No,' I said doubtfully. 'No, I don't think he would.'

'You know perfectly well he wouldn't.'

'Yes, I suppose I do – but it isn't the same.'

'It's exactly the same. If you don't go with me to Limbourne the whole thing is off.'

'Why don't you go by yourself and —'

'No!' cried Simon. 'If I were to go to Limbourne alone and – and get accepted by my grandfather it would mean a break with you and the twins. I'd belong to Limbourne in future. I won't have that at any price. I won't have it!' cried Simon desperately. 'It's all or nothing, Mums. Don't you understand?'

'Yes, I see what you mean; but you could go by yourself this time and explain. Then, if he's willing to be friends with me —'

Simon shook his head. 'No general worth his salt would give up a strong position without making favourable terms – and this is the right moment to make terms.'

'I don't want to go! It would be frightful!'

'Absolutely frightful,' agreed Simon.

'Well, then —'

'Mums,' said Simon earnestly. 'I don't blame you for being bewildered. You see I've had lots of time to think, because I haven't been sleeping well. Ever since Wednesday when I got the letter I've been lying awake and thinking. I've had hours and hours to think it all out and decide what to do. At first I couldn't see the way, it was like a fog, and then I thought of Dad and it was all quite clear. You've always told me to think of Dad – and what he would do – haven't you?'

The shadows beneath Simon's eyes were explained; he certainly had done a lot of thinking. I began to realise that his conclusions were reasonable; I began to see that I should have to face the ordeal. It would be frightful, but I should have to bear it – for Simon's sake.

'But perhaps he won't want me to go,' I said with a sudden gleam of hope.

'Then I don't go either,' said Simon promptly. 'I shall make that perfectly clear when I write to my grandfather.'

3

'Do we clear up now or leave it till the morning?' asked Simon looking at the remains of his repast.

'Leave it,' I replied. 'It's too late. We'll sit down quietly for a few minutes and then we'll go to bed.'

As we went into the sitting-room and took our places on the sofa I began to think of plans.

'When are we to go?' I said. 'We've got the cottage for August. Perhaps we could go to Limbourne in September.'

'Let's get it over, Mums. We'll enjoy the hols much more if we haven't got it hanging over us. I thought it would be a good plan for you to come south at the end of July and meet me in London – Barstow breaks up on the twenty-seventh – then we could go down to Limbourne together. Aunt Liz would have the twins, wouldn't she? We shall have to stay for a week – not longer – then we come back here, pick up the twins and make tracks for Craig-an-Ron.'

Obviously he had thought it all out. I could find no fault in his plan except that it brought the dreaded visit much too near. I would rather have put it off until September in the hope that something might happen to prevent it from taking place.

'Much better to get it over and done with,' said Simon who, apparently, had read my thoughts.

I sighed. 'Who lives there? Did Sir Mortimer tell you? He doesn't live there alone, does he?'

'Aunt Florence lives with him; she's a widow with a son and a daughter. The son is at Cambridge, but he'll be at Limbourne when we go . . . and there's an old lady, Sir Mortimer's sister. I suppose she's my great-aunt. She lives there too.'

The idea of so many people was terrifying – all strangers and rich – with lovely clothes. They would gaze at me to see what I was like. 'I haven't anything fit to wear,' I exclaimed.

'Rubbish, it doesn't matter what you wear.'

'Of course it matters – and for you, too. We may be poor relations but we can't go to Limbourne in rags.'

'M'm, I see what you mean. We shall have to keep our end up. I suppose they'll dress for dinner, which means I shall have to launch out into a dinner-jacket. I shall take the money out of my Post Office Savings. That's what to do.' He smiled and added, 'I've been saving up to buy a gun. You didn't know that, did you?'

All the evening I had been feeling that there was something different about Simon and now, quite suddenly, I knew what it was. 'You're very sure of yourself,' I said.

He nodded. 'I've grown up, that's why. It's a funny

sort of feeling to grow up suddenly. This time last week I was thinking about cricket, wondering if I'd be chosen to play in the Haileybury Match, but now it doesn't seem to matter awfully. It's because I've done such a lot of thinking. I've grown up,' repeated Simon. 'When we go to Limbourne I shall call you Katherine.'

'You can't!'

'Yes, I can. Listen,' said Simon earnestly. 'You're only eleven years older than I am, so —'

'Twelve,' I said firmly. 'I was nearly nineteen when I married your father and you were seven.'

'Call it twelve if you like. The point is you look very young indeed so it would be absurd for me to call you "Mother." I shall call you Katherine.'

I was too tired and bewildered to argue with him.

'Poor darling, you're half asleep,' said Simon. 'Off you go to bed. I'll tidy up and shut the windows.'

I went meekly. It seemed as if Simon and I had changed places.

CHAPTER 10

The next day was Saturday so there was no need to get up early and see the children off to school, but I had to phone to Alec and put off our jaunt to Moffat for about the sixth time. I explained that Simon had been given the week-end by Mr. Desborough.

'Lucky young dog,' said Alec. 'We didn't get week-ends off when I was at school. No, of course you can't come.'

'I'm frightfully sorry, Alec. You'll go to Muirfield, won't you?'

'Yes, don't worry, I'll get a game all right.'

It was after nine when we sat down to breakfast. Simon appeared in pyjamas and dressing-gown. I had intended to let him sleep but he said the smell of frying bacon had wakened him.

Den and Daisy welcomed him with enthusiasm as usual and as usual Simon was delightful with them. He produced two little parcels from the pocket of his dressing-gown – a knife for Den and a little red purse for Daisy.

'Cheap and nasty,' said Simon to me, *sotto voce*.

They were cheap, of course, but the children were charmed with the presents.

There was a lot of chat at breakfast. The children wanted to know if Simon had been chosen to play in the first eleven.

'Not definitely,' he replied.

'Will you be chosen?' I asked.

'It depends on Mark – we're both in the running. I'm erratic, sometimes I can hit up a pretty good score; Mark is steady and a bit stodgy. They'd rather have Mark, really, but he has a groggy elbow. If Mark's elbow is better by Wednesday week I'm out. That's the position at the moment.'

'I hope Mark's elbow won't be better!' exclaimed Daisy.

Simon smiled. 'I hope it will,' he said. 'At least . . . yes, I hope it will. As a matter of fact I've been rubbing it for him every night with some stuff the doctor gave him.'

'Good!' I said.

'Oh well, he's a good pal,' said Simon.

Later, when Simon had dressed, the three went out together to pay a visit to the Castle. They wanted me to go with them but I was still feeling tired and I had a lot to do. I reminded Simon that Aunt Liz would be expecting us to lunch and he promised to be back in time.

I was busy in the kitchen when Aunt Liz arrived.

'Well, has he come?' she asked.

I kissed her and said, 'Yes, late last night.'

'Has he run away from school, or what?'

'Mr. Desborough gave him permission to come.'

'What has he been up to?'

I looked at her as she stood there, frowning balefully, and realised that what Simon had said was true. Aunt Liz didn't like him.

'What has he been up to?' she repeated. 'Some silly scrape, I suppose.'

'That isn't fair!' I exclaimed. 'You haven't heard yet —'

'I can see you're worried,' she interrupted.

'Yes, I'm a bit worried. I want to tell you about it and ask your advice.'

I made some coffee and carried the tray into the sitting-room.

'Well, let's hear all about it,' said Aunt Liz more amiably.

Aunt Liz had been a rock of strength to me since I was a small child. I was very fond of her and I admired her integrity. She was prickly at times, but if you were in any kind of trouble she would stand by and see you through so it was not difficult for me to tell her 'all about it.'

She sat there, listening intently, drinking coffee and smoking a cigarette in an expendable cardboard holder. It was a pleasant sight to see Aunt Liz smoking, she looked comfortable and happy; many of her friends had given it up but Aunt Liz said she had smoked for forty years and she saw no reason why an old woman should deny herself small pleasures.

When I had told her everything she sat in silence for several minutes.

At last she said, 'Kit, I don't like it.'

'Neither do I, Aunt Liz.'

'I wonder what Gerald's reaction would have been.'

'But, darling, if Gerald were here there would be no problem at all.'

'I didn't mean that,' she explained. 'I meant what would he have advised you to do under the present circumstances.'

I was silent.

'Don't you understand?' she said earnestly. 'He knew his family – which we don't. He must have spoken to you about them and told you what they were like.'

'He seldom spoke of them – they had cast him off, you see – he never blamed them or said anything bitter about them.'

'He never regretted the breach? Never showed any desire to revisit his old home?'

'We were happy,' I said defensively. 'We were – we were sort of complete with each other and the children. He was interested in his work and . . .'

'Go on,' said Aunt Liz.

'Well, it's just something he said. I had forgotten about it but you've made me remember. It was one night in winter, the wind was howling in the chimney. The children were in bed and we had made up a lovely fire. We sat and chatted; Gerald always told me about his research, it was terribly interesting, you know. Then suddenly Gerald said, "I've never been so happy in my life."'

'He wasn't happy when he was young,' said Aunt Liz thoughtfully.

I swallowed the lump in my throat and said, 'No, not happy.'

'Why?'

'He was odd-man-out in his family. Henry and Florence were much older than he was and there was another brother – much younger and rather spoilt. Nobody appreciated Gerald. He wasn't good at games or shooting or hunting or – or anything like that. They all thought he was cowardly and stupid. It was only when he went to Oxford that he discovered he was short-sighted.'

'Do you mean Gerald didn't know he was short-sighted?'

'He never realised that other people could see better than himself.'

'How extraordinary!' exclaimed Aunt Liz.

I nodded. It had seemed extraordinary to me. Gerald had never discovered before that the reason he couldn't shoot or hunt or play games like the rest of his family was because of his poor eyesight. He had discovered it one day when he was out for a walk in the country with Antony Finch. Antony had said suddenly, 'Good lord, look at that chimney-pot! It's as crooked as sin. It'll topple over on to someone's head if they don't have something done to it. I wonder if the people know. We'd better go in and tell them about it.' Gerald had followed Antony up the path and had stood there while Antony explained. The owner of the house came out into the garden, followed by his wife and son. They all looked up at the chimney-pot and talked about it and decided to ring up the builder.

'What on earth is the matter with you?' asked Antony as they walked on. 'You never opened your mouth. Are you dumb?'

'I've just discovered that I'm blind,' replied Gerald.

At first Antony couldn't believe that Gerald had been unable to see the chimney – or at least had seen it only as an indefinite blur – but when he found that his friend really was myopic he took him to London to see a famous oculist in Welbeck Street. Gerald told me that when he got his spectacles it was a revelation. The world suddenly became large and incredibly beautiful. 'But it wasn't only *that*,' Gerald had explained when he was telling me about it. 'The best thing of all was that I realised why I was such a hopeless duffer at everything. I wasn't really stupid, I was only blind.'

When I had explained all this to Aunt Liz she said again, 'How extraordinary!' and added. 'I can scarcely believe it.'

'Well, it's true. His spectacles not only changed the world for him, they banished the inferiority complex which had ruined his life; they gave him confidence in himself.'

'Oh, I can understand that, of course. I'm quite idiotic without my spectacles. What I can't understand is why his disability wasn't discovered before. His parents can't have taken much interest in him.'

'They didn't. I've told you that already.'

Aunt Liz pulled herself together. She said, 'Well, we must decide whether you're to go or not. Is Sir Mortimer ready to be friendly with you?'

'That isn't really the point,' I replied. 'The point is Simon won't go without me. He says his father wouldn't have gone without me.'

'You told me that,' nodded Aunt Liz. 'To me the point is whether or not Simon should go near the place. Gerald got away and never wanted to go back, so he can't have liked it much. Would Gerald have wanted his son to go to Limbourne?'

We seemed to have come round to the beginning of the argument; I could find nothing else to say.

'There must be something queer about the whole set-up,' declared Aunt Liz as she stubbed out the end of her cigarette. 'It's useless for you to ask my advice; I can see you've made up your mind to go. I only hope you won't regret it. What about clothes?'

'I thought my blue would do for the evenings if I had it cleaned and pressed.'

'It won't,' said Aunt Liz firmly. 'If you're determined to go to that place you must have decent clothes; two evening dresses and some cotton frocks. You can have your tweed suit cleaned and pressed – it doesn't matter if tweeds are slightly shabby – but you had better have a couple of new shirts. I shall give you the outfit.'

I began to thank her.

'There's no need for all that nonsense,' declared Aunt Liz. 'You've got to have decent clothes; I don't want you to disgrace our family . . . which, in its own way, is every bit as good as theirs.'

CHAPTER 11

Simon was obliged to go south on Sunday; I sent him by train; I could not bear the idea of him 'hitch-hiking' all over the country. After he had gone I thought of all sorts of things that we should have discussed and arranged . . . but there had been so little time. There had been no time for Simon to answer Sir Mortimer's letter. We had made several rough drafts – none of which seemed satisfactory – and eventually Simon had stuffed them into his pocket and said he would write when he got back to school. 'Mark will help me,' he said. 'Mark is a whizzer at letters.'

The week passed slowly; I was restless and depressed. One moment I found myself hoping that Sir Mortimer would agree to receive me at Limbourne, the next moment I found myself hoping that he would not.

On Friday night Alec rang me up to ask if to-morrow was all right for Moffat and at last I was able to say yes.

'Yes,' I said. 'Unless something frightful happens in the night.'

'It won't,' said Alec. 'I have a feeling in my bones that we'll make it this time, and the weather forecast is good.'

He rang off and I put the receiver down. Immediately the bell rang again – and it was Simon.

'Mums, can you hear me?' he said. 'Mr. Talbot is letting me use his phone. It's all right about Limbourne. Can you hear me?'

'Yes, of course I can hear you. Do you mean you've had a letter from Sir Mortimer?'

'Yes, this morning. It's a nice letter – I'll send it to you – he says he will be very pleased to have you. That's good, isn't it?'

'Yes, very good,' I said, without enthusiasm.

'You sound awfully far away,' said Simon's voice rather sadly.

'It's all right,' I told him. 'I shall be seeing you quite soon – meeting you in London as we arranged. What about the match? Is Mark's elbow better?'

'Yes, it's better – and I'm glad.'

2

There was rain in the night and it was a cloudy morning, but before Alec called for me the clouds were clearing and the sun had begun to shine warmly. He had opened his car and, as he tucked me in with a light rug, he asked if it would be all right.

'If you feel too much draught I can easily shut it,' he said.

I told him I liked lots of air.

He was in good spirits and I wished that I felt more cheerful; poor Alec had waited so long for this famous run that he deserved a high-spirited companion. I did my best to respond adequately but my efforts did not deceive him.

'Something wrong, Katherine?' he asked.

'Not really; just silliness,' I said. 'Simon rang up last night and my fate is sealed. Sir Mortimer has asked me to Limbourne.'

'It won't be as bad as you think.'

'Perhaps it will be worse.'

'Nonsense, Katherine!'

We talked about it off and on as we wended our way through the busy streets. I had told Alec the whole story and he thought I was doing the right thing. He pointed out that our position was strong – as Simon had said – and that, putting aside all questions of feeling, it was to the advantage of the inhabitants of Limbourne to be friendly with the heir to the property.

'But I'm not the heir,' I said doubtfully.

'If they offend you, they offend Simon; so, unless they're perfect fools, they'll all be extremely kind and pleasant to you.'

Being a lawyer Alec took a lawyer's point of view, serious and matter-of-fact, and I found it comforting after listening to the vague and gloomy prognostications of Aunt Liz. By the time we had passed Fairmilehead and were out in the country I was feeling a great deal better. We took the road to West Linton and fairly whizzed along the straight stretch across the moor . . . but after that Alec slowed down as he wanted me to enjoy the scenery.

'Mark's elbow is better,' I said.

'Oh,' said Alec in a disappointed tone.

'It's good, Alec. Simon is glad, which makes it splendid.'

'Friendship is better than cricket, you think?'

'A hundred times better.'

We had taken a left-hand turn at West Linton and were now drifting with effortless and noiseless ease along a winding road which led past meadows full of buttercups and placidly grazing cows.

'When are you going to Limbourne?' asked Alec.

'Much too soon. In other words the end of this month when Barstow breaks up. Then we come back to Edinburgh to collect the twins and all go off to the cottage for August. It's awfully kind of Zilla to —'

'August!' exclaimed Alec. 'But you're going to Craig-an-Ron in September. Zilla has let it to the Mitchells for August.'

'No, Alec. It's August – really it is.'

He was silent for a few moments, negotiating a hairpin corner which led on to the main road.

'Are you certain?' he said at last. 'You see Zilla told me it was September. I thought you would be in Edinburgh in August and made plans accordingly.'

'Plans?'

'Yes, I planned to be in Edinburgh. I thought we could have some expeditions – picnics with the children – and Simon could have more coaching. I could arrange for him to play in a match; I was making plans about that. But if you're to be away —'

He sounded so disappointed that I felt sorry. I explained the reason Zilla was allowing us to have the cottage in August, making the story as amusing as I could.

Alec was not amused. 'Oh, I know she was annoyed about the dogs and I wondered why she was letting them have it again.'

'She isn't.'

'No. But why did she tell me a . . . I mean why did she say what she said?'

Perhaps I could have answered his question, or perhaps not. 'Don't let's worry,' I said. 'Let's enjoy ourselves. This is a delightful little village.'

'Broughton. Yes, it's pretty, isn't it?' said Alec gloomily.

Soon we came to the youthful River Tweed, sparkling and glittering joyously in the bright golden sunshine. Some of the peaceful reaches of the little river were incredibly blue, reflecting the sky. I pointed this out to my companion and added that if somebody painted a picture of that gorgeous colour people would say it was unreal.

The road wound along beside the river, going uphill all the way until we came to its source, then we passed over the top. All around us were the rolling hills, one behind the other as far as eye could see; they were like huge green billows in a rough Atlantic gale, which had suddenly frozen into a state of immobility. Later they would be clad in heather, purple as the robes of a king. A turn in the road brought us to The Devil's Beef Tub. Then we drifted slowly downhill and the valley opened before us, a pleasant peaceful vale in which the Annan wandered gently on its course. Far away in the distance, so hazy and indefinite that they looked like clouds, were the English Hills.

'Moffat,' said Alec, pointing down at the little town nestling in snug comfort on the floor of the valley, the spires of its churches half-hidden in trees.

3

Presently we found ourselves in the wide High Street and looked about us for a place to have lunch.

'I know nothing about the hotels, I'm afraid,' said Alec. 'Which do you fancy? Shall we say "Eeny, meeny, miny, mo"?'

We said it, laughing at the joke, and soon we were sitting at a small table in a pleasant dining-room enjoying a simple but well-cooked meal.

There was still a little cloud on Alec's spirits and I was sorry for this. He had been looking forward to the day so much that I wanted him to forget his disappointment and enjoy himself. I was grateful to him for making plans for Simon; I was grateful for the good advice he had given me and last but not least for this delightful day. I was enjoying it tremendously and, if I could manage it, Alec should enjoy it too, so I set to work to entertain him. It was not very difficult. I soon had him laughing at my silly jokes.

The dining-room was fairly full but not overcrowded. I

was sitting with my back to the wall so I had a good view of our fellow diners. Half-way down the room there was a couple who caught my interest, chiefly because they seemed to be interested in me. The man was middle-aged with a bald head and a very red face, the woman was younger. Her face was dead-white with large brown eyes and orange-coloured lips. She would not have attracted attention in London, where heavy make-up is fairly common, but here in this country hotel she was completely out of place; as foreign to her surroundings as a bird of paradise.

'What are you looking at?' asked Alec.

'Two people,' I said. 'They seem interested in me, but I never saw them before. The look sort of Londony – if you know what I mean.'

'I expect they are admiring you, which isn't surprising.'

'It would be very surprising indeed,' I retorted. 'The lady looks as if she had just emerged from a beauty parlour. Don't look, Alec.'

'I don't want to look; she doesn't sound my type. You'll have coffee, won't you?'

'Yes, please,' I said.

A few minutes later the 'Londony' couple got up and went away.

The afternoon was not so warm, there were big clouds coming up from the west, but the country was beautiful – perhaps even more beautiful than in blazing sunshine. Alec took a different road back to Edinburgh, a lovely road up the narrow valley of Moffat Water where high steep hills rose up on either side. We stopped at The Grey Mare's Tail and walked up a rocky path to look at the waterfall splashing down into a dark and somewhat sinister-looking pool. Then on we went to St. Mary's Loch; its large expanse was dark, reflecting the cloudy sky, and little waves were whispering on the shore. Half-way down the loch we left it, turning up the hill called Paddy Slacks, a delightful name, then down through the ancient town of Peebles and so back to Edinburgh and home.

PART TWO

CHAPTER 12

Simon had made all the plans for our visit to Limbourne and they worked out well. On leaving Barstow he had spent two nights at Wimbledon with the Butterfields so that he could do some necessary shopping in London. I had come south by the night train and we had met at Harrods for lunch. We were now seated in a first-class compartment of the afternoon train to Wandlebury.

The first-class tickets seemed to me an unnecessary extravagance.

'It isn't,' said Simon firmly. 'They'll probably meet us at the station. You said we weren't to go to Limbourne in rags.'

After that we were silent.

The compartment was empty except for ourselves so we could have talked quite comfortably, and there were all sorts of things I wanted to ask Simon, but I was unable to speak a word. Simon also was dumb; was he as frightened as I was? I began to wonder what would happen when we arrived at Wandlebury. Sir Mortimer had said we would be met at the station, but I had no idea how far it was or when we would arrive; worst of all, if any of Simon's relations came to meet us how should we know them?

The train slowed down and stopped.

'Come on, Mums! It's Wandlebury. I'll get a porter,' exclaimed Simon, opening the door and leaping out.

I saw to my dismay that it was a large station, thronged with all sorts and kinds of people hurrying hither and thither, jostling each other in their endeavour to keep clear of trucks laden with luggage. How could we possibly find anyone in this chaos? The only thing to do was to collect our belongings and get out of the train. I had just managed to drag one suitcase off the rack when an oldish man in chauffeur's uniform appeared at my elbow.

'Allow me, madam,' he said and took the suitcase out of my hand.

'Oh, thank you!' I exclaimed in surprise. 'Are you —'

'I'm Nitkin, madam. It's a bit of a crowd to-day. I doubt if Mr. Simon will be able to get a porter but we'll manage all right ourselves. There's a big meeting at the town hall, that's what all the fuss is about. I did ought to have brought Hurrell along to help with the luggage but I never thought. . . .'

Nitkin had got all the things out of the compartment when I saw Simon, shouldering his way through the crowd.

'No porters anywhere!' he declared.

'We can manage ourselves, Mr. Simon,' said Nitkin and, taking a suitcase in each hand and a large cardboard box (belonging to Simon) under one arm, he set off down the platform. He was a wizened little man with spindly legs so he must have been stronger than he looked.

'Who is he? How did you get him?' asked Simon.

There was such a noise now – doors banging, people shouting, whistles blowing – that I couldn't reply. Besides I hadn't the slightest idea how I had got him. For all I knew he had materialised out of thin air. I signed to Simon to pick up his kit-bag and we followed as quickly as we could.

A Daimler was waiting in the station-yard. Nitkin stood beside it. He opened the door as we approached. 'I'm sorry there wasn't no porters,' he said. 'There usually is. Sir Mortimer would be vexed if he was to know you'd carried the luggage. I did ought to have brought Hurrell. . . .'

'It's all right, don't worry,' said Simon cheerfully.

'Nitkin,' I said, 'how did you know us in all that crowd?'

He smiled. 'Easy. I've bin at Limbourne most of my life. When Mr. Gerald came home for the holidays I always met him – if I could. Mr. Gerald liked me to meet him. When he was going away he used to say, "You'll meet me, won't you, Nitkin?" Sometimes I couldn't (if Sir Mortimer wanted me for something) but I managed it usually. When I saw Mr. Simon jump out of that there door onto the platform I thought it was him for a minute – gave me quite a turn, it did.'

Simon and I got into the car and Nitkin drove off.

There was no glass between us and Nitkin; it was not that kind of car. I put my mouth close to Simon's ear and murmured, 'He doesn't want us to tell Sir Mortimer that you had to carry your kit-bag.'

Simon grinned and replied in the same manner, 'We'd be stinkers if we let on, wouldn't we?'

We drove a long way through pleasant, wooded country and lush meadows and small villages. There were old-fashioned cottages with gardens full of flowers. Nitkin chatted as we went along, pointing out various objects of interest (I was tired after the night journey so I lay back in my corner and let Simon reply). Nitkin asked after Mr. Denis and Miss Marguerite and seemed pleased to hear they were in good health.

'You did ought to have brought them along with you, Mr. Simon,' he said. 'But you'll bring them next time. It'd be nice to see children about the place again. I could pick up a couple of nice ponies for them – quiet ones, you know. I like children. We never had none of our own. Me and my wife lives in a little cottage in the stable-yard. It's convenient for looking after the horses but not very up-to-date. My wife complains a good deal, she thinks we did ought to have one of the other cottages – me having bin here forty years – but I don't know as I'd like to change.'

'Horses – for riding?' asked Simon eagerly.

'Bless you, yes, Mr. Simon! Two nice hacks, but Mr. Lance and Miss Anthea don't care for riding so it's a job to keep them exercised. Time was when we had six in the stable – Sir Mortimer was keen on hunting in his younger days – but it's different now. Major Wentworth likes a ride when he comes down from London but he doesn't often get leave.'

'Major Wentworth?' asked Simon.

'Your Uncle Peter, Mr. Simon,' explained Nitkin. He added, 'The horses are really my proper job. It's Hurrell that drives the car – usually, that is.'

Simon glanced at me and winked.

'That's Hurlestone Manor,' said Nitkin as we swept past a tall, stone gateway with curious-looking stone beasts sitting on the tops of the pillars. 'The D'Artingtons are a very old family – came over here with William the Conqueror, they say. It's only about six miles before we get to Limbourne. I expect you'll be glad to get there, Mr. Simon, after your long journey.'

Simon had not had a long journey, but he did not explain this.

Presently the road ran up a steep hill and then turned sharply along a ridge from which we could look down upon parklands set with fine old trees.

Nitkin stopped and pointed. 'There, Mr. Simon,' he said. 'That's Limbourne.'

The house lay in a hollow; we looked down upon it as if from the air. It was built in the form of the letter L; the roof was gabled and there were rows of tall chimneys; rows of tall windows, shining in the afternoon sunshine.

'How old is it?' asked Simon after a little silence.

'Well, I don't rightly know,' admitted Nitkin. 'There's been a house there for hundreds of years and it's always belonged to the family but it was rebuilt in Sir Mortimer's grandfather's time so there's only a bit of the old house left. My grandfer used to talk to me about it when I was a lad – he remembered the building. He said it was foreigners that came; they set up camp and built it.'

'Foreigners?' asked Simon.

'That's what they called them in the village. They weren't blacks or such-like, Mr. Simon. It was just that they didn't belong to this part of the country. Very narrow the village people were in those days,' added Nitkin with a pitying smile.

We drove on down the hill. The village lay on our right; to the left were big wrought-iron gates which opened of their own accord as we approached.

'Oh, I say!' exclaimed Simon in amazement.

'It's sort of mysterious,' agreed Nitkin with a chuckle. 'Sir Mortimer had them made like that so he doesn't have to wait for them to be opened. It's a neat contraption. Sir Mortimer likes to have everything just right. You should see the Home Farm, Mr. Simon. It's a model – really it is.'

'Does my grandfather run it himself?'

'Not to say *run* it. There's Mr. Marsh, you see. Mr. Marsh looks after all the farms – estate agent, they call him – but Sir Mortimer keeps an eye on things and woe betide if things aren't just O.K. Mr. Marsh is a very capable gentleman but he's getting on in years and there's talk in the village that he's to have an assistant – some say it's to be Mr. Lance. The village is an awful place for gossip.'

While Nitkin had been talking we had been running smoothly along the avenue, with a hedge of rhododendron bushes on one side and a wide expanse of parkland on the other; we were now in sight of the entrance. There were three broad steps up to the door with a pillar on either side.

'Here we are, Mr. Simon,' said Nitkin; he gave a little toot with his horn, the door opened and a man ran down the steps to fetch the luggage.

In the doorway there was a tall thin woman with grey hair. She came forward and said, 'Good afternoon, Mrs. Wentworth. I'm Mrs. Sillett, the housekeeper. I hope you had a good journey. Good afternoon, Mr. Simon.'

We shook hands with her.

Mrs. Sillett chatted in a friendly manner as she led me up the broad staircase; she explained that Mrs. Godfrey always rested in the afternoon and that tea would be ready in half an hour. I had not much time to look about me but I saw thick carpets and beautiful old furniture. The walls were hung with oil paintings, chiefly portraits. I stopped suddenly in front of one, which depicted a tall elegant man with powdered hair; he was wearing a brocade coat with wide skirts and there was a sword at his side.

'That's the fifth baronet,' said Mrs. Sillett. 'It's a beautiful picture, isn't it?'

'Beautiful,' I agreed . . . but it was not the beauty of the picture which had arrested me, it was the amazing resemblance to Gerald.

Mrs. Sillett walked on and opened a door. 'This is your room, Mrs. Wentworth. I hope you'll be comfortable here. If there's anything you want just ring the bell. The head housemaid is out this afternoon but Betty is a very nice girl.'

It was a lovely room with tall windows looking out over a flower garden and beyond to the park which sloped upwards to a wooded hill.

Mrs. Sillett opened another door and disclosed a bathroom. 'I'm afraid you'll have to share it with Miss Anthea,' she said apologetically. 'But Miss Anthea isn't at home just now and we aren't sure what day she'll be coming.'

'Would there be time for me to have a bath before tea?'

'Yes, of course,' she replied. 'You needn't hurry. It won't matter if you're late for tea. Sir Mortimer is very particular about punctuality, but he doesn't bother about tea and Mrs. Godfrey won't mind. Just come down to the drawing-room when you're ready.' She paused at the door and added, 'Mr. Simon's room is at the other end of the passage; Bassett is looking after him.'

CHAPTER 13

The bathroom was luxurious; I spent some time in the scented water, soaking the tiredness out of my limbs, so when I had found a frock and dressed and brushed my hair it was later than I expected. However I felt a great deal better and Mrs. Sillett had said I needn't hurry.

When I was ready I went out onto the landing and had another, more careful, look at the portrait of the fifth baronet. Yes, it was exactly like Gerald. Gerald in fancy dress! Somehow the sight of Gerald's portrait hanging on the wall in this strange house gave me confidence. The house had not been strange to Gerald; he had been born here and had lived here when he was young. Sad to say he had been unhappy here . . . but perhaps he would be pleased if he knew that some day it would belong to his son.

I went downstairs and found my way to the drawing-room and opened the door quietly; tea was laid on a round table near the window and before it sat a small plump woman with fluffy grey hair. She was eating a large piece of chocolate cake with obvious enjoyment and was so intent that she did not hear me come in. She was Mrs. Godfrey, of course.

For a few minutes I hesitated, then I went forward and said, 'I'm Katherine.'

'Oh!' she exclaimed. 'Oh yes, of course! How do you do?'

We shook hands solemnly.

Her eyes were pale blue, slightly protruding, and she had a double chin. Could this woman really be Gerald's sister? It was almost incredible.

'I expect you're tired,' she said vaguely. 'Where would you like to sit? The boys had a cup of tea and went out together. I hope you aren't annoyed about it.'

'Of course not! I'm sorry I'm late for tea, but —'

'Well, I told them they had better wait and ask you if you minded, but Lance doesn't pay any attention to what I say.' She poured out my tea, offered me a cucumber sandwich and helped herself to another piece of chocolate cake. (It crossed my mind that Mrs. Godfrey would soon be the possessor of a third chin.)

'I don't mind in the least,' I assured her. 'It will be nice for Simon to have a walk with his cousin.'

'Oh – yes – they're cousins!' she said – as though it were a new idea to her. 'Lance is very clever,' she added.

'How nice,' I said. It was an idiotic thing to say, but I was nervous and uncomfortable.

Mrs. Godfrey seemed quite placid and unperturbed. She continued to munch her cake in silence.

At last I said, 'What is Lance going to do?'

'He's at Cambridge.'

'Yes, but afterwards?'

'Oh, he's coming home. He's going to manage the estate. It was Henry's wish. Henry was very fond of Lance. Henry was a widower, you know; he had one son . . . but Morty was killed two years ago in a plane accident. It was a great grief to us all when Morty was killed.'

'Yes, it must have been.'

'But of course you know all about it, don't you?'

'No, I'm afraid I don't know much about the family.'

'Oh, how funny!' said Mrs. Godfrey. 'I thought you would have heard about poor Morty. It was after Morty was killed that Henry came to me and said he would look after Lance. Those were his very words, "you needn't worry, Florence, I'll look after Lance." I knew he meant Lance was to take Morty's place.'

Mrs. Godfrey had finished her tea by this time. She took out a large work-bag and began to work at a piece of tapestry with coloured wools.

'It was all very sad,' she continued. 'There was a good deal of trouble about it. You see Papa had an idea that he ought to find out whether Gerald had any children (I mean after Morty was killed), but Henry said to wait. Henry was thinking of getting married again, and she was young, so they might have had children. Then poor Henry had a heart attack. It was very alarming – very alarming indeed – but he recovered and seemed quite well. Then he had another . . . and died.'

'How dreadful!'

'Yes, dreadful,' said Mrs. Godfrey, taking out her handkerchief and wiping her eyes. 'He worked too hard. He was a barrister, and very clever, so of course he had lots of briefs. I was very fond of Henry. Henry and I were always friends; we were friends when we were children.

Gerald was quite different; he liked to go his own way. Papa was very angry when he wrote to say he was going to marry that Italian girl.'

I had listened half-dazed to all this information, which had been poured out so rapidly that there was no chance for me to reply . . . but now she paused for a minute while she scrabbled about in a tangle of wool to find the colour she needed.

'Why shouldn't Gerald marry her?' I exclaimed.

'It was a *mésalliance*,' she replied. 'Of course some Italians are well-born, but that girl was just a peasant. Papa made inquiries.'

'They were very happy,' I said defensively.

'He should have married Rosamund Ferrars,' declared Mrs. Godfrey. 'That's what Papa wanted him to do. If he had married Rosamund and settled down and looked after the estate none of this would have happened.'

Here was plain speaking indeed, but the extraordinary thing was I could not be angry with the woman. There she sat, scrabbling about in her tangle of wools like a kitten, saying unforgiveable things in her vague wuffly voice . . . and I was not angry.

I said quite calmly, 'No, I suppose it wouldn't; and it wouldn't have happened if your family hadn't broken off all relations with Gerald.'

'How could you expect anything else?' asked Mrs. Godfrey in mild surprise. 'He couldn't have brought that Italian girl to Limbourne. *Noblesse oblige*, that's what Papa always says. If you belong to a family like ours you can't do exactly as you like. I was in love with a young man when I was eighteen, but Papa wouldn't have it, and afterwards I saw he was right. You see poor Tom had no money so we should have been very uncomfortable. Then I met Lawrence. It was all done properly. Papa arranged it and we were married. Lawrence had a beautiful place in Essex – not as large as Limbourne, of course, but very delightful – and we lived there happily till Lawrence died. Unfortunately he wasn't a very good business man – Lawrence I mean – so when he died the place had to be sold. By that time Mamma was an invalid so I came home. The children were young and Papa was a little strict so it was difficult at first.'

'It would have been nicer for you to have a house of your own, wouldn't it?'

'Oh, no! You don't understand. I couldn't have afforded to have a nice house. Henry explained it to me and said it would be much more comfortable for me to come home.'

'I like to be independent,' I told her.

She had been stitching industriously, but now she raised her head and looked at me in astonishment. 'Independent?' she said as though she had never heard the word before.

'I like to live my own life,' I explained. 'My aunt asked me to live with her, but I refused because I wanted to bring up my children in my own way. You can't do that if you live in somebody else's house.'

'It's Papa's house,' said Mrs. Godfrey. 'You haven't seen Papa yet, have you? When you see him you'll understand. He's very kind if people do as he says. Perhaps it's just as well to warn you,' she added, looking at me with her faded blue eyes.

There was a short silence.

'Children are different nowadays,' continued Mrs. Godfrey. 'Lance and Anthea never listen to me, but we were brought up to obey our parents. It says in the Bible, "Children obey your parents" so that was what we did . . . all except Gerald, who was rather queer.'

I had not been angry before but now, suddenly, I was angry – so angry that if I had said anything I would have said a great deal. Sometimes a sort of devil gets inside me. He was inside me now and I was forced to wrestle with him. I reminded myself that it would be the height of folly to quarrel with the woman; Simon and I had come here to make friends with these people and for Simon's sake I must try.

'I don't know why these wools get into such a tangle,' said Mrs. Godfrey peevishly. 'I never can find the colour I want.'

My devil was vanquished now, so I said, 'Shall I disentangle them for you?'

She smiled and handed me the tousled mess.

'Tell me about your daughter,' I suggested as I began my task.

'Wait till you see her!' exclaimed Mrs. Godfrey. 'She's so pretty – just like me when I was eighteen and poor Tom fell in love with me. Anthea is staying with some old family friends but she rang up a little while ago and said she was coming home to-morrow afternoon. I asked if she wanted to be fetched but she said someone would bring her. Poor Anthea is a little unsettled just now; she wants to go to an art school in London – she's very good at painting – but of course that would be quite absurd. Papa says it will be much better for her to stay at home and learn how to manage a house. Mrs. Sillett will teach her. It will be so useful when she's maried.'

'Is Anthea engaged?' I asked.

'Well, not exactly. Papa thinks she's a little too young. There's Giles D'Artington, of course. He's a good deal older than Anthea but it would be very suitable. Hurlestone Manor is quite near; you must have passed it on your way from Wandlebury. Then there's Edward Ferrars – that's where Anthea is staying now. I expect he will bring Anthea home to-morrow, so you'll see him. Papa would like her to marry Edward, but there's no hurry, of course.' She threaded her needle with rose-coloured wool and added, 'I think it would be a good plan for her to marry Simon.'

'Simon!' I echoed in amazement. 'You don't mean – Simon?'

'Why not?' she said vaguely. 'It would settle everything so comfortably, wouldn't it?'

'Simon is just a child!'

'Oh, I don't mean at once – Anthea is only eighteen, you know – I just mean some day. I don't want Anthea to marry for *quite* a long time.'

'It's out of the question, Mrs. Godfrey – it's absurd – Simon is only sixteen and very young for his age. He hasn't a thought for girls or – or anything like that.'

'Oh,' she said thoughtfully. 'Yes, perhaps he is a *little* too young for Anthea – and of course they're cousins, aren't they?'

'We needn't discuss it,' I said firmly. 'It isn't – sensible. When Simon is old enough to marry he shall choose for himself.'

'He couldn't have anyone nicer than Anthea,' said Anthea's mother complacently. She added, 'I expect Papa will choose someone nice for him when he's old enough.'

It was ridiculous to allow myself to be upset by her foolish prattle! All the same I was so upset that my heart was thumping madly. They intended to absorb my Simon into their family; they intended to choose a suitable wife for him. They had failed with Gerald, they were going to try the same thing with Simon. Mrs. Godfrey was the silliest woman I had ever met, but she was an echo of the Wentworth family.

'It's so nice for us to have had this little chat,' said Mrs. Godfrey. 'We've got to know each other, haven't we? I suppose I shall have to call you Katherine; you're my sister-in-law, aren't you? It seems funny.'

It seemed very funny indeed. I looked at her and wondered if I could ever manage to call her Florence.

She folded up her work and put it into the bag. 'Dinner is at eight and Papa likes us to be down in plenty of time. I always rest before dinner. Just ask Mrs. Sillett for anything you want.'

Obviously I was supposed to retire to my room.

2

There was plenty of time before dinner so I unpacked and dressed in a leisurely manner. I wondered where Simon was and what he was doing.

Presently there was a tap on my door and Simon came in; he was ready except for his tie.

'Goodness!' I exclaimed in amazement.

'Am I all right?' he asked, surveying himself in the long mirror.

He was very much all right. The formal evening clothes became him admirably and fitted him like a glove.

'Where did you get them?' I asked. 'They must have cost the earth.'

'Hired,' he replied, grinning mischievously. 'It was far too expensive to buy evening clothes, besides I shall probably grow. Mark came with me and helped me. We went to a place where they had dozens and dozens of suits. I tried on six jackets before the chap was satisfied with the fit. Pretty good, isn't it?' he added, turning round slowly to give me a view of his back.

'Wonderful,' I said.

He held out the black tie and I tied it for him. I had often done the same little service for Gerald. It seemed strange to be doing it for Simon.

'I had a very interesting time,' he said. 'Lance took me for a look round. It's a lovely place, Mums. Everything is in apple-pie order. Lance has a super motor-bike, he showed it to me.'

'Have you seen your grandfather?'

'Not yet. Lance said that he spends a lot of time in the library and nobody must disturb him "on pain of death." Lance calls him "The Bart" – but not to his face, of course. He seems a bit of a Tartar.'

'Yes, I gathered that.'

'Lance is frightened of him, but I'm not going to be frightened,' declared Simon defiantly. 'Why should I be frightened? He asked me to come here – and I've come. You aren't frightened, are you?'

I didn't answer.

'Don't be silly, Mums. He can't eat us.'

I smiled and replied, 'No, he can't eat us . . . and you look simply marvellous in those clothes. If he isn't proud of you he ought to be.'

'Yes, I see what you mean,' agreed Simon. 'It's all awfully funny, isn't it?'

Funny was not the word I should have chosen.

'Have you got a nice room?' I asked.

'Not as nice as this, but very comfortable. It looks out onto the yard. I suppose you had tea with Mrs. Godfrey – I mean Aunt Florence – she's a frightful ass, isn't she?'

CHAPTER 14

When we went down to the drawing-room Sir Mortimer was there alone. He was standing on the hearth-rug with a glass of sherry in his hand – a tall old man with dark eyebrows and a jutting nose. His hair was thick and grey; it looked as if it was powdered. I had a feeling that he was out of place in the modern world.

Sir Mortimer greeted us courteously; he gave us each a glass of sherry and inquired if we had had a comfortable journey. Simon had declared that he was not going to be frightened of his grandfather but I could see by his heightened colour that he was not very comfortable. I had expected to be terrified – but was not. In fact I found myself talking to the ogre quite naturally, answering his questions about the children and explaining that I had left them with my aunt.

'Denis and Marguerite,' he said. 'Why didn't Gerald give them family names?'

'I don't believe he ever thought of it,' I replied.

There was a slight constraint in the air. (Perhaps Sir Mortimer realised that I had almost said, 'Why should he have given them family names?')

'You must bring them with you next time you come,' he said.

I smiled. 'That's very kind, but you might find them rather much for you, Sir Mortimer. They're quite young and not very civilised.'

'They're natural children,' declared Simon, rushing to their defence. 'They're full of beans and very amusing – especially Daisy – nobody could help liking them.'

Sir Mortimer turned, 'You're fond of your half-brother and sister?'

'Yes, of course. We're a whole family, you see. We're . . . sort of complete,' declared Simon, becoming very red indeed.

'Ho, you're "sort of complete," are you?'

'Yes, sir,' said Simon.

Sir Mortimer was staring at Simon with his dark piercing eyes. 'You're like your father,' he said at last.

'I'm glad,' declared Simon. 'I couldn't be like anybody better – or finer.'

There was a short silence while they stood and gazed at each other. Simon was nervous but he stood his ground. I realised that he had determined to say what he had said; to make it perfectly clear from the very beginning that we were 'a complete family' and that he admired his father more than anybody else on earth. Those were Simon's terms, he had stated them plainly, Sir Mortimer could accept or reject them . . . but in reality Sir Mortimer had no choice. After a short silence he turned and picked up his glass.

'Lance took me for a walk round,' said Simon. 'We saw the horses. Nitkin said to ask you if I could ride.'

'Most certainly. Order them whenever you please, but Nitkin had better go with you. Tell him I said so.'

'Oh, thank you! Yes, I'll tell him,' said Simon, smiling

with delight. 'I haven't ridden for some time, but Nitkin said one of the horses was fairly quiet so I had better have the quiet one – just until I get used to it.'

'Nitkin will see to that,' returned Sir Mortimer with a twinkle in his eyes.

It was encouraging to see that the ogre had a sense of humour.

We chatted for a few minutes longer, then Sir Mortimer glanced at the clock on the chimney-piece; he took from his pocket a thin gold watch and compared them. 'It's eight o'clock,' he said. 'Ring the bell, Simon.'

The bell should have been a long bell-pull, hanging from the ceiling – or so I felt – instead of which it was a modern electric push-bell. Simon did as he was told and a few moments later an elderly manservant opened the door and announced that dinner was served. Sir Mortimer offered me his arm and we went in.

As we took our places at the table Lance appeared and slid into his chair as unobtrusively as possible. 'I'm sorry, Grandfather,' he murmured.

'Where is your mother?'

'Mother was – delayed. She'll be down in a minute.'

This was my first glimpse of Lance – it was not the moment for an introduction. He was tall and slender with a small head and a pointed nose. His hair was light brown and sleek, brushed back from his forehead. Unlike the rest of the family, Lance was not memorable, he could have passed unrecognised in a crowd.

We had just begun our soup when Mrs. Godfrey came in, looking hot and flustered. 'Oh dear, am I late?' she said. 'I couldn't help it, Papa. Anthea rang me up to say she's coming home to-morrow afternoon. We needn't send for her, someone will bring her – Edward, I expect. That's what delayed me.'

'How strange,' said Sir Mortimer acidly.

'What is strange, Papa?'

'Strange that Anthea's telephone call should have delayed you. She rang up at four o'clock. I heard you speaking to her in the morning-room as I was crossing the hall.'

There was silence. The soup plates were removed and fish was served.

It was a strangely uncomfortable meal. Mrs. Godfrey twittered to me in a low voice, trying to explain that the telephone call from Anthea had delayed her because she had been obliged to speak to Mrs. Sillett about Anthea's room. I pretended to believe her. Lance and Simon conversed spasmodically in almost inaudible murmurs. Sir Mortimer was silent, he seemed to be lost in a trance. The food was delicious. (I was glad to see that Simon thought so too.)

'What did you say, Simon?' asked Sir Mortimer suddenly.

'Oh!' exclaimed Simon in surprise. 'Oh – well – I was just t-telling Lance that I'd like to go to Peru. That's all, sir.'

'Why Peru?'

'To see those temples and things.'

'What do you know about them?'

'Not very much, really. I'd like to know more about those Maya people who built them. There was a book in the school library; that's where I read about them, and I just thought . . .' His voice died away.

'What did you think?' inquired Sir Mortimer.

'I thought I'd like to see those temples. They looked enormous in the pictures.'

'Well, go on,' said Sir Mortimer. 'They looked enormous – was that why you wanted to see them?'

'There were carvings in stone, beautiful carvings and very intricate; there were jade axe-heads and brooches inlaid with turquoise. I wondered how the people made them without proper tools. They had no wheels either. People in other parts of the world had wheels. It seems funny.'

'Funny?' inquired Sir Mortimer with a puzzled frown.

'I mean strange,' said poor Simon. 'I mean they were so clever at building and carving; why didn't somebody invent wheels?'

'Hmph,' said Sir Mortimer – and that was all.

Absolute silence descended upon the dinner-table.

Fortunately for everyone the meal was nearly over. The table was cleared and a decanter of port was placed before Sir Mortimer. Mrs. Godfrey looked at me and we rose.

'You can stay, Simon,' said Sir Mortimer.

Lance opened the door for his mother and me. He followed us out and shut it firmly behind him. 'Phew!' he exclaimed. 'Simon stuck his neck out, didn't he?'

'I'm afraid Papa is a little displeased,' said Mrs. Godfrey.

I was speechless. The whole thing was quite absurd. It was cruel to lead the child on and then leave him floundering.

I should have liked to rush back into the dining-room and rescue Simon . . . but of course I couldn't. I was obliged to follow the others into the drawing-room and sit down as if nothing had happened. I took the tangle of wool from Mrs. Godfrey's work-bag and continued the task of sorting out the colours.

Lance brought my coffee cup and put it on the table beside me. 'It isn't my fault,' he said. 'I warned Simon to be careful. The Bart likes leading you up the garden path and making you look a fool. It's just one of his endearing little ways. When we're alone like this it doesn't matter so much, but it's rather painful if we happen to have guests. It isn't any good to be angry with me, it was Mother's fault.'

'My fault!' cried Mrs. Godfrey.

'You were late and you made it worse by that silly lie. If you tell a lie to the Bart it has to be a good one – absolutely watertight.'

'Really, Lance —'

'I'm not angry with anyone,' I said loudly.

'Good,' said Lance, smiling at me. 'Let's consider the subject closed. I want to ask you something: am I supposed to call you Aunt Katherine – or what?'

I smiled and said he could call me what he liked.

'Simon calls you Katherine, so I suppose —'

'Nonsense!' exclaimed Mrs. Godfrey. 'I never heard of such a thing.'

'You would have heard if you had listened,' declared Lance. 'When we were talking at tea-time Simon referred to his step-mother several times by her Christian name. The odd thing about you is that one never knows whether you're listening or not. Sometimes it's a bit awkward.'

'That isn't the point,' said Mrs. Godfrey.

'I thought it was,' replied Lance in injured tones. 'I thought it was obvious that if Simon is permitted to call her Katherine – which incidentally is a delightful name – there is no reason why I shouldn't do so.'

'She is your aunt,' said Mrs. Godfrey stubbornly.

'But she doesn't look like an aunt,' complained Lance.

'That doesn't matter, dear. An aunt is an aunt. You've never heard me call Aunt Prissy anything but Aunt Prissy.'

'Aunt Prissy looks like an aunt. Incidentally where is Aunt Prissy? I haven't seen her all day.'

'She was feeling a little out of sorts so I advised her to stay in bed,' explained Mrs. Godfrey. 'She is going away for a little holiday on Wednesday – as you know. We want her to be quite well before Wednesday. She would be so disappointed if she couldn't go.'

'I doubt it,' said Lance. He turned to me and explained. 'You see, Katherine, Aunt Prissy wanted to go to a large hotel at Eastbourne for a fortnight, so my grandfather arranged for her to go to a small hotel in Tunbridge Wells.'

'It will be much more peaceful and quiet for her,' said Mrs. Godfrey hastily.

'Oh, definitely,' Lance agreed. 'Only Aunt Prissy doesn't want peace and quiet – she gets enough of it at home – she wants to see a bit of life.'

'It's a very comfortable hotel,' declared Mrs. Godfrey. 'Aunt Prissy will enjoy her visit and it will do her a great deal of good.' She added in a low voice, 'Lance dear, just peep out and see if Grandpapa and Simon are still in the dining-room.'

'They aren't,' he replied. 'I don't have to peep. I heard them come out a few minutes ago. They crossed the hall and went into the library.'

'Lance has such sharp ears,' said Mrs. Godfrey complacently. 'He has always had sharp ears. When he was a baby we had to creep about on tiptoe; he wakened at the slightest sound.'

'I'm going out,' said Lance. 'Good night, Katherine, you're wasting your time trying to disentangle Mother's wools; she'll have them in a worse mess in half an hour.'

'Lance, where are you going?' cried his mother.

But Lance had gone.

2

The hour I spent with Mrs. Godfrey in the drawing-room was extremely trying. She twittered on interminably about the difficulties of running the household, at one moment complaining bitterly that Lance and Anthea never listened to her and the next moment assuring me that they were the height of perfection. Lance was so good at rowing that he was sure to be chosen to row in the Cambridge boat and Anthea was so pretty that she was certain to make a good marriage. I was worried about what was happening to Simon – shut up in the library with his grandfather – and could scarcely listen to what she was saying. Luckily she could talk incessantly without any intelligent reply.

At last I could bear it no longer and told her I should like to go to bed, explaining that I had travelled south from Edinburgh the night before.

'Didn't you sleep well?' asked Mrs. Godfrey in surprise. 'I always think sleepers are so comfortable.'

'No, I didn't sleep well,' I replied (omitting to add that I had sat up all night in a crowded second-class compartment).

'Oh, what a pity! It's only ten o'clock. Papa will be coming in later; he'll be surprised if he finds you've gone to bed.'

'Papa's' feelings did not affect me in the least. I said good night and escaped.

My head was aching intolerably. I drew back the curtains and opened the window and sat there looking out. The garden was bright with moonlight; across the lawn lay a shaft of silver and beyond, beneath the trees, it was dark as black velvet. A bed of white flowers glimmered like stars and their heavy scent was wafted up to my window in an occasional puff of air.

At first I was too upset to notice the beauty of the night. I felt quite desperate. We had come here for a week – but we couldn't stay. A week of this would be unbearable. How could we escape? Should I wire to Aunt Liz and ask her to ring up and say we must go home at once? It seemed the only way.

3

For a long time I sat at my window looking out, and gradually the peacefulness of the moonlit scene soothed me. My head ceased to ache and I began to feel better. I had no idea what time it was – probably very late – but I did not want to go to bed until I had seen Simon. If I had known where his room was I could have gone there – but I didn't know and I couldn't go wandering about this strange house looking for him.

I was still sitting there, wondering what to do, when there was a tap on my door and Simon came in.

'All in the dark!' he exclaimed.

'It isn't dark. The moonlight is lovely – and peaceful. Simon, this is a dreadful house.'

'Dreadful?' he asked in surprise. 'Oh, you mean dinner? Yes, I was rather silly, wasn't I? But Grandfather didn't really mind. You see he knows a lot about those Maya temples, he's actually been there, Mums. Isn't it amazing? He took me into his library and showed me books about them. He lent me this one to read.' An enormous tome was dumped upon my lap. 'Look, Mums! Look at the pictures! I'll turn on the light so that you can see them properly. Aren't they interesting? Here's a gorgeous piece of carving! Grandfather actually saw it when he was there – saw it with his own eyes – and here's another. . . .'

When I had admired the pictures sufficiently, and listened to an account of Sir Mortimer's adventures in Peru, I inquired whether anything else had been discussed. 'You were with him for hours,' I pointed out.

'Yes, I know. You see he started talking about Limbourne and the family; he's terribly keen on the family. It goes right back to Henry Wentworth who lived in Ireland and was made a baronet by James the First. Then later the family came to England and were given these lands by Charles the Second – and they've been here ever since. In the old days the place was called Limbourne Royal because it was the gift of a king. He showed me the family tree – they were nearly all called Mortimer or Henry or Gerald, but in seventeen-five there was a Peter who did something very important. I'm a bit vague about it all,' admitted Simon. 'There was such a lot of it – and Grandfather doesn't like you to ask questions – but I'll study it some time and get it clear. I shall have to,' he added with a sigh.

'I suppose you will.'

'Mums,' said Simon. 'All the time we were talking I was thinking of Dad and wishing he were here. It's too much for me all of a sudden like this. It's a sort of – a sort of burden. If Dad were here he could have shouldered it all right, and I could have learnt it gradually. That would have been the natural thing.'

'I know, darling. It would have been the natural thing. You're too young, that's the trouble. Try not to let it be a burden. Sir Mortimer will probably live for years so you needn't think about it too much.'

'But that's just it,' explained Simon. 'He wants me to think about it. He wants me to come here when I leave school and learn all about it from Mr. Marsh.'

'Simon!' I exclaimed in dismay.

'Don't you like the idea, Mums?'

'No,' I cried. 'Besides, you can't do it, can you?'

'You mean Butterfields?' said Simon doubtfully. 'But Mr. Butterfield said I needn't decide about that until I left school . . . and it seems sensible, doesn't it? You see all this will belong to me some day. I can't really believe it,' declared Simon with a dazed air. 'I simply can't believe that all this – will belong – to me.'

I couldn't really believe it either.

'So you see,' he continued, 'if it's all going to belong to me – some day – then I ought to learn to look after it properly. That's what Grandfather said.'

'Yes, I suppose you ought. The only thing is . . .'

'What?'

'Well, Mrs. Godfrey seems to be under the impression that Lance is going to help Mr. Marsh and learn to manage the property.'

'Oh, I know! Grandfather explained that. It would have been quite a good plan while Uncle Henry was alive. Lance could have managed it for Uncle Henry. But now that it's going to belong to me – some day – I'm the person who ought to learn to manage it. You needn't worry about Lance because he doesn't want to.'

'How do you know?'

'He told me this afternoon when we were walking in the grounds. I asked him what he was going to do and he said, "I've got to do what I'm told. When I leave Cambridge I've got to come home and trot round after Marsh." I said, "But what do you want to do?" and he laughed and said, "Not that, anyhow."'

'Do you want to do it, Simon?'

'Oh goodness, I don't know!' cried Simon in perplexity. 'How does a fellow know what he wants to do? I thought Butterfields sounded an interesting business; it seemed a good opening and it would have been fun to be with Mark . . . but now this has happened.'

'Yes, this has happened.'

'It seems sensible, Mums.'

I was forced to agree.

'Grandfather was very decent. At first I thought he was an absolute monster, but he isn't, really. You've just got to be careful not to put his back up. He explained what I shall have to do when I come here; I shall get a salary as assistant to Mr. Marsh and I can have a couple of hunters – he was mad on hunting when he was young. I can have a car, too, if I want. Well, I should jolly well think I'd want a car if I could get it!'

Here was bribery.

Simon laughed excitedly. 'Who wouldn't want a car? I could buzz up to Edinburgh and see you whenever I liked, couldn't I?'

'Yes, you could.'

'And that wasn't all,' continued Simon. 'I told him about Den – and how clever Den was – and he said he would pay for Den's education. Of course he ought to pay for it. He's Den's grandfather, isn't he?'

'Yes,' I said wearily.

Simon looked at me in surprise. 'You don't like it, Mums?'

'Not awfully, Simon. It seems so strange. For years and years he took no notice of us; he didn't even bother to find out whether we existed – and now he seems all over us.'

'Because I'm his heir, that's all. Because when he's dead Limbourne will belong to me. That's why he's doing it. Limbourne means a lot to him; it has belonged to the Wentworths for hundreds of years. It isn't because he has taken a liking for me or anything like that; it's because he wants to do the best thing for Limbourne . . . and obviously the best thing for Limbourne is to have its future owner here on the spot, learning about the best ways to take care of it.'

This was all true. Perhaps it was foolish of me to feel so unhappy.

Presently Simon rose to go. 'I hope it'll be fine tomorrow,' he said. 'I'm going to ride. Grandfather has made arrangements with Nitkin to take me at ten.'

'That will be nice.'

'Lovely,' said Simon. He kissed me and said good night.

CHAPTER 15

Nitkin brought the horses round at a few minutes before ten and I went out to have a word with him and to explain that Simon was not an experienced rider.

'That's all right,' said Nitkin. 'I'll look after Mr. Simon. Don't you worry, madam.'

I was not really worrying; I trusted Nitkin. As a matter of fact he was the only person at Limbourne that I trusted. I had liked him yesterday; this morning I liked him even more. Yesterday I had felt there was something slightly comic about the little man in the chauffeur's coat and cap, but to-day he looked absolutely right in his well-cut breeches and gaiters and ancient bowler hat. Horses were really his job.

Simon came out attired in riding-breeches and boots which he had borrowed from Lance. He was excited and happy. We stood and chatted for a few minutes and admired the horses. Simon produced an apple from his pocket and asked Nitkin if he might give it to one of them.

Nitkin smiled and cut it in half with his penknife. 'Fair's fair, Mr. Simon,' he said.

When Simon had given them the apple he mounted nimbly enough and Nitkin altered his stirrup leathers. 'This is Dark Rosaleen and that's Postiche,' said Nitkin. 'I call them Rosie and Posie – it's easier. We'll go through the plantation and back by the village, it's a nice ride and not too far for your first day. We don't want you stiff as a board to-morrow.'

Simon laughed and trotted off down the avenue.

'He's got a good seat,' declared Nitkin. 'It's just practice he wants. My, he *is* like Mr. Gerald! I taught Mr. Gerald to ride and he liked riding, but he was always a bit nervous. I wouldn't say your young gentleman was nervous.'

I watched them ride away. Nitkin had said they would come back by the village; that was because he wanted 'the village' to see him out riding with Simon!

When I had watched them out of sight I began to wonder what I was supposed to do. Mrs. Godfrey had not appeared at breakfast – did she expect me to hang about and wait for her? It was a lovely morning, sunny and breezy; the country lay before me, green and pleasant. I decided to go for a walk and explore. I went through the park and discovered a little path which led through a grove of oak trees, and presently found myself on the hill which I had seen from my bedroom window. Here the wind was stronger, ruffling the grasses, creaking and groaning amongst the scattered clumps of trees. I climbed up steadily; larks rose from the ground and soared into the sky, singing joyfully; sheep stopped cropping the grass and gazed at me in mild surprise. The wind blew through my hair.

Soon I had reached the top and finding a sheltered nook between two boulders, sat down upon the turf. I had come so quickly that I was breathless . . . it was only then that I realised that my morning walk had been a flight.

Yes, quite definitely it had been a flight from Limbourne. I had rushed to the hill-top to get away from the place. The atmosphere of Limbourne was unhealthy. I had had a glimpse of what lay beneath the surface and a glimpse was enough. There was physical comfort in abundance, the house was full of beautiful things, but there was no love, no kindness, there was none of the gentleness and consideration which makes the smallest cottage a home.

I thought about Gerald. What Nitkin had said was true: he had lacked self-confidence. Gerald had been passed over and treated as of no account; he had been 'a hopeless duffer' at hunting and shooting, useless at games. Now that I had seen his home I understood Gerald better; I saw why he had escaped and rushed into marriage with a girl who could give him love. I saw why he had never wanted to come back. Gerald had been gentle in spirit.

There was gentleness in Simon, also, but Simon's upbringing had been very different, he had been surrounded with love from his earliest days, so he had developed naturally and was happy and fearless . . . but was it right that he should come and live here?

Although the hill where I was sitting was not very high it gave a bird's-eye view of the country; there were little woods and meadows and fields of different colours separated by green hedges. There were several farms, neat and well-cared for, with outbuildings and huge stacks in orderly rows. Limbourne itself stood in its green park with fine trees; the gardens were a blaze of colour, the glass panes of the greenhouses glittered in the morning sunshine. To the left was the village, a cluster of little cottages and one or two larger houses surrounded with gardens. The church was Norman with a square tower and a flagstaff, it stood in a green churchyard with the vicarage close by.

For a long time I sat and looked at the peaceful English scene, wondering how much of it belonged to the Wentworth family.

The sky had been blue and clear but now a white cloud appeared from behind the woods; it grew larger, towering higher and higher, changing shape every moment, until it became so huge that it seemed to dwarf the landscape. The wind was colder now and I found myself shivering in my thin cotton frock and cardigan; I sighed and rose and went slowly back to Limbourne down the hill.

2

The path by which I had come led through the wood, but I went back by a shorter way through the vegetable garden, and when I opened the gate I saw Sir Mortimer sitting on a wooden seat near the greenhouses. It would have been natural to go forward and speak to him, but the whole atmosphere of Limbourne was unnatural and it was affecting me. For a moment or two I hesitated, wondering whether I should go back; then he saw me and waved.

He rose as I approached and asked if I had enjoyed my walk.

'Yes, it was lovely,' I replied. 'I went to the top of the hill. There's a fine view from there. I wondered how much of it belongs to you.'

'Most of it,' he said, smiling. 'You can see Hurlestone Manor behind some trees, if you know where to look, and of course the village and the church are on D'Artington property – they were here long before we came – but all the lands to westward are ours: farms and woods and plantations.' He looked at me with his piercing eyes and added, 'I'm glad you've seen it, Katherine, because now you can realise better that there's a great deal of valuable property to look after. Did Simon tell you my plans?'

'Yes, he did . . . but he's very young, Sir Mortimer. He

feels that it's rather too big a responsibility, coming suddenly like this.'

'I'm glad to hear it. A boy should have a sense of responsibility.'

'I don't want him to feel it a burden.'

'A burden? No, he should feel it to be a privilege.'

'He's very young,' I repeated.

'Of course he's young, but he will grow older. Simon is still at school and will remain there for another eighteen months at least. All I want is for him to come to Limbourne when he leaves school and learn about his family and the property, so that when the time comes he will be ready to step into my shoes. I'm a perfectly fit man . . . it may be years before Simon has any of the responsibilities which you seem to dread.'

'Yes, of course! I didn't mean —'

'Is it unreasonable to want Simon to be trained to carry on the family traditions? I venture to think it is eminently reasonable.'

'I suppose it is, but I'm not – not happy about it.'

'Not happy? I very much doubt if you have the power to prevent Simon from accepting my offer.'

'Oh, I shan't try!' I cried. 'You don't understand, Sir Mortimer. I want the best possible life for Simon. It's just – it's just that it all seems – so strange.'

'Come now, Katherine,' said Sir Mortimer, smiling at me kindly. 'I want you to be happy about it, because it will be so much better for everyone concerned. Think about the matter seriously, pull yourself together and face the facts. What do you want for Simon?'

I was silent. I did not know what I wanted.

'You see,' said Sir Mortimer. 'You can't answer that. Simon told me about his idea of going into Butterfields and working in their warehouses; it's a sound firm, I admit, and probably would have been a very good opening for a young man without any prospects, but in Simon's case it would be the height of folly. He would learn nothing there that would be of use to him in later life. Surely you realise that what I propose is the best possible plan for Simon?'

Put like that, nobody could fail to realise it. 'Yes,' I said. 'Yes, I realise that. But – but you'll be good to him, won't you, Sir Mortimer?' I smiled and added, 'He's very precious, you know.'

'That won't be difficult,' he replied. 'I like Simon; he's a fine boy.'

'I'm glad you think so.'

'Meantime we'll say nothing about our plans . . . to anyone. You understand, Katherine?'

I understood perfectly. 'I don't like secrets, Sir Mortimer.'

'Just for the present,' he said firmly. 'Later I shall explain the whole matter to my daughter, but not now. I have my reasons.' He hesitated for a few moments and then continued, with mounting fury, 'Florence is a fool. She wanted Lance to go to Cambridge because his father had been there. I should never have given my consent – never. What is Lance doing at Cambridge? Wasting his time and my money! Work is anathema to Lance, he does as little as he possibly can. He rows!' said Sir Mortimer scornfully. 'His chief aim in life is "to get into the boat" and even that miserable goal is beyond him because he can't be bothered to train. Lance is too fond of his creature comforts. He's soft. He'll never be any good at anything. If he had gone in for cricket I could understand it better – but rowing! Sitting in a contraption they call a boat with other young men as brainless as himself – rowing! Is that a proper sort of training for life?'

'Rowing requires skill and endurance and – and discipline, doesn't it?' I said uncomfortably.

'Discipline!' exclaimed Sir Mortimer. 'Lance doesn't know the meaning of the word. He should have gone into the Army – as I wanted him to do – Sandhurst would have knocked him into shape.'

Sir Mortimer had become so red in the face with rage that I thought it best to change the subject. 'Shall we see Major Wentworth while we're here?' I asked.

'Peter? No, I'm afraid not. He's at the War Office at present. I wrote and told him that you and Simon were coming and I wanted him here, but he can't get away. Absolute nonsense! In the old days an officer was treated as a gentleman, not tied to his desk like a clerk. Of course Peter comes down to Limbourne when he can. He loves the place and he's interested in the family.'

Quite suddenly I realised that if it had not been for Simon the baronetcy and the property and all the rest of it would have gone to Peter . . . and obviously, from the way he had spoken of his youngest son, Sir Mortimer would have liked that. Peter had always been his father's favourite. Only Simon stood in Peter's way. But no, there was Den. The thought of Den relieved my mind, though why it should do so I could not imagine.

'Peter always manages to come for the pheasant shooting.' continued Sir Mortimer. 'He's a very fine shot – takes after me in that. I don't suppose Simon has done any shooting?'

'No.'

'Just as well,' said Sir Mortimer cheerfully. 'He won't have any bad habits to unlearn. Perhaps you would like to walk through the greenhouses, Katherine. I want to have a look at the orchids and speak to Medlam about the vine.'

We went through the greenhouses, which were extremely warm and full of exotic plants. The orchids were very strange, more strange than beautiful in my humble opinion. Sir Mortimer gave some directions to the head gardener, then he took out his thin gold watch and looked at it.

'Twelve o'clock,' he said. 'I shall have to go in. Marsh wants to see me about one of the plantations. I suppose you think me a gentleman of leisure, Katherine, but I can assure you there is a great deal to do in a place like this. I like to see everything in perfect order. When I go over to Hurlestone Manor it annoys me to see the property going downhill. The D'Artingtons have no excuse for their neglect, they have plenty of money.' He turned to the gardener and added, 'Show Mrs. Wentworth the rose-garden and cut some good specimens for her.'

With these words Sir Mortimer walked away quickly and disappeared into the house.

3

Like everything else at Limbourne, the rose-garden was a model of tidiness. There were grass paths between the beds – paths of velvet smoothness – and there was not a weed to be seen. I thought suddenly of my daughter and her remark: 'Funny sort of garden with no daisies!' She would think this a very funny sort of garden, there was no doubt of that.

The roses grew in orderly array, each little bush perfect in shape, bearing perfect blooms. I asked Medlam how he managed to attain such perfection and he explained that there was a nursery behind the beech hedge so that any bush which was not perfect could be replaced.

'It's beautiful, isn't it, ma'am?' said Medlam, looking round with complacency. 'It's the best rose-garden in the country.'

It was beautiful of course – roses are always beautiful – but to my mind it was too tidy and neat. The roses did not look happy; perhaps they were aware that if they failed in their duty to their owner they would be rooted out, thrown on the rubbish heap, and replaced by another rose-bush from the nursery garden behind the tall beech hedge.

Although Medlam had received orders to 'cut some good specimens' for me he seemed reluctant to carry out his task. He stood there fingering his knife and looking round in a doubtful way.

'What about cutting them in the nursery garden?' I suggested.

The idea commended itself to Medlam . . . but still he hesitated.

'I expect there are lovely roses there too.'

'Oh yes,' he agreed. 'Lots of them, but Sir Mortimer sed as how I was to cut them in the rose-garden – that's the trouble.'

'But the nursery garden is really a part of the rose-garden so it would be just the same, wouldn't it?'

His brown leathery face crinkled into an enormous grin, and without another word he escorted me through a gate in the hedge. Here there were more roses, dozens and dozens of little bushes, their exquisite flowers filling the air with fragrance. There were red and white and pink and yellow roses in prodigal confusion.

'I'm afraid it isn't very tidy, ma'am,' said Medlam apologetically. 'It isn't really for show, you see. We just plants them here temporary until they're wanted.'

'I like it,' I said. 'The roses here look natural and happy and their scent is far sweeter.'

Medlam did not deign to reply to this piece of nonsense. He set about cutting my bouquet without more ado.

CHAPTER 16

Mrs. Godfrey had expected Anthea to arrive at three o'clock and had been restless and miserable since half past two. It was half past four and we were all having tea in the drawing-room (with the exception of Sir Mortimer, who despised afternoon tea) when a car was heard approaching. I was sitting near the window so I saw a red sports car drive up to the door with a girl and a young man in it.

Mrs. Godfrey rushed into the hall to meet them. Lance strolled over to the window and looked out.

'Hallo, it's Oliver Wade!' he said. 'That won't be popular with the parent. She was banking on Ferrars bringing Anthea over from Minston. I wonder what happened.'

I said nothing. I had listened for hours to Mrs. Godfrey's eulogies of Edward Ferrars, of his passion for Anthea and of his suitability as a husband for her child. 'So rich, you know, and such a lovely place. Of course the family isn't very old – Edward's grandfather made his money in jam – but that doesn't matter so much nowadays, does it?'

In a few minutes the new arrivals came in and were introduced. I had heard so much about Anthea that I was interested to see her. She was a pretty creature – small and fairy-like with dark curls and brown eyes – but her prettiness was a little spoilt by a curious wavy sort of mouth outlined in brilliant carmine.

'I expected you at three,' said her mother. 'I was very worried, Anthea. I thought something must have happened.'

'Three?' asked Anthea. 'Why three? I didn't say three, did I?'

'I thought you said three.'

'You must have muddled it. I couldn't possibly have said three. The Ferrars had a luncheon party. I shouldn't be here now if Oliver hadn't rescued me.'

'So kind of you, Oliver,' murmured Mrs. Godfrey. 'Perhaps you would like to stay to tea.'

'Of course he's staying to tea,' said Anthea as she sank into a chair. 'He had better stay to dinner too – if there's anything fit to eat.'

'Yes, that will be lovely,' agreed Mrs. Godfrey in tepid accents.

'Can't be done,' declared Mr. Wade.

'Oh, Oliver, why not?' asked Anthea.

'No clothes.'

'It doesn't matter —'

'It does matter,' interrupted Mr. Wade. 'Sir Mortimer likes his guests to be properly clad. I shall never forget the occasion when I appeared at the baronial table arrayed in tennis gear.'

'Well, never mind,' said Mrs. Godfrey hurriedly. 'You must have a good tea, Oliver. Where would you like to sit?'

Rather surprisingly Mr. Wade chose to sit down beside me on the sofa near the window. He said, 'Anthea has been telling me about you, Mrs. Wentworth. It must be interesting coming to Limbourne for the first time. How does it strike you?'

'It's a beautiful place.'

'Yes, and so well kept. Most of the Stately Homes of England are a bit dilapidated these days, aren't they? My home used to be stately, but it's going downhill fast.'

'What a pity! Can't you do anything about it?'

'My father says I must marry money,' said Mr. Wade. 'It sounds all right, of course, but so far I haven't been able to carry out his suggestion. There isn't much money walking about ready to be snapped up by an impecunious land-owner . . . and, if you do happen to meet it, ten to one it's extraordinarily unattractive in other ways. Don't you agree?'

I smiled at this nonsense and said, 'I'm afraid I don't know anything about it.'

'In the old days it was different,' he continued. 'In the old days if a gentleman needed a little money to bolster up his estate he could do a spot of buccaneering on the high seas. It was the done thing, nobody thought any the worse of him. As a matter of fact – strictly between ourselves – that was how my ancestor made his pile. He built a large and extremely inconvenient mansion and founded the family.'

'In the days of Queen Elizabeth?' I suggested.

'Those were the days,' agreed Mr. Wade with a sigh. 'But nowadays buccaneering is out of fashion.'

'How right you are! Nowadays all that a high-spirited gentleman can do to mend his fortune is to write a best-seller.'

'Is that what you're doing?'

Mr. Wade nodded gravely. 'I haven't really got down to it yet but it shouldn't be too difficult.'

'I should think it might be very difficult indeed.'

'Not if you go about it properly. Obviously the right way to begin is to buy all the best-sellers and study them carefully.'

'A best-seller must be original, Mr. Wade.'

'You dismay me, Mrs. Wentworth,' he declared. 'I have laid out money I can ill afford on these books; surely if I study them carefully I shall discover what it is that makes them sell like hot cakes.'

I couldn't help laughing. 'Why not make hot cakes?' I suggested.

So far his face had been serious, but he actually laughed at that. We were both laughing when Lance came towards us with a plate of sandwiches.

'You seem to be having a good joke,' said Lance.

'Mrs. Wentworth has been advising me how to write a best-seller,' explained Mr. Wade.

'I've told you how not to write it,' I pointed out.

'Yes, that's true. There has been nothing constructive about her advice. I believe Mrs. Wentworth is of the opinion that piracy or highway robbery would be more lucrative.'

'Nonsense!' I exclaimed. 'I told you to make hot cakes.'

'You're both mad,' said Lance as he offered me the plate of sandwiches. 'Don't have one of these, Katherine,' he added. 'Mother told me to hand them round, but I've just had one and they're very nasty.'

'Thanks for the warning,' said Mr. Wade. 'I don't want a nasty sandwich either. You can go and get us two large pieces of chocolate cake. Hurry up about it, Lance, or your mother will finish the lot.'

Mr. Wade and I went on talking; he was clever and amusing, there was something curiously attractive about his personality. We were still talking – half sense and half nonsense – when Anthea came across the room and sat down beside us on a pouffe.

'Oliver, listen,' she said, breaking into the conversation. 'It's all right about dinner. The Bart is going over to Hurlestone Manor to play chess with Lord D'Artington so he won't be here and nobody else minds about your clothes. You will stay, won't you?'

Anthea had made it obvious by her manner that I was *de trop* so I rose and gave her my place on the sofa. She took it without a word of thanks and as I moved away I heard her say earnestly, 'Do stay to dinner, Oliver. We could have a club meeting to settle about next week.'

2

In the absence of Sir Mortimer, dinner was a different sort of meal. The three young people talked incessantly about various friends and acquaintances and laughed heartily at jokes which were incomprehensible to a stranger. Simon and I were obliged to sit in silence.

Mrs. Godfrey was silent too, and I could see that she felt ill at ease. At first I thought she was distressed at the bad manners of her son and daughter, but presently she leant forward and whispered to me, 'Papa wouldn't like it.'

'Wouldn't like what?' I asked.

'Oliver . . . but I couldn't help it, could I? Really, it's rather naughty of Anthea.'

'You couldn't help it,' I agreed. 'You can explain to Sir Mortimer how it happened.'

'Oh no!' she exclaimed in an alarmed whisper. 'Oliver must go away before Papa comes home. I've told Anthea that he must slip away directly after the meeting. That will be best. You must warn Simon not to mention Oliver, it would never do to distress Papa.'

I thought it unlikely that Simon would mention Mr. Wade's visit to his grandfather but Mrs. Godfrey was not satisfied until I had promised to warn him. 'Is it a tennis club meeting?' I asked.

'No, I don't think so,' replied Mrs. Godfrey vaguely. 'It's some sort of club, you know. Perhaps if you asked Anthea she would tell you.'

The club did not really interest me; I had only asked Mrs. Godfrey about it as a means of changing the subject. Certainly I had no intention of asking Anthea.

The conversation between Lance and Anthea and their guest continued in a sprightly manner. Simon, at the other end of the table, remained silent, eating steadily through the excellent meal. The food was always good at Limbourne but to-night it seemed even better than usual and I felt pretty certain that the banquet had been ordered to do honour to Edward Ferrars.

So far I had not met 'Aunt Prissy' but when we went into the drawing-room for coffee she was there; a tall thin woman with white hair, and bearing a remarkable resemblance to her brother.

'Oh dear, I didn't know you were coming down!' exclaimed Mrs. Godfrey in a flustered manner. 'The children are having a meeting to-night upstairs in the nursery.'

'The children?' inquired 'Aunt Prissy,' looking round the room inquiringly.

'I mean Lance and Anthea and – and a friend,' explained Mrs. Godfrey. 'Oh, they've gone,' she added in relief.

They had vanished swiftly and noiselessly directly their eyes had fallen upon old Miss Wentworth.

'Well, it doesn't matter,' said that lady. 'I came down to meet Katherine and Simon. These are they, I suppose.'

'Yes, of course,' agreed Mrs. Godfrey. 'I should have introduced them properly but it isn't really necessary, is it?'

Simon and I shook hands with Miss Wentworth and I sat down beside her to talk. It seemed the right thing to do but I found it exceedingly difficult. I was glad to see that Simon had taken upon him the task of handing round the coffee cups.

'That's a handsome boy,' said Miss Wentworth, in approval. 'He's a great deal better-looking than Lance.'

This statement, made in a clear contralto voice, produced an embarrassed silence. It was broken by Mrs. Godfrey, who murmured uncomfortably, 'You mustn't mind Aunt Prissy; she's deaf, you know.'

'What did you say, Florence?' inquired the old lady.

'Nothing, really. Nothing important, I mean.'

'You have never learned to produce your voice correctly,' declared her aunt. 'Young people nowadays mumble and mutter in an indistinguishable manner. I remember telling your mother many years ago that you required elocution lessons but my advice was ignored. How old are you, Simon?'

'Sixteen and a half – nearly,' replied Simon loudly.

'Well-grown for your age,' said Miss Wentworth, adding in a slightly lower voice, 'Obviously a Wentworth. I shall tell Mortimer that it is unnecessary to make any further inquiries about his paternity.'

It was clear that the implications of this remark were

lost upon Simon. He remained unruffled, but Mrs. Godfrey was so perturbed that she knocked over the cream-jug.

'Oh dear!' she exclaimed. 'Look what I've done! Aunt Prissy gets such funny ideas – it's because she's deaf, of course – all that lovely cream wasted! Ring the bell, Simon. Bassett must bring a cloth or something. . . .'

'You are very clumsy, Florence,' said her aunt.

'Yes, dreadfully clumsy,' shouted poor Mrs. Godfrey, trying to wipe up the mess with an inadequate lace handkerchief. 'I don't know what made me do such a silly thing – but Bassett will clean it up. I think you should go to bed, Aunt Prissy,' she added.

'Did you say go to bed?' asked Miss Wentworth in surprise.

'I'm sure you're tired,' declared Mrs. Godfrey loudly and clearly. 'You look very tired indeed. Remember you are going away to-morrow and you'll have a long day's journey.'

'Three hours' drive in the car.'

'More than that,' said Mrs. Godfrey earnestly. 'You don't like Hurrell to drive fast.'

'Past where?' asked Miss Wentworth.

'Fast,' shouted Mrs. Godfrey. 'You don't like driving FAST.'

'There is no need to shout like that, Florence,' said Miss Wentworth reprovingly. 'But perhaps I am a little tired. I shall say good-bye to Katherine and Simon and go upstairs. You had better come with me. Clara is having her supper and I require a little assistance.'

We all rose and said good-bye. Simon ran to open the door and the two went out together.

When they had gone Simon and I escaped to the garden and, finding a seat in a sheltered corner, we sat down and talked about all that had happened during the day. It had seemed a very long day – more like a week – and I was glad it was over.

CHAPTER 17

Several days passed. To tell the truth they all seemed long to me but Simon was quite happy. He rode with Nitkin in the morning and usually went out with Lance in the afternoon. Anthea had a studio in the attic where she painted and Sir Mortimer seldom appeared, except for meals, so I was left to the mercies of Mrs. Godfrey. She had told me to call her Florence and I was beginning to manage it.

Luckily for me Florence was fond of bed; she got up late in the morning and always rested in the afternoon. After lunch – and coffee in the drawing-room – she would rise and collect her various belongings and say, 'I think we should rest, Katherine.' She said it as if it were quite a sudden idea.

At first I had said I would rather go for a walk, but she argued with me about it, saying a doctor had once told her that every woman over a certain age should rest in the afternoon. It was useless to tell her that I was not over a certain age – whatever that might mean – she still continued with her persuasions. I found it easier to agree with her and follow her upstairs. Once she was safely in her room I was free to do as I wanted. I could put on my walking shoes and go out by myself.

Usually I went up the hill, which I had climbed my first morning at Limbourne, and took deep breaths of fresh air to rid myself of the curious oppression which lay like a damp blanket upon my spirits, but one afternoon I wanted postcards to send to the children so I walked down the long avenue into the village and bought some coloured ones at a little shop.

It was very warm and there were few people about. Some children were playing on the village green and an old man was sitting in the sun in a cottage doorway. He said good day to me and I stopped for a few moments and admired the little garden, which was bright with old-fashioned flowers. He seemed pleased and said a good deal, waving his hand, but unfortunately I couldn't understand a word.

'Yes, they're lovely,' I said. 'I never saw better pansies and your hollyhocks are marvellous.' Then I walked on.

Presently I came to the lych-gate, which led into the churchyard, so I went in. I had seen the church from the hilltop – it was a simple Norman building of grey stone with a square tower. Trees grew about it amongst the head-stones; great oaks, some of them so old that they were mere skeletons, hollow inside, but still bearing green leaves. I was standing looking at one of these ancient giants and marvelling that anything so old should be capable of producing new foliage when the vicar came out of the side door of the church. He was a small thin man with pale, clean-cut features; the sun shone on his thick silver hair turning it to gold.

'I think you must be Mrs. Gerald Wentworth,' he said.

I smiled and said, 'Yes.'

We shook hands.

'John Heath is my name. My wife heard that you and your stepson were staying at Limbourne. I have been here for over thirty years and of course I knew your husband – I knew him well – so I have been hoping to meet you. Would it interest you to see the church, Mrs. Wentworth?'

'Oh, yes, I should like to, but – but I've no hat or scarf or – or anything,' I said.

'Do you think God will mind?'

'No, I just wondered if you would.'

Mr. Heath looked at me in a surprised sort of way. 'How interesting!' he said. Then he opened the door and held it for me to go in.

It was dim and shadowy in the little church, after the glare of the sunshine, and I stood for a few moments looking round. The walls and floor were of stone – the floor uneven, worn into channels by the passage of many thousands of feet – the roof was barrel-shaped, crossed by great oaken beams. The windows glowed like jewels and threw coloured patterns on the stones. Over the doorway was a wooden screen and carved upon it were the words, 'O come let us worship and bow down; let us kneel before the Lord our Maker.'

It seemed to me good advice. I knelt down in the nearest pew and prayed that Simon might be guided aright through all the dangers and difficulties of his life. When I rose I felt happier and more relaxed.

Mr. Heath smiled at me in a gentle way and began to talk about the history of the little church and to show me round. He knew all about it and loved it. He told me that the D'Artingtons were a Norman family, descended from a certain Gilles D'Artagnon who had come over soon after the Norman Conquest and been granted lands; it was the grandson of this man who had built the church. As in the case with many old families, their name had been anglicised to a form easier for their neighbours to pronounce. There was still a Giles D'Artington at Hurlestone Manor, said Mr. Heath proudly. He was very old – but his son was another Giles.

Mr. Heath showed me the effigy of a knight in armour, carved in stone and lying on a stone slab. A beam of yellow light from one of the windows showed every detail of his fine features. His sword lay upon his body, his hands were crossed upon it and his legs were crossed at the knees.

'Wilfrid Giles D'Artington,' said Mr. Heath. 'No doubt you are aware that the curious position – with crossed hands and knees – indicates that he took part in two crusades. A mighty warrior, indeed!'

'Yes,' I said. 'Gerald made a study of the crusades – so I knew.'

'Of course you're more interested in the Wentworth family,' said Mr. Heath. 'Compared with the D'Artingtons they are newcomers.'

'Newcomers? But I thought —'

'They came over from Ireland in the seventeenth century, and were granted lands by Charles the Second.'

I looked at Mr. Heath and saw that he was perfectly serious. Three hundred years seemed nothing to him.

'The title of baronet is of fairly recent origin,' continued Mr. Heath. 'You are aware of that, of course. King James the First created the rank and bestowed it upon landed gentlemen in Ireland. He found it a convenient way of augmenting his exchequer.'

'Do you mean they paid for it?'

Mr. Heath smiled. 'Do you find that so horrifying?'

'It's rather – disappointing. I always thought it was given for valuable services.'

'Ah, perhaps you're thinking of "banneret" from which the word is derived. That title is of very much older origin and was bestowed by a sovereign upon a knight who distinguished himself in battle. It was bestowed then and there on the field of victory. The pennon which the knight had carried was converted into a banner by the sovereign himself tearing off the points of the pennon with his own sword and thereby converting it into a square banner.'

'I'd like to have seen it done!'

'So should I,' agreed Mr. Heath. 'It must have been an impressive sight. If you're interested in heraldry I shall be delighted to lend you a book on the subject.'

I thanked him, but said that I was only here for a week.

He left that and moved on. 'This is a very fine window,' he said. 'It was given by Sir Mortimer's grandfather as a memorial to his wife. These pews beneath the window are the Wentworth pews. The D'Artington pews are opposite.'

There were three pews on each side, facing each other across the aisle.

'The Wentworth pews are always empty now,' said Mr. Heath regrettfully. Then he added, 'But perhaps you will be here on Sunday?'

'Yes, I'd like to come,' I said – and then I changed my mind. 'No, I couldn't, Mr. Heath. I'm very sorry but I couldn't face it. I couldn't sit there all by myself with everybody staring at me. Perhaps if you would let me sit at the back in an ordinary pew —'

'My dear young lady, you may sit anywhere you like.'

We went all round the church. We looked at brass tablets commemorating long-dead D'Artingtons and Wentworths and various other families in the neighbourhood. We looked at a large stone slab bearing the names of sixty-nine people who had died in the Great Plague. Mr. Heath took me into the vestry and showed me an old yellow parchment with names of parishioners who had given money to repair the church after its partial destruction by Cromwell's Roundheads.

It was all very interesting indeed, but very tiring; I was not sorry when at last we came out together into the sunshine and Mr. Heath invited me to tea at the vicarage, saying that it would give his wife a great deal of pleasure if I would come. I saw he really meant it, so I accepted. There was no need to hurry back to Limbourne; it was a relief to escape from the uncomfortable atmosphere of the Wentworth family and to talk to somebody kind and pleasant and good.

'My wife will be delighted,' said Mr. Heath joyfully. 'This way, Mrs. Wentworth – through this little gate – I take a great deal of pleasure in my garden. Roses are my hobby.'

Unfortunately I could not take pleasure in Mr. Heath's garden, nor even admire his roses, because I had suddenly begun to feel very queer indeed. I sat down upon a conveniently placed seat and tried to pull myself together.

'Oh dear!' exclaimed Mr. Heath, looking at me in alarm. 'I'm afraid I've tired you, Mrs. Wentworth. I'll run and fetch my wife.'

He trotted away rapidly towards the house; I heard him shouting, 'Helena, Helena!'

The seat was in the shade and I was beginning to feel better when Mr. Heath reappeared, followed by a large stout woman with a round kindly face. 'It was most inconsiderate of me,' he was saying. 'You know what I'm like, Helena, when I begin to talk about the church! I have tired Mrs. Wentworth, I have exhausted her. Oh, dear me, how very thoughtless!'

Mrs. Heath had brought a bottle of smelling-salts with her. 'Tea is ready,' she said. 'I could bring it here on a tray. Perhaps that would help. A cup of freshly made tea is very reviving.'

'I'm all right now,' I told her, trying to smile. 'It was just the hot sun – or something. Terribly silly of me!'

It took some minutes to convince the kind people that I really was better and quite able to walk to the house. Presently we were sitting in the vicarage drawing-room: a cool room, shabby and threadbare, but with a curious old-world dignity of its own; Mrs. Heath poured out tea into lovely old Wedgwood china cups and Mr. Heath hurried away to fetch a tin of glucose.

'I'm afraid it's rather nasty,' said Mrs. Heath apologetically. 'I always think it spoils a good cup of tea, but John has great faith in glucose; it will please him if you allow him to give you a little. John is so interested in the church that he doesn't realise how tiring it is to be shown round.'

'I was very interested indeed,' I assured her. 'I'm all right now, so please don't worry. As a matter of fact I've been having rather a difficult time lately.'

Mrs. Heath nodded. 'Yes, I expect you have. We don't go to Limbourne very often – only occasionally, when Sir Mortimer thinks it his duty to ask us to lunch – but I'm always very glad when it's time to come away. It's a tragic family, Mrs. Wentworth.'

'Tragic?'

'Yes, I think so. They have so much . . . and yet nothing. They have none of the really important things, if you know what I mean.'

There was no time to say more; Mr. Heath returned with the tin of glucose and spooned some into my cup. 'It produces energy,' he explained. 'You know, Helena, I really think Mrs. Wentworth is looking better. Of course you are unable to judge, because you didn't see her when she arrived at the church. She had such a pretty colour. So when she suddenly became very pale it gave me quite a shock – the more so because I felt myself to blame.'

It was time to change the subject. 'Have you a large parish, Mr. Heath?' I inquired.

'Yes, large and very scattered. Too large and scattered for me to visit as frequently as I should wish; I have only a push-bike, you see. However, our son, who is a first lieutenant in the Navy, is coming home shortly on leave from Singapore; he has a small car which is reposing in our garage at the moment, and he has promised to take me to some of the outlying farms while he is here.'

'The church is very well filled on Sundays,' put in Mrs. Heath.

'Yes, that is so,' agreed the vicar. 'People are very good in coming – even on wet days – and although the Wentworth and D'Artington pews are empty both families are generous in giving. Some time ago when we had a case of vandalism Sir Mortimer and Major D'Artington paid for things to be put right.'

'Vandalism – in the church?'

'It was in the churchyard. Some of the headstones were daubed with yellow paint. It was quite a costly business getting it removed.'

'Another night we had a ghost,' said Mrs. Heath, smiling. 'Tell Mrs. Wentworth about that.'

Mr. Heath shook his head. 'Not a real ghost, of course.

It was merely a sort of scarecrow set up on one of the tombs and covered with luminous paint. Several people who were coming to Evensong were alarmed, and I must admit it was a disturbing sight . . . in the dark, you know. The figure appeared to be emerging from the grave. Fortunately I was on the spot in a few minutes with a powerful torch and I soon had "the ghost" in pieces on the ground.'

'Did you inform the police?'

'Yes, indeed we did. Two of them came to see me and took notes, but that was as far as they got. One of my choirboys was suspected but I was able to clear him. He comes to me for coaching in Latin and was with me at the time.'

'It was ridiculous to suspect poor Cyril,' Mrs. Heath put in.

'Yes,' agreed the vicar. 'Cyril is a thoroughly good boy, it would never have occurred to him to play such a cruel trick, but of course the sergeant did not know Cyril as we know him. One must remember that, Helena.'

'You would find excuses for the devil himself!' exclaimed Mrs. Heath.

'Helena, my dear! What will Mrs. Wentworth think of us?'

'We needn't bother, John,' replied Mrs. Heath, smiling sweetly. 'Mrs. Wentworth is one of those people who understand *everything*. I knew that the moment I saw her.'

I couldn't help laughing; if I did not understand 'everything,' I certainly understood the Heaths. They were darlings.

'For my part,' continued Mrs. Heath, 'I can find no excuse at all for the sergeant. He's rude and stupid. Why can't he catch those hooligans who are doing all the damage in the district?'

'Do you mean there have been other cases of vandalism?' I asked.

'Yes, I'm afraid so,' replied Mr. Heath unhappily. 'Not actually in our village but farther afield. The police seem unable to trace the culprits.'

'Wait till Adam comes home,' said Mrs. Heath confidently. 'Adam has more brains than all the police put together. Adam will catch them.'

After that we talked about other things. They wanted to know all about Simon – which was not unnatural – so I told them what I could.

'Cricket!' exclaimed Mr. Heath, beaming with satisfaction. 'He's fond of cricket, is he? That's excellent. We shall have him in the village team; he will be a great asset. We are badly in need of new blood.'

I was enjoying myself so much that the time passed quickly and presently Cyril arrived for his lesson in Latin, so Mrs. Heath said she would walk home with me. There was no necessity for this kindness – I was perfectly well – but it was pleasant all the same. As we walked along together I asked her about the D'Artingtons, for I had heard enough about them to make me eager to hear more, and Mrs. Heath was quite ready to tell me all I wanted to know.

'Lord D'Artington is very old,' she explained. 'He's practically an invalid now so of course he never comes to church, but Major D'Artington comes when he can. When John said the Wentworth and D'Artington pews were always empty I think he really meant they were comparatively empty. Years ago, when we first came here, they were both quite full. You understand, don't you?'

'Yes, of course.'

'Major D'Artington is a widower,' continued Mrs. Heath. 'He has an only son who is at Eton. Wilfrid is a dear boy, he often drops in to see us during the holidays. Major D'Artington was very badly wounded in the war, he got the D.S.O. and the M.C. as well. Tom Coles (who's the son of the blacksmith in the village and was in the same regiment – I think it was the Coldstream Guards) says that it ought to have been the V.C. Tom Coles says the Major is as brave as a lion. Major D'Artington is very kind and generous, he always heads the subscription list when John wants money for anything, but he isn't very friendly – if you know what I mean. We've known him for years and years, of course, but you never seem to get to know him any better. John says it's his Norman blood.'

'Perhaps it is.'

'Yes, but simple faith is better than Norman blood, isn't it? He may have simple faith for all I know,' added Mrs. Heath with a sigh.

'He sounds very interesting.'

'Yes,' agreed Mrs. Heath doubtfully. 'I expect he is interesting – if you could get to know him. He's very popular in the village, of course. The people are all terribly proud of him; they feel he belongs to them. I've seen him talking and laughing in the blacksmith's with Tom Coles and other men in a very friendly way.'

'Sir Mortimer sometimes goes over to dinner at Hurlestone Manor and plays chess with Lord D'Artington.'

'Oh yes, the two families are quite friendly,' agreed Mrs. Heath. 'But of course there is no Mrs. D'Artington now, so they don't entertain. I sometimes feel it's rather a sad house for a young boy like Wilfrid. There's talk in the village that the Wentworths would like Miss Godfrey to marry Major D'Artington, but I'm quite sure he has never thought of such a thing for a moment. He was devoted to his wife, and although he isn't really old in years (about forty-five, I suppose) he seems to have become old and settled in his ways. It may be because he was so very badly wounded – I think he still suffers a good deal of pain – or it may be the death of Mrs. D'Artington. At any rate I should be very much surprised if he were to marry again. I hope you don't think I'm a dreadful gossip, Mrs. Wentworth. We hear these things, you see. The women who come to the work-party at the vicarage talk about them. John thinks I shouldn't listen, but I can't shut my ears, can I?'

'Of course you can't,' I agreed.

Although I knew a little more about Mrs. Godfrey's plans for her daughter. I decided to hold my tongue. Mrs. Heath was a dear kind creature but she certainly was a talker.

CHAPTER 18

My afternoon with the Heaths had been so enjoyable that I felt strengthened and encouraged; I was further encouraged by letters from home which arrived the following morning. Aunt Liz had written in her usual terse manner, informing me that the children were good and happy and eating well; Bella was enjoying their company and had given them tea in the kitchen one afternoon as a treat. Aunt Liz had taken them to the Zoo and had arranged to take them to tea at West Linton with some friends of hers the following day. The friends had three grandchildren staying with them and were the possessors of a delightful garden. She enclosed a short letter from Den – very nicely written – and a highly-coloured picture of Noah's Ark, drawn and painted by Daisy.

There was also a letter from Alec:

My dear Katherine,

This is just a hasty scribble as I am writing in the office and have not much time. I hope you had a good journey and that you are finding Limbourne more comfortable than you expected. I feel sure I was right when I told you that your 'in-laws' would be pleasant and kind. It is to their own advantage to be friendly. Remember that you are in a strong position – and keep your end up.

Unfortunately I shall not be here when you return to Edinburgh on Monday. I had hoped to see you and hear a full account of your experiences, but Zilla is very anxious for me to take her to London, where she is to join her friends the Carews and stay with them at their flat for a few days before starting on their tour of France. Zilla dislikes travelling alone so I feel I ought to take her, especially as she has not been well lately. She had another of her heart attacks last night and I was so alarmed that I decided to take your advice and see her doctor. I have made an appointment for him to-morrow. He may be able to suggest some treatment.

It is most unfortunate that I shall be here in Edinburgh all August while you are in the north. I could easily have arranged to take my holiday in August, as it is a very slack time at the office, but somebody must be on the spot in case anything unexpected turns up. I thought I had arranged things rather cleverly when I volunteered for the job but my well-laid plans have 'gone agley.' To tell the truth I am feeling very depressed – so you must excuse this stupid letter – the future looks bleak and 'the grasshopper is a burden.' If you could find time to write me a few lines it would cheer me up a bit.

Your affectionate friend

ALEC

It was kind of Alec to write when he was so busy. I was delighted to receive his letter and especially glad of the reminder that I was 'in a strong position.' When I thought about it seriously I realised that I was allowing myself to be intimidated by Limbourne. Although Sir Mortimer was always polite and pleasant to me he took it for granted that everybody beneath his roof would conform to his wishes. Florence was his faithful slave and expected me to be the same; Lance did not bother about me, except occasionally when he felt inclined to exercise his humour. I had tried to make friends with Anthea but she was uninterested – not only in me but in everything. When she was not upstairs in her studio, painting, she mooned about the garden or sat in the drawing-room turning over the pages of a fashion magazine in a listless manner. I thought the girl seemed unhappy and said so to her mother, but Florence assured me that dear Anthea was perfectly happy; she was very very sensitive and highly-strung. 'Just like me when I was eighteen,' said Florence complacently.

The whole atmosphere was discouraging and had a lowering effect upon my spirits, so Alec's advice to keep my end up had come at the right moment.

So far so good, but the last few sentences of Alec's letter were disturbing. I was very fond of Alec so I was sorry to learn that he was depressed. Naturally he was annoyed at the miscarriage of his holiday plans, but it seemed to me that his depression must have some deeper origin. Alec was a sensible man, not given to exaggeration; he would not have said that the future looked bleak unless he felt seriously unhappy about it. I wondered what could be the matter. I decided that I must write to him and try to cheer him up a bit – as requested.

2

On Saturday morning I went out to the rose-nursery; I had been there several times since Medlam had shown it to me; it had become a refuge. This delightful spot was the only place in the vicinity of Limbourne where there was the disorder which I had come to associate with freedom. Better still, I could be certain of solitude – nobody came to this part of the garden – I could sit amongst the roses upon an up-turned wheelbarrow and think my own thoughts, secure in the knowledge that I would be undisturbed by

Florence or Anthea or Sir Mortimer – or even Mrs. Sillett. Mrs. Sillett often wandered round with one of the gardeners to pick flowers for the vases in the house, but she never came here.

To-day, however, the rose-nursery was not deserted; Medlam was there, engaged upon the task of budding roses. I had never seen this done before so I watched with interest. Medlam seemed pleased to see me and explained the whole matter in detail; he was kind enough to allow me to try my hand at the operation, showing me how to cut a bud from one of the tea-roses, to insert the stem in a sturdy briar and to bind it together securely.

'That's good, that is,' he declared. 'I'll put a label on it and next time you comes to Limbourne you'll see your own rose.'

I felt inclined to tell him that my own rose would have died of old age before my next visit – but I refrained.

'Now you'd like a booky,' said Medlam, taking out his knife and looking round.

Although I did not really want a 'booky' (I had nowhere to put it except in my bedroom) it was impossible to refuse the offering so I accepted the enormous bunch of beautiful roses with suitable gratitude.

What should I do with the roses? Should I take them to the church and see if Mrs. Heath would like them? It seemed a good idea.

Mrs. Heath was in the church doing the flowers, she was delighted with the roses and asked me to stay and arrange the alter-vases. We did it together, very happily, and then sat in the porch and chatted for a while.

'It makes such a difference having lovely flowers,' said Mrs. Heath. 'Those roses are perfectly beautiful. Of course the Limbourne rose-garden is known all over the country. I didn't know that Sir Mortimer ever allowed them to be picked – except when they are fading.'

'Medlam cut them for me in the nursery-garden,' I explained. 'There are lots of roses there.'

'There are lots of beautiful flowers, besides roses, aren't there? I wanted John to ask Sir Mortimer if we could have some now and then, but he won't do it. He says it's better to have flowers for the church from people who want to give them – even if they aren't so beautiful. Sometimes the flowers are very straggly,' she added with a sigh.

'I agree with Mr. Heath.'

'Yes, I thought you would. You're like John in thinking that ideas are more important than things. John says you gave him an idea for a sermon.'

'I did?' I asked in surprise.

She nodded. 'It was something you said about not having a hat to go into church. John said it was very revealing; it showed you had faith in God and consideration for the feelings of your fellow creatures.'

I couldn't remember what I had said.

'Well, never mind,' said Mrs. Heath. 'John gets ideas for his sermons in all sorts of ways. One day when I was baking a cake for John's birthday an old man called at the door and asked for a piece of bread. I gave him a ham sandwich and a glass of milk. I was so sorry for the poor old thing that I quite forgot the cake, and when I remembered to look in the oven it was burnt to a cinder. You wouldn't think that a good idea for a sermon, would you?'

'No, indeed!' I said, laughing.

'It was an excellent sermon. John said we should never expect rewards for kind actions . . . and so on and so forth. Of course he never mentioned the cake – but that was what gave him the idea. I'm glad I've seen you to-day,' she continued. 'I've been thinking a lot about you and about the "difficult time" you said you were having. I told John and we both feel we should like to help you in any way we can. So if there's anything we can do – no matter what – we should like you to let us know.'

I thanked her sincerely – she really meant it – and although I did not see how the Heaths could help me, except by talking to me in a friendly way, it was good to know that I had made two friends.

After that Mrs. Heath talked about her son: they had just heard that he was flying home from Singapore, so probably would be arriving quite soon.

'I wish you could see him, Mrs. Wentworth,' she said. 'Of course I know I'm rather silly about Adam, but he really is a son to be proud of. He isn't very tall but he's tremendously strong and very good-looking – with fair hair and blue eyes and a ruddy complexion – and he's brimming over with energy and vitality. You mustn't mind me talking about him like this; we haven't seen him for two years so I'm terribly excited.'

'No wonder you're excited! It will be lovely for you to have him on leave.'

Mrs. Heath nodded. 'Yes, there's only one thing I don't like about having Adam home on leave.'

'You feel as flat as a pancake when he goes away.'

'How did you know?' she asked in surprise.

I laughed. 'Because that's how I feel when Simon's holidays are over.'

3

On Saturday night when I was dressing for dinner I felt remarkably cheerful; in fact I was happier than I had been for some time. I had dreaded this visit to Limbourne and it had been exceedingly unpleasant – though not in the way I had expected – but now it was nearly over. We were going home on Monday.

Only one more day, I said to myself as I sat before the mirror, brushing my hair. Only one more day!

When Simon came in I was nearly ready. He came to my room at this time every evening for me to tie his tie and to chat about the events of the day. It was the best time for a private talk; indeed it was the only time when we could be sure of being together without interruption. Although I was now quite used to seeing him 'all dressed up,' his appearance gave me a little thrill of pleasure. The wretch knew this and grinned at me mischievously.

'Not too bad,' he said, surveying himself with satisfaction in the full-length mirror. 'I can't see myself properly in my own room.'

'Just like a waiter,' I said teasingly.

Simon laughed. Then he turned and put his arm round my waist. 'Listen, Mums. Would you mind if we stayed on a few days longer?'

'We can't!' I cried in dismay.

'You mean you don't want to?'

'I couldn't – even if I wanted to. We *must* go home on Monday. Aunt Liz is flying to Copenhagen on Tuesday, so she can't keep the children any longer . . . and there are all sorts of things I must do before we go to Loch

Ron. It's all settled, Simon. We're going to Loch Ron on Thursday. You know that as well as I do.'

Simon was silent.

'Do you want to stay on?' I asked him.

'I do – rather,' he replied apologetically. 'The fact is there's going to be a treasure hunt. I shouldn't tell you, really, because it's a dead secret, but you won't let on, will you?'

'Why has it got to be a secret?'

'Oh, you know what Aunt Florence is like. She would fuss about it and spoil everything.'

This was perfectly true.

'A treasure hunt is rather fun,' continued Simon. 'We had one at school on a Saturday afternoon – it was good sport. There were hidden clues and you had to guess them. Of course we just ran, you know. It will be much more exciting at night with cars.'

'At night with cars!'

'They've done it before; they often do it. You needn't worry, Mums.'

Of course I was worried. The idea of my precious Simon tearing about the country in the middle of the night with Lance and Anthea and their friends was extremely alarming.

'It's all right, darling,' said Simon, giving me a little hug. 'They're all a lot older than I am. As a matter of fact they said at first that I was too young but Lance managed to persuade Oliver to let me come.'

'Oliver Wade?'

'Yes. It's a sort of club and Oliver is the president. He manages the whole thing. Lance had an awful job persuading him. It was decent of Lance, wasn't it?'

'Simon, do you really want to?'

'Yes, I do – really,' said Simon earnestly. 'You don't mind, do you?'

I minded quite a lot but I realised that I should have to give in. It was impossible for me to stay at Limbourne any longer, but there was nothing to prevent Simon from staying. He could come north later and join us at the cottage. I reminded myself that Simon was sixteen – and very sensible. Aunt Liz said I kept him in cotton-wool and perhaps there was truth in her accusation. He had been small and delicate as a child so he had needed a lot of care. Now that he was no longer small and delicate I must cease to fuss about him . . . and anyhow what could happen to Simon here? These people were his relations: his grandfather, his aunt and his cousins.

Simon had walked to the window and was standing there, looking out. He said, 'Say honestly, Mums. If you don't want me to stay on I'll come north with you on Monday. It doesn't matter about the treasure hunt.'

'Of course you must stay on if you want to.'

'Sure?'

'Yes, certain,' I replied. 'You'll be sensible, won't you?'

He laughed. 'Yes, of course – frightfully sensible. Lance will take me as his "observer." We go in couples, you see. As a matter of fact it's very decent of Lance to take me, because I shan't be much help to him – not knowing the ropes – but he says he doesn't mind.'

'You like Lance, don't you?'

'Yes, of course. Don't you like him?'

'I don't feel I know him very well.'

'Perhaps he is a bit difficult to know,' agreed Simon. 'But he's awfully decent to me. Lots of chaps, so much older, wouldn't bother to be decent. He isn't like Mark, of course.'

'People are all different,' I suggested.

'Yes, but I don't mean that, exactly. Mark has a frightfully high standard.'

'And Lance hasn't?'

Simon smiled. 'It's funny, isn't it? He doesn't think it wrong to tell lies.'

I knew that already but it didn't seem 'funny' to me. 'I can't bear lies and secrets and deceit,' I declared emphatically.

'I know – neither can I – but people are all different. You said that yourself, didn't you? Don't worry,' added Simon. 'Lance will never be my very special friend, like Mark, but it's better to take people as you find them . . . and he really is very kind indeed. He and Anthea are going to Austria to ski in the Christmas hols and he said I could join the party if I liked. It would be tremendous fun – absolutely terrific! Of course I told Lance I couldn't go unless my expenses were paid, but he said the Bart paid for everything – so that would be all right, wouldn't it?'

'Yes,' I said. I was trying hard to feel pleased and happy about this new plan, but it was difficult. I had never been able to give Simon pleasures, and now they were being showered upon him by his relations. It was not that I was jealous; quite honestly I would have been pleased and happy for Simon's sake if these people had been good and wholesome. Simon had said that it was better to take people as you found them, and this was true – to a certain extent – but was it possible for a boy like Simon to mix with these people and maintain his integrity?

'What are you worrying about?' asked Simon.

'Nothing much,' I said. 'Give me your tie. Who is going to tie it for you when I've gone?'

He smiled. 'I'll get Bassett – or somebody.'

After that we talked of other things. I told Simon that I intended to go to church the following morning at eight o'clock and he said he would come with me if I wakened him in time.

CHAPTER 19

Simon was awake when I went to call him. The big, beautifully furnished house was very still – not a mouse seemed to be stirring. We dressed and crept downstairs as quietly as we could.

'I feel like a burglar,' whispered Simon as he eased back the bolt of the front door.

There was something in the atmosphere of Limbourne which gave one a feeling of uneasiness – as if one were doing wrong. (I had thought that Simon was free from this curious obsession but obviously he was not.)

Once we were outside in the sunshine the feeling vanished.

'Lovely, lovely morning,' said Simon in his ordinary voice. 'It's so fresh and new, isn't it? Why don't we always get up early? I think I shall tell Nitkin that I want to ride before breakfast every morning.'

'Yes, you should,' I said.

Simon took my arm and we walked down the avenue together and into the road. As we neared the church we saw several people at the lych-gate; a man came forward and opened it for us while his companions waited for us to go through. We both said good morning and they all smiled in a friendly manner and returned the greeting.

I hesitated at the church door. 'Simon,' I said, 'shall we sit at the back or in the Wentworth pew?'

'The Wentworth pew, of course. Do you know where it is?'

'Mr. Heath showed me.'

Perhaps he was right. In fact I knew he was right; it would have been foolish to shrink from the ordeal. I led the way up the aisle and went into the pew. Simon followed.

I had known it would be an ordeal – and it was. I could not help noticing the stir and rustle of people coming in and finding their seats; I could not help feeling that everybody was looking at us. It was difficult to fix my mind on my prayers. I glanced across the aisle at the D'Artington pew . . . a man was sitting there alone. It was Major D'Artington of course – it couldn't be anybody else – but the strange thing was that I knew him. I had seen him before, quite recently, but I could not remember where.

Presently Mr. Heath came in and the service began. It was a very simple service; there was no music; just the beautiful prayers in Mr. Heath's quiet, clear voice. I was swept away, soothed and comforted, I forgot the other people. For all I knew there might have been nobody else in the lovely old building.

Unfortunately when the service was over the queer uncomfortable feeling returned and once more I was aware of the interested glances. I noticed that the little congregation were sitting quietly in their seats. They were waiting for Major D'Artington to go out first. He was lame and walked slowly with a stick. Simon was about to pass him, but I put my hand on his arm and he understood at once . . . and waited. We followed him slowly down the aisle; it was not until we reached the door that the other people rose and came out after us.

Major D'Artington's car was standing at the lych-gate, but before getting in he turned and spoke to us . . . and, now that I saw him in the sunshine, I knew where I had seen him before. I had seen him carved in stone, lying on a stone slab. The stern features, the look of suffering, the Norman nose and firm mouth were identical. He was the living embodiment of his crusading ancestor. I was so surprised at this discovery that I was moonstruck.

When I came to myself I heard Simon saying, 'Yes, sir. I'm at Barstow. I'm staying at Limbourne for a few days longer, but my stepmother is going north to-morrow. Perhaps I should – introduce you – or something,' he added doubtfully.

Major D'Artington smiled and replied, 'Perhaps I should introduce myself, Wentworth. Then you could perform the introduction correctly.'

'Oh, I know who you are, sir!' exclaimed Simon.

'In that case no introduction will be necessary,' declared Major D'Artington with a little chuckle. 'I always think introductions are a terrible bore.' He turned to me and added, 'Gerald was a great friend of mine, so I'm delighted to have this opportunity of meeting you. It's a pity you're going away so soon but you'll be coming back, of course.'

I smiled at him. It was difficult to reply because I had no intention of returning to Limbourne if I could possibly avoid it.

'Now, let's see,' said Major D'Artington, turning to Simon. 'My son is coming home to-morrow. He's a little older than you are, I think.'

'I'm sixteen, sir.'

'Yes, well, Wilfrid is seventeen – but I dare say you may find quite a lot in common. I don't make engagements for him but I'll tell him you're here and he can ring you up. That's the best way.'

'Yes, I should like to meet him. I mean we're neighbours, aren't we?'

'You are indeed, so the sooner you get to know each other the better. Perhaps you could come over to Hurlestone and spend the day. Have you got a bicycle?'

'I could ride over,' said Simon eagerly. 'My grandfather said I could have a horse whenever I liked.'

'Good,' said Major D'Artington. 'We'll arrange something.' He shook hands with us; his chauffeur helped him into his car and drove away.

'He's nice, isn't he?' said Simon. 'It will be fun to ride over to Hurlestone Manor. I wonder what Wilfrid is like.'

As we walked home together I told Simon all that I had heard about Major D'Artington; how he had been badly wounded in the war and had won distinction for his courage; how the villagers felt he belonged to them in a special sort of way because of his ancestry, and were fond of him because of his kindness and generosity.

'Yes,' said Simon thoughtfully. 'He's like a king, isn't

he? What a good thing you grabbed hold of me and prevented me from passing him in the aisle!'

'It would have been a bad start,' I agreed.

'It would have been frightful,' said Simon emphatically.

2

There was nobody about when we returned to Limbourne – except the servants, of course – so we had breakfast together in the dining-room. Sir Mortimer came down later, and Lance and Anthea appeared when we had nearly finished. Neither Simon nor I mentioned our visit to church; we had not agreed upon this, but obviously Simon thought – as I did – that it was better to be silent on the subject. Nobody would know whether we had been or not – nobody would care – that was my idea. It appeared that I was wrong.

The morning sunshine had vanished behind heavy clouds and it had begun to rain by the time we had all finished breakfast, so I took a book and sat down in the drawing-room to read. I had been sitting there for about half an hour when Florence's maid came in and said Mrs. Godfrey would like to see me.

'Now?' I asked in surprise.

'As soon as convenient,' replied the woman.

It was a new experience to visit Florence in bed. She was propped up with coloured cushions and was wearing a pink lacy bed-jacket and a white Shetland shawl.

'Oh, good morning, Katherine,' she said.

'I hope you aren't ill!' I exclaimed.

'No, perfectly well. I always have a little longer in bed on Sunday mornings. You went to church, I believe.'

'Yes, I like going to the eight-o'clock service.'

'Papa is not pleased.'

'Not pleased!' I echoed in astonishment.

'Oh, of course he has no objection to your going to church, but you should have told me so that I could order the car.'

'But I went early! I didn't want to bother anybody.'

'Hurrell is there to carry out Papa's orders.'

'I know, but I didn't want the car. It was a lovely walk; I enjoyed it.'

'Papa knows that you're fond of walking, and of course he doesn't want to prevent you from taking walks, but if you're going to church he wishes you to go in the car. Hurrell can be told the night before. Papa is not angry,' explained Florence. 'He knows it's difficult for you, Katherine. He just asked me to explain that it is more *comme il faut* for members of the Wentworth family to go to church in the car. Papa wishes you to use the car.'

This was intended to be the last word, but Alec had told me to keep my end up. 'I prefer to walk to church,' I said firmly. 'And anyhow I shan't be here next Sunday.'

Florence looked surprised. She said, 'Oh, you're going north to-morrow, aren't you? But of course you'll be coming to Limbourne again quite soon, so it's just as well for you to know what Papa feels about the matter.'

For a few moments I was angry and then the humour of it struck me. Florence was exactly like the White Queen, sitting there in bed with her round face and popping eyes and the little fleecy shawl about her shoulders – so, instead of saying angrily that it would be a very long time before I paid another visit to Limbourne, I smiled and thanked her for giving me the message.

3

On Sunday evening Simon came to my room before dinner as usual. I was leaving Limbourne early the next morning so there were several matters to be arranged. I had calculated carefully how much money Simon would require for tips to the Limbourne staff (a difficult and delicate matter), for his railway fare to London and from London to Inverquill . . . and various incidental expenses. Fortunately I had brought plenty of money with me so I produced a sheaf of notes and counted them out on my dressing-table.

'It's costing an awful lot!' exclaimed Simon in dismay.

It was costing a great deal more than I had expected – or could afford. I saw the new curtains for my sitting-room and new winter blankets for the children's beds vanishing into space. 'It can't be helped,' I said with a sigh.

'Are you pleased to be going home to-morrow?' asked Simon as he took the notes and stowed them away carefully in his pocket-book.

'Yes, very pleased,' I replied, without much enthusiasm (if Simon had been coming with me my heart would have been soaring like a lark).

'You aren't worrying about me, are you?' he asked.

'No, of course not. I'll see you on Friday at Inverquill. If you let me know what time you arrive I can send a car to meet you.'

'It won't be Friday, Mums. I was just going to tell you that. You see they've had to put off the treasure hunt till Friday night, and there's to be a cricket match next week. They asked Lance to play in the village team but he doesn't want to – he's a wet blob, of course – so he said I could take his place. I'm not sure what day it will be. Then there's Hurlestone Manor – I want to go over there if they ask me. Will it be all right if I let you know what day I'll be coming north?'

'Yes, quite all right.'

Simon put his arm round me and gave me a hug. 'You're sure?' he asked anxiously. 'You don't mind, Mums? You see, the cricket match would be good fun. All the local chaps play – and they're frightfully keen, Lance says.'

'Of course you must play,' I said.

As I went down to dinner I paused, as I always did, and looked up at the picture of the fifth baronet. To me he had become Gerald and I addressed him silently: What do you think about it? Are you pleased that Simon is being absorbed into Limbourne?

There was no reply, of course – how could there be? – but the words of Aunt Liz came into my mind. 'Gerald got away and never wanted to go back, so he can't have liked it much. Would Gerald have wanted his son to go to Limbourne? . . . There must be something queer about the whole set-up. I only hope you won't regret it.'

My last evening at Limbourne was spent with Florence in the drawing-room, listening to her reminiscences and disentangling her wools. (I had done this several times during my visit but to-night they were in a worse tangle than ever.) Lance and Simon had gone to see a film at West Barstead and Florence seemed to be under the impression that Anthea had gone with them. I knew that Lance had taken Simon on his motor-bike, but I did not bother to contradict her. It did not matter to me where Anthea had gone.

'I hope you won't think it rude if I don't come down in the morning to see you off,' said Florence. 'You're leaving early, aren't you? It always upsets me dreadfully to be wakened early.'

'Of course not,' I told her. 'You mustn't think of it, Florence. I'll say good-bye to-night. If you don't mind I'll just say it now; I've got my packing to do.'

'Packing is dreadfully tiring,' complained Florence. 'I remember once when we were in Paris . . .'

I listened patiently to the story, reminding myself that it would be a long long time before I should have to listen to another, and then I said good-bye – and good night – and went upstairs.

4

It was quite late, I had finished my packing and was lying in bed reading, when there was a light tap on the door leading into the bathroom which I shared with Anthea. I was surprised that she should want to come in and see me, but perhaps she had decided she had better say good-bye.

'I saw your light,' explained Anthea. 'I wondered if you had any aspirin.'

As she came forward into the circle of light thrown by the bedside lamp I saw she was wearing a blue evening frock. She was flushed and her eyes were shining. I had never seen her look like this before; she seemed to have come alive.

'Aspirin?' I said. 'Yes, of course. Are you feverish, Anthea?'

'Yes, feverish,' said Anthea in a queer excited way. 'I shan't sleep a wink unless I can have something to take. Have you any sleeping pills?'

'I've got aspirin – that's all. I'll get the bottle out of my case.'

'Don't bother, it isn't really aspirin I want.'

'What's the matter, Anthea?'

She sat down on the end of my bed. 'There's nothing the matter – or everything. Sometimes I feel life isn't worth while.'

'You want to go to London and study painting, don't you?'

'I wanted to do that – but they wouldn't let me – it's too late now.'

'Anthea,' I said earnestly. 'It isn't too late. Why don't you go to your grandfather and speak to him seriously about it? Tell him —'

'Tell him!' she exclaimed. 'You've been here a week; surely you know who does the "telling" in this house! Besides, I don't want it now.'

'You don't want it?' I asked in surprise. 'I thought you were very keen on your painting.'

'I'm bored with it. I'm no good, you know. I don't suppose I shall ever be any good.'

'If you had lessons —'

'I've told you I'm bored with painting. I want – I want something quite different.'

'What do you want?'

'I want – the moon!' she cried. 'That's funny, isn't it? Why don't you laugh, Katherine?'

'Listen, Anthea,' I said as firmly as I could. 'If you don't tell me what's the matter I can't help you, can I?'

'I don't want help!'

'Then why did you come?'

'I don't know,' said Anthea piteously. 'I had to talk to someone and there was nobody else. Talk to me, Katherine. Talk about anything – it doesn't matter what – I can't go to bed feeling like this.'

Anthea had said I was to talk to her but I could think of nothing to say. I gazed at her helplessly.

'Talk about anything,' she repeated.

'Have you been to a party?' I asked – it was the first thing that came into my head. 'You look as if you had been to a party. You're wearing a very pretty frock.'

'No, not a party; just out for a drive with – with someone.'

'With Oliver Wade?'

'How did you know?'

'I didn't know. I just thought he was a friend of yours, that's all.'

'Why shouldn't I go out with him?' she demanded. 'He can't come here – they're beastly to him. They're beastly to him,' she repeated furiously. 'You saw how beastly they were the day he came to lunch. He had to creep out by the side door in case the Bart saw him and kicked up a row. You liked him, didn't you, Katherine? You were laughing and having jokes with him; he's amusing and – and attractive, isn't he?'

'Yes, very.'

She leant forward and lowered her voice. 'He's wild and dangerous, that's why I like him.'

'Dangerous?'

'He drives like a madman – it's terribly exciting – it's terrifying! His car goes like a rocket, rushing through the darkness; the wind whistles in your ears. Then suddenly he stops and switches off the lights. . . .'

'Anthea, you shouldn't —'

'Oh, yes, he's dangerous,' she continued breathlessly. 'You never know what he'll do next. I could tell you – but I won't. I've told you too much already. I'd better go to bed.'

I took her hand and said earnestly, 'Listen to me, Anthea. I'm older than you are and much more experienced —'

'I don't want a sermon!' she exclaimed, snatching her hand away and rising and going towards the door.

'Be careful, Anthea.'

'Be careful!' she echoed scornfully. 'That's what everyone says: be careful – slow down – this hill is dangerous – fasten your safety belt! But I say, let's have a jolly good time while we're alive. When the bomb falls we'll all be blown up together; safety belts won't be much good.' She opened the bathroom door. 'Good night, Katherine,' she said – and shut the door firmly behind her before I could reply.

I was half-way out of bed to go after her when I heard the key turn in the lock. So that was that.

Anthea's troubles were beyond me. She had taken me by surprise; perhaps I might have done more to help her if I had been prepared. I had tried to warn her, but she had thrown the warning back in my face. I felt I had mismanaged the whole thing.

For a long time I lay and thought about Anthea and wondered what on earth I could do. I had thought she was unhappy; I saw now that she was desperate. I was sorry for her – terribly sorry – and worried. Something ought to be done – but what? Should I go round to the other door and try to make her listen to me? I knew it would be useless. It would be absolutely useless to go to her mother; I knew that. I wondered if I should tell Sir Mortimer what was happening – that would blow everything sky-high – but somehow I couldn't bring myself to betray Anthea's confidence and deliver her into his hands. Perhaps that was what I should have done – but I couldn't do it.

At last I gave it up in despair; there was nothing I could do, absolutely nothing.

5

Simon came downstairs in the morning whilst I was having breakfast. He sat and talked to me and drank a cup of tea. I had not slept for more than a couple of hours so I was tired and depressed; it was difficult to appear cheerful.

Then, just as I was leaving, Sir Mortimer came down to say good-bye. We shook hands and I thanked him for his hospitality.

'Your visit has been too short, you must stay longer next time,' he said. 'At Christmas, perhaps, when this young man is in Austria. Arrange that, Katherine.'

Simon was kissing me, so I could not reply. 'Take care of yourself, Mums,' he was saying. 'I'll be coming soon.'

Hurrell was waiting at the bottom of the steps with the door of the car open. I ran down the steps and got in.

'Good-bye, Mums!' cried Simon, waving his hand.

As the car moved off down the drive I looked back and saw the two figures standing in the doorway; Sir Mortimer had his hand on Simon's shoulder.

PART THREE

CHAPTER 20

'Help, you're strangling me!' I cried.

The twins released me from their embrace. 'But you don't mind being strangled – for love,' said Daisy.

I didn't really mind . . . but it is a trifle disturbing to be wakened early in the morning (after a long journey the day before) by four arms wound tightly round your neck. As a matter of fact I had dreamt that I was in the toils of an octopus, but I was awake now and the dream had given place to reality. I had arrived at the flat the night before and was here in my own bed with my own rather shabby but dearly-loved furniture all around me. It was late when I arrived, the children had been asleep, but Aunt Liz had been here to greet me and to assure me that all had gone well. She had then taken her departure and said good-bye, for she was flying to Copenhagen the following morning with a friend.

The twins had wakened early – as they always did – and here they were, sitting upon my bed and strangling me – for love.

'No, I don't mind,' I said and hugged them close.

'You won't go away again, will you?' said Den.

'Not for a long, long time anyhow.'

'Never,' said Den firmly.

'But you've been quite happy with Aunt Liz, haven't you?'

'We haven't been miserable,' admitted Daisy.

'She has been very kind to you,' I pointed out. 'She took you to a party at West Linton; you've had fun with Bella; you've been to the Zoo and —'

'But you've been away such a long, long time,' complained Den.

I didn't argue the matter for, although I had been away for only a week, it seemed a very long time to me. 'Well, I'm back now,' I said cheerfully. 'And the next thing is to get everything ready for Thursday.'

'We'll help you to pack,' said Daisy.

I knew that I should have to get up in a few minutes and prepare breakfast, but I put off the task as long as I could by telling them some of my adventures and making them as interesting as possible.

'Are we going to Limbourne some day?' inquired Daisy.

'I don't think you'd like it much.'

'Because we'd have to be good all the time,' said Den, nodding to show that he understood.

'Yes, every single minute,' I said firmly. 'You'd have to be as quiet as mice and do what you were told and never, never argue.'

'But Simon likes it,' Den pointed out. 'If Simon hadn't liked it he would have come home, wouldn't he?'

'Yes,' I said – and sighed.

'When is Simon coming?' asked Daisy anxiously.

'Soon,' I replied. 'He'll come when we're settled at the cottage.' Then I hugged them again and kissed their soft cheeks and got up to make their breakfast.

It was a busy day, washing and ironing and packing, but although I had so much to do I was happy (I felt like a woman who has just been released from prison). After tea I went out to engage seats in the train for our journey on Thursday and to get the tickets, leaving the children alone in the flat. It was not often that I left them alone – and never at night, of course – but they were quite sensible so I was not worried. They were delighted at the idea of being on their own and assured me that there was no need for me to hurry back.

The errand took a little longer than I expected – I was away for nearly three-quarters of an hour – so I ran up the stairs as quickly as I could and put my latch-key in the door.

Immediately, the door was flung open and they fell upon me with shrieks of delight – as if I had been away for days.

'Guess who's been here!' cried Daisy.

'What do you mean?' I asked.

'We've had a visitor,' said Den.

'Guess who!' cried Daisy.

'She'll never guess,' declared Den.

'She'll never guess!' sang Daisy, capering round in her usual crazy way. 'She'll never guess – so we'll have to tell her. It was Uncle Arly.'

'Uncle who?' I asked in bewilderment.

'That's what he said we were to call him,' explained Den. 'It wasn't his real name, of course.'

They were in such tearing spirits that I thought the whole thing was a joke. I took off my jacket and went into the kitchen to prepare an omelet for supper . . . but the two pursued me, Daisy chattering and Den putting in a word or two when she paused for breath.

'All right,' I said. 'It was a good joke but it's over now.'

'It isn't a joke,' declared Den. 'He was here for nearly half an hour but he had to go.'

'He had to go,' echoed Daisy, laughing merrily. 'He had to go and sit on a heap of barley.'

'Do be quiet and tell me properly!' I said.

'Which?' asked Den. 'If we've got to be quiet we can't tell you.'

'He was in a joky mood,' said Daisy. 'He said it was because he was free to do what he wanted. He said he'd just got out of school – but that was silly. Old people like him don't have to go to school.'

'Who was it?' I asked as I broke the eggs into the bowl and stirred them gently.

'Uncle Arly of course,' said Daisy. 'We wanted to make tea for him, but of course we couldn't because we'd promised not to light anything while you were away – and he said, "Quite right, I'll have a drink of water."'

'We gave him orange juice,' put in Den.

'He said it was very refreshing,' added Daisy.

'Who was it?' I repeated. 'Did he leave a message?'

'He wrote his telephone number on the block,' said Den. 'He said you were to ring him up between eight and nine o'clock to-night. There, that's the message.'

'He said we could all fit in,' declared Daisy, chuckling. 'He said to me, "You're a bit overweight of course, but we'll squeeze you in somehow." And when I said, "What about the luggage?" he said, "Yes, all except the grand piano." That was a joke,' explained Daisy. 'He knows we haven't got a grand piano and, even if we had, we wouldn't want to take it to the cottage.'

'Daisy!' I exclaimed. 'I don't know what you're talking about.'

'Uncle Arly, of course. He was sitting on a heap of barley with a railway ticket in his hat. It's a poem and we're going to learn it so that we can say it to him and —'

'Daisy!' I cried. 'Will you be quiet and let Den explain!' I said it in my 'no nonsense' voice which they knew must be obeyed.

'It was Mr. Maclaren,' said Den soberly. 'He's going to take us to Loch Ron on Thursday in his car. You've to ring him up and fix the time.'

I was struck dumb with surprise. Alec! What was he doing here? He was to have gone to London with Zilla. I had imagined him in London. At last I found my voice. 'Are you sure?' I asked.

'Of course I'm sure,' replied Den. 'I told you the message. He wrote his number on the block. It's his club. He'll be there between eight and nine o'clock.'

'Won't it be fun?' cried Daisy. 'No horrid old trains! His car goes like a bomb. It went like a bomb when he took us to Queensferry. Isn't it gorgeous, Mums?'

I made the omelet quickly and the children helped me to carry in the plates. All the time I kept on wondering why Alec had changed his plans. Why hadn't he gone to London with Zilla? Why had he offered to take us to Craig-an-Ron in his car? Why had his mood suddenly changed from deep depression to high spirits? I should know the answers to all these questions when I rang him up, of course. I decided to refuse his offer to take us. The children would be disappointed but that could not be helped. I must tell Alec that our plans were all fixed to go by train, our seats engaged and the tickets bought. I must tell Alec that there was no need for him to bother.

2

It was half past eight before I had got the children off to bed and was free to ring up Alec's club. He must have been waiting, for they found him at once.

'Alec,' I said. 'What have you done to my children? They're quite crazy.'

He laughed. 'We were all crazy togther; it was fun. I'm Uncle Arly – did they tell you?'

'Why Uncle Arly? It's Lear, isn't it?'

'Yes, I've forgotten most of it but I'm going to look it up for them. I shall give half a crown to the one who says it best.'

'A shilling will be ample.'

'Sweated labour!' exclaimed Alec, chuckling.

'Alec, listen. Why didn't you go to London with Zilla?'

'But I did,' declared Alec's voice in reproachful accents. 'I said I would go to London with Zilla – so of course I went. I couldn't stay in London because my lungs aren't adjusted to breathing petrol fumes and diesel oil. I came back this morning by plane. When your lungs rebel you feel extremely ill.'

'You don't sound ill. In fact you sound particularly full of beans.'

He gave a hollow cough. 'I'm very ill,' he said. 'That's why it's essential for me to have a breath of pure Highland air.'

'You aren't really going to Loch Ron?'

'Yes, on Thursday. Didn't they tell you?'

'Alec, please be sensible. There's no need for you to take us. I've bought our tickets to Inverquill and engaged seats in the train.'

'British Railways will refund the money.'

'And I've engaged a car to meet us at Inverquill and take us to the cottage,' I said desperately. 'It's all arranged, Alec.'

'You can disarrange it.'

'Alec, listen. You can't stay at the cottage.'

'Of course not. I shall put up at the inn in the village for a few days until I recover.'

'Zilla said the inn was dreadfully uncomfortable.'

He laughed. 'Zilla probably said, "My dear, it's frightful . . . an outside lavatory and no bath."'

'Something like that,' I admitted.

'But I don't mind,' explained Alec. 'I can swim in the loch every morning. As for the other inconvenience —'

'Quite,' I said hurriedly. 'I just thought if you were ill —'

'Lungs,' he reminded me. 'Rebellious lungs.'

'It sounds horrid.'

'Air is what I want; lovely fresh Highland air and lashings of cream to my porridge. You understand, don't you?'

'Yes, perfectly. It's terribly kind of you, Alec.'

'What is kind?'

'To take us, of course – and our luggage – with the exception of the grand piano.'

He laughed and said, 'Do they tell you everything?'

'They told me that, anyhow.'

'Katherine, I want to see you. Can I come along now?'

'No,' I replied firmly. 'I'm tired. I'm going to bed.'

'Just for a few minutes to arrange what time we should start.'

'You can tell me now. I'm listening.'

'But, look here, I shall have to stop talking. There's a fellow making faces at me through the glass. Perhaps he thinks I've been talking too long, or something.'

'You've been talking much too long. Just tell me what time you want us to be ready on Thursday morning and then ring off.'

'Oh, well, we can't start until about half past eleven because I've got to look in at the office first. I'm afraid it will make us a bit late at the other end but it can't be helped.'

'We'll be ready at half past eleven.'

'I might be delayed,' said Alec's voice doubtfully.

'Just come when you can. We'll be ready,' I told him.

I put down the receiver and sat there, wondering. He had sounded unlike his usual self – excited, irresponsible. Daisy had said he was in a joky mood, because he was free . . . free to do what he wanted. I had intended to refuse his offer to take us to Loch Ron, but he had made it impossible for me to refuse. Quite honestly I didn't want to go with Alec in his car – and I didn't want Alec at Loch Ron. I wanted to get right away and have a peaceful time with the children. I wanted to be quiet and think things out; there were so many things, all tangled up in my mind like Florence Godfrey's wool. The children were not exactly peaceful companions but they didn't make demands upon my thoughts. I could dream my own dreams and attend to the children with the surface of my mind . . . but now Alec was coming! I couldn't attend to him with the surface of my mind. Alec was invading my stronghold – yes, invading was the word – and I had to be on my guard to keep him out.

Alec was a very good friend – that was what I wanted – the other sort of relationship was over and done with as far as I was concerned.

I realised suddenly that I was very very tired, so I rose and went to bed.

CHAPTER 21

The weather conditions on Thursday morning were not propitious – clouds were rolling in from the east and a light drizzle was falling – but in spite of this the children were in tremendously high spirits.

Alec was ten minutes late in calling for us, he arrived in a fluster full of abject apologies.

'It's all right,' I said soothingly. 'You couldn't help being delayed. Don't worry about it, Alec.'

He looked at me in surprise and I realised that if he had kept Zilla waiting her reaction would have been different. The idea made me smile.

We had several large suitcases and two kit-bags – and of course the children had discovered various odds and ends which could not possibly be left behind. However, there was plenty of room in Alec's car and everything was stowed away comfortably except the children's bicycles which I had arranged to send by train to Inverquill.

It was unfortunate that we had not a better day for the run, the drizzle continued steadily and there was mist on the hills. We stopped somewhere on the road and had lunch in the car; Alec had brought a picnic basket prepared for us by Ellen.

'This isn't a proper picnic,' began Daisy in disapproving tones. 'When you go for proper picnics —'

'Of course not,' I said firmly. 'This is an *al fresco* meal. Wasn't it kind of Ellen to make such lovely sausage rolls?'

Den was munching happily. He said, 'I liked Ellen, she was fat and smiley. She said we had nice manners and she made meringues even better than Bella.'

'I'm afraid there aren't any meringues to-day,' said Alec apologetically.

'They would be quite unsuitable for an *al fresco* meal,' I declared with conviction.

Daisy was squashed. She said no more about 'proper picnics' but set to work upon the sausage rolls and salad and cheese-cakes and various other good things with her usual gusto.

'*Al fresco*,' said Den, who was always interested in new

words. 'When we have lunch like this in Clara it's an *al fresco*, but when we have lunch outside it's a picnic. Is that right, Mums?'

It wasn't, of course, so I had to explain.

We had hoped that the day would improve but there was mist and rain nearly all the way. Here and there the clouds lifted a little and we caught glimpses of moors and lochs and craggy mountains but for the most part there was nothing to be seen but grey mist and driving rain.

'This is frightfully disappointing,' said Alec at last. 'It's such a lovely run in fine weather. You would have enjoyed it.'

'You can't control the weather,' I pointed out.

'I know, but all the same I feel I ought to have been able to provide a fine day for your visit to Craig-an-Ron – and I'm afraid we shall be a bit late in arriving because I can't risk going at a decent pace. The visibility is so poor. Would you like to stop somewhere for tea or shall we push on?'

'Let's push on,' I said. I was beginning to feel very tired and all I wanted was to get to our destination as soon as possible.

At first the children had been good and happy, but presently they became restless and kept on asking how much farther we had to go, so we stopped and I got into the back seat beside them and told them stories.

It was nearly seven o'clock when Alec said, 'Look, this is Loch Ron village! That's the little inn where I'm going to stay. We haven't far to go now.'

'But aren't you going to stay with us at the cottage?' asked Daisy in surprise.

'No,' replied Alec.

'Why not?' inquired Den. 'It would be much nicer.'

'There won't be room for me at the cottage.'

'But you could have Simon's room!' exclaimed Daisy. 'Mums, he could have Simon's room, couldn't he? It would be much cheaper for Uncle Arly to stay at the cottage.'

Poor Daisy! She was used to counting the pennies so she could not understand why I did not extend a pressing invitation to 'Uncle Arly' to come and stay with us at the cottage. She continued to argue about the matter, backed up by Den, until we arrived at Craig-an-Ron.

The rain had stopped, but it was a dull misty evening

so we could see little of our surroundings. All we could see was the small whitewashed building with its lighted windows. The door opened as we arrived and a man and a woman came out.

'Here are Mr. and Mrs. MacRam,' said Alec cheerfully. 'They'll look after you all right.'

'Yes, indeed,' declared Mrs. MacRam. 'Supper is ready. The poor wee children will be ferry tired and hungry. Och, it has been an awful day of rain! It has never ceased for a minute. I have a fire in the sitting-room – it is nice there. Will Mistress Wentworth come in and warm herself?'

'Yes, go in, Katherine,' said Alec. 'Don't hang about in the cold. I won't wait now. I'll see you to-morrow.'

By this time Mr. MacRam – a silent man – had finished carrying in the luggage so Alec got into his car and drove away.

Zilla had said the cottage was 'primitive' and 'a wretched hovel,' but to me it seemed charming. The two good bedrooms were large and airy; the bedrooms on the top floor (which Zilla had described as 'monkish') were small and had sloping ceilings but, in spite of this, were perfectly comfortable. The children wanted these rooms – chiefly because the stair up to them was like a ladder – and I agreed. (Simon, when he came, could have the larger bedroom next to mine.)

We had supper and unpacked and I put the children to bed. By this time I was absolutely dazed with fatigue. I had been tired when I left Limbourne – tired and worried – and I had spent two strenuous days washing and ironing and packing. The long motor-run in the rain had finished me. I refused Mrs. MacRam's offer of a bath, stripped off my clothes and fell into Zilla's extremely comfortable bed with a sigh of relief.

2

When I opened my eyes next morning I gazed round in bewilderment. I had been dreaming about Limbourne so I had expected to see the luxuriously appointed room with its polished furniture and tall windows and long crimson curtains . . . instead of which I saw the smaller, simply furnished room and low casement windows with flowery cretonne curtains moving gently in the breeze.

Then I remembered and glanced at my watch. It was ten o'clock!

What on earth could have happened? I had told Mrs. MacRam to waken me at eight and we would have breakfast at half past; for, although I was so weary that I felt I could sleep for a week, I knew that the children would be up early, merry and bright – and hungry.

For a few minutes I lay and listened. There was not a sound to be heard: no babble of children's voices, no patter of feet. There was no sound at all except the distant cry of a curlew – so faint and far-off that it was scarcely distinguishable.

I put on my dressing-gown and ran downstairs. The sitting-room was spick and span – and empty. The front door was open and for a moment I stood there, in the hall, quite breathless at the beauty of the scene framed in the doorway. The stretch of smooth green turf sloped down to the shore of the loch which lay still and clear like a mirror reflecting the hills. Beyond that were the hills themselves, towering into mountains, their outlines cutting a jagged slice out of the bright blue sky.

I was standing there entranced, when I heard a movement behind me and turned to see Mrs. MacRam emerge from the kitchen premises, padding softly in carpet slippers.

'Och, and I was hoping Mistress Wentworth was sleeping!' she exclaimed in her gentle musical voice.

'I'm terribly late —'

'But you were ferry weary. It was a long, long way to come – and the packing up and everything.'

'The children —' I began.

'Children waken early like the birds. They took their porridge and boiled eggs and have gone away out to explore.'

'I never heard a sound!'

'There was no sound to hear,' explained Mrs. MacRam with a happy smile. 'It was just a little game we had – the children and me – to be very quiet and not waken Mother.'

'How kind of you!'

'Och, it was not kind at all. I am very happy with children.'

'Where have they gone? Will they be all right?'

'They will be quite safe,' she replied placidly. 'I have

said they must not go near the loch – and they are very biddable. There is nothing to hurt them on the hill, just the sheep and the birds and the little burns amongst the heather. Mistress Wentworth need not worry.'

I was not worrying. There was something sweet and peaceful about this little spot – and Mrs. MacRam was sweet and peaceful too. I had been too tired last night to look at her properly, but now I saw that she was plump and rosy with dark smooth hair and brown eyes. Her voice was delightful and her slight Highland accent attractive; it was part of her make-up. She had said, 'It wass chust a little game we had' and 'I am ferry happy with chiltren.' Mr. MacRam's accent was much more noticeable and one had a feeling that English was really a foreign language to him. Afterwards, when I knew them better, I discovered that when they were alone they always spoke to each other in Gaelic.

Mrs. MacRam tried to persuade me to return to bed, but I wanted to go out, so I had a quick bath in Zilla's super bathroom, dressed hastily and ate my breakfast in the sitting-room near the widely open window.

When I had finished Mrs. MacRam gave me a tartan plaid and told me to spread it in the shade of a little grove of rowan trees beside the loch.

'The grass will be a little damp this morning,' explained Mrs. MacRam, 'but it is a nice thick plaid and it will be restful for Mistress Wentworth to lie there in the shade.'

'Yes, lovely,' I agreed, 'but what about food? Perhaps we should arrange what to have.'

'Och, it will be easier for me to do the catering. I am used to children, good plain fare is what they need.'

'Do you mean you'll order everything?' I asked in surprise.

She nodded. 'There is a ferry good butcher in the village and other shops as well. The grocer is a cousin of Mister MacRam so he will bring all we need in his van. I have only to send a message with the postie. It is all quite easy – if that will suit.'

It suited me admirably. I had been wondering how we were going to get supplies but now I realised that I need not have bothered; I was only too glad to leave the matter in Mrs. MacRam's capable hands. As I spread the plaid in the shade of the trees I could not help smiling. Despite her gentle manner there was a strange sort of strength in the woman – it was not surprising that she had found the children 'biddable.'

The turf was short and soft, the rowan leaves spread a flickering shade over my head. It was absolute peace. I had lain there for some time when I saw a shadow move across the grass and looked up to see Alec standing there.

'I hope I didn't wake you,' he said.

'I wasn't asleep – just lazy.'

'Am I disturbing you?'

'Of course not! Come and sit down, Alec.' I moved to make room for him on the rug and added, 'This is a perfectly heavenly place; it's so blissful to have nothing to do.'

He smiled and sat down beside me. 'Yes, you're looking better already; I was awfully worried about you yesterday. I didn't want to say anything while the children were there, but you looked so strained and miserable. Did you have a troublesome time at Limbourne? I can't believe they were disagreeable to you.'

'They weren't. They were really very kind, but – but I didn't like them much, I'm sorry to say.'

'And Simon?'

'Alec,' I said, 'I want to tell you about it. I want a solid, sensible man's opinion about the whole thing.'

He smiled at me. 'Well, I'm solid all right and I hope I'm fairly sensible.'

'Could you bear it if I told you everything?' I asked, sitting up and looking at him. 'It will take a long time but unless I tell you everything it's no good.'

'Not the slightest good,' agreed Alec. 'Tell me everything. Time doesn't matter in this place; that's what makes it so peaceful. Begin at the very beginning and go on till you get to the end.'

So that's what I did. I told Alec all about Limbourne, its absolute tidiness and perfection, which extended to the rose-garden where every little bush had to obey its owner's rule. I told him what everybody had said and done – as far as I could remember – finally I told him about Sir Mortimer's plans for Simon.

When I had finished there was quite a long silence.

At last Alec said, 'You mustn't allow it, Katherine. It isn't the right thing for Simon.'

'Not right!' I exclaimed in surprise. 'I thought you'd say it was sensible.'

'You feel it's the wrong thing, don't you?'

'Yes, but I feel it's wrong to – to feel it's wrong,' I explained. 'It's sensible for Simon to learn to look after the estate. My feelings about it are stupid.'

'Your feelings aren't stupid. Simon is too young and immature to be thrown into deep water and left to sink or swim.'

'Yes, it's deep water – muddy water – with undercurrents.'

'Dangerous,' said Alec thoughtfully. 'Not right for Simon. The right thing for Simon would be to go to Cambridge – and grow up. It would be time enough after that for him to go to Limbourne and learn about the management of the property. Do think of this seriously, Katherine.'

'Think of it!' I exclaimed. 'There's no need for me to think of it! It's what I've always wanted for Simon – it's what Gerald wanted for his son. Gerald used to say that a thoroughly sound education was never wasted; it didn't matter what you were going to do in life, even if you were going to be a dustman. . . .'

'He had the right idea.'

'But I can't afford it!'

'I could afford it.'

'Of course you could, but I can't, so it's no use thinking about it any more. As a matter of fact it's no use talking about it, because it's settled. Simon is going to Limbourne when he leaves school.'

'Does Simon want to do that?'

'At first he was a little doubtful, but he has decided now that it's the right thing to do.'

'Quite definitely?'

I nodded. 'Perhaps I shouldn't have bothered you about it and asked your advice but I was sure you would say it was the sensible thing and I was silly to worry. I hoped you'd say that, Alec.'

Alec sighed. 'I can't say that, but if it has been decided definitely we shall have to leave it in the meantime. Here's a piece of advice which may be helpful. Shelve the whole problem. Simon will have two more years at school so leave off bothering about his future; shelve it, Katherine. It's quite a sound way of dealing with future problems. I've discovered that. I had a problem and I worried myself into fits about it. Then, when the time came, everything changed and it solved itself. So just pack up future problems and put them on the top shelf and forget about them – see?'

'Yes,' I said doubtfully. 'But what will change? Two years from now everything will be the same.'

'How do you know? Two years is quite a long time. All sorts of things can happen in two years.'

Alec had meant it kindly but to me the words had a sinister meaning. I was silent, thinking about all the things that might happen in two years. . . .

'Katherine, don't look like that!' Alec exclaimed.

'Like what?'

'Tragic. You're afraid you'll lose Simon, aren't you?'

'Not altogether,' I said slowly. 'But – but those people have different values, a different way of living. Simon will spend part of his holidays there. If it would be better for Simon I could bear it – I could even be happy about it.'

'They won't be able to take him away from you.'

'Do you mean they'll try?'

'You think so, don't you?'

'Yes.'

'They won't succeed. You won't lose the boy.'

I said in a low voice, 'He has been promised a lavish allowance – a car of his own – two hunters – ski-ing in Austria. What boy could say no to all that? And Simon has had nothing!' I was almost in tears. 'He's had nothing, Alec. He's never known what it is to have enough money in his pocket; we've always had to count every penny. Perhaps I'm being selfish. Perhaps I'm jealous – possessive – I can't be sure.'

'You are none of these horrible things,' said Alec, putting out his hand and patting my knee. 'Don't torture yourself, Katherine.'

We were silent for quite a long time after that. I was thinking about Alec's advice to 'shelve the problem' and deciding that I must do my best to take it. Perhaps before the time came for Simon to leave school something unexpected would have happened and he would be able to go to Cambridge after all . . . and 'grow up,' as Alec had put it.

'Alec,' I said at last, 'I've sometimes wondered why you went to Cambridge.'

He smiled and said, 'To read Law.'

'But English Law is different. I suppose you must have had to read Scots Law as well.'

'Yes, I had to take a degree at Edinburgh University. As a matter of fact it's a case in point – the case of your dustman. Everybody told me that if I intended to practise in Edinburgh it was a waste of time to go to Cambridge and everybody was wrong.'

'You know both kinds now. That's useful, of course.'

He laughed. 'Well, I wouldn't put it quite like that, but you've got the idea. To study something worth while is never a waste of time . . . and there were other things at Cambridge besides work. There was the way of life, there were friends and good talk; last but not least there was cricket. I wouldn't have missed Cambridge for anything. That's why I want it for Simon.'

I did not reply. I, too, wanted it for Simon but I could not give it to him.

Alec rose. He said, 'Shelve it, Katherine. Don't worry. That's my advice.'

He was walking away and then suddenly turned and came back. 'What an ass I am!' he exclaimed. 'I came over on purpose to say that I'd take the children out in the boat after tea – and you, too, if you feel inclined.'

'Don't you want to fish?' I asked in surprise.

'Obviously you aren't a fisherwoman,' he replied, laughing.

This time he strode off briskly and did not look back. I watched him until he had disappeared into the wood.

CHAPTER 22

The sky remained blue and cloudless; the loch was like a sheet of glass, there was not the slightest whiff of wind to ruffle its calm surface. I had discovered by sounding Mrs. MacRam in a tactful manner that blue skies and calm, clear water was not the weather for fishermen. 'They are very clever, the fish,' she explained. 'If they see a boat and a line they go away down to the bottom. Thunder is bad too. Maybe there will be grey skies and a nice breeze soon and then Mistress Wentworth will get a trout for her breakfast.'

This information relieved my mind. Fishing was hopeless to-day, so Alec was not giving up his sport to take us out in the boat.

Another thing I discovered from Mrs. MacRam was the name of the village – which Zilla had omitted to tell me.

'The loch is Loch Ron,' she said in answer to my question. 'So the village is chust called Loch Ron . . . and the cottage is called Craig-an-Ron because of the big cliff behind. If you walk up the path by the burn you can see how pretty it is, with the bell-heather in bloom and little ferns in the crevices of the rocks. It is a pretty walk to the village too, through the woods and across the moor, or you can go along by the side of the loch – but that way is longer. It is longer still if you go by the road. I am glad you are going out in the boat after tea, the children will enjoy it. The boat belongs to Mister MacRam but the arrangement is that Mister Maclaren can have it when he likes. There is a boathouse round the promontory where the boat is kept. Mistress Wentworth can have the use of it while she is here.'

'Oh, thank you.'

'There is no need for thanks. It is the arrangement,' explained Mrs. MacRam.

When we had finished tea we went out and sat on the grass, waiting for Alec to come, and I pointed out to the children that the hills and the trees and the jagged rocks on the opposite shore of the loch were all reflected faithfully in the calm water.

'How funny! It's just like a mirror,' said Den.

Daisy rose, and standing firmly with her back to the loch looked at it between her legs. 'No, you can't,' she said breathlessly – her figure was not the kind that bends easily from the waist.

'Can't what?' asked Den.

'Tell the difference,' she replied. 'Try it, Den. It's the same whichever way you look.'

They were both looking at the loch upside down when Alec came in sight, rowing round the little promontory.

'What's going on?' he asked as he pulled in to the shore.

'It's an experiment,' explained Den.

'Come and try it, Uncle Arly!' cried Daisy. 'It looks the same both ways – the rocks and trees and everything. Mums won't try it, but you're sporting, aren't you?'

'Extremely sporting,' he replied and, leaping out of the

boat, he assumed the correct posture for the experiment.

At this moment Mr. MacRam came out of the wood and was petrified with astonishment. Unfortunately his dog was not petrified, but immediately rushed at the three strange figures, barking furiously. Daisy fell flat on her face, Den fled for his life and Alec stood up looking flushed and sheepish.

'Och thiss iss dreadful!' exclaimed Mr. MacRam, as he seized the dog by the scruff of the neck and cuffed it vigorously. 'I haff neffer seen Pruce do such a thing pefore, Mister Maclaren. I am thinking the teffel hass got into him.'

'It was a game,' explained Alec. 'The children were looking at the reflection upside down and wanted me to try it – quite silly, of course – no wonder Bruce thought we'd gone mad. Don't beat him, Mr. MacRam, it wasn't his fault.'

I had been wrestling with giggles; but now, having overcome them, I was able to speak so I rose and joined in the conversation, saying how greatly we were enjoying our stay in the cottage and the delicious food Mrs. MacRam was providing for us.

'Och, she iss not a pad cook at all,' he agreed proudly. 'She iss baking cakes sometimes for the W.R.I. and getting prizes for them. She iss saying it iss a pleasure to be cooking for Mistress Wentworth and the chiltren.'

By this time Den had appeared from behind the shelter of a boulder so, after a few more complimentary exchanges, we embarked and Alec rowed off with fierce strokes which sent the little boat tearing through the water at a terrific pace.

'Alec, you'll make yourself terribly hot. It isn't a race!' I exclaimed.

He laughed and slowed down. 'There's nothing better than rowing for letting off steam. Gosh, what a fool I felt! It must have been damn' funny for an onlooker.'

'It was,' I admitted.

'These people are so dignified, that's the trouble. Mr. MacRam will never have any respect for me again.'

'Uncle Arly, row us to the island,' said Daisy. 'Mr. MacRam says there are bits of an old castle on the island where people used to live long ago.'

'There aren't many "bits",' Alec told her. 'There's just

a piece of wall. Some day they're going to excavate but meantime the whole place is thick with nettles and brambles. The piece of wall is the remains of an old fort; it's vitrified – if you know what that means – but it isn't particularly interesting, unless you're an archaeologist, of course.'

This was far above Daisy's head, but fortunately she had become interested in a family of swans so she did not demand an explanation.

There are few pleasures more delightful than to lie back upon a cushion and to be rowed with long slow strokes upon the calm bosom of a Highland loch. The skies were blue; the sun was golden; the murmur of the water against the sides of the boat was soothing. Alec rowed along the edge of the loch where tall rushes swayed gently in the ripples and the damp scent of marsh herbs filled the air with a strange astringent smell. Presently we came to a broken-down landing-stage behind which some tumbled walls and a rowan tree proclaimed the fact that there had once been a cottage in this out-of-the-way spot. The children wanted to land and 'explore,' so Alec pulled the boat shorewards and helped them out.

'Can we be long?' asked Den anxiously.

This curious request was the outcome of the usual injunction from grown-ups: 'Don't be long.' I was about to explain it to Alec, but there was no need.

'You can be as long as you like,' he replied, settling himself comfortably in the bottom of the boat and taking out his pipe.

They ran up towards the ruined cottage and disappeared.

It was very peaceful when they had gone. We did not speak for some time. I was thinking how good Alec was with the children, how kind and understanding. Few men would have sat there doing nothing peacefully and looking happy about it.

Suddenly Alec looked up at me and smiled, 'I know what you're thinking,' he said. 'As a matter of fact I often know what you're thinking. You don't mind, do you?'

'What was I thinking?'

'Just feeling a bit surprised because I'm happy doing nothing. Is that right?'

'Yes.'

'It's because I'm with you, that's all. Quite simple, really.'

'We're friends,' I said quickly. 'That's what we are, Alec – good friends.'

'Yes, I know,' he agreed. He smiled and added, 'I'm "solid and sensible."'

'That – and more. It's wonderful to have a friend like you,' I told him.

He did not speak.

'You're happier now, aren't you?' I said. 'When you wrote to me you seemed terribly depressed and wretched.'

'It was a foolish letter, wasn't it? "The grasshopper was a burden" – that's what I said, didn't I?'

'But the grasshopper has ceased to be a burden?'

'Yes, I'll tell you about it some time – but not now. Here come the victors laden with spoils.'

Here they came, leaping down the slope, their hands full of flowers which they had found in the neglected garden: trails of honeysuckle fresh and fragrant, little moss-roses tightly packed in their little green sheaths, all mixed up with meadow-sweet and bluebells and spikes of lavender. It was a queer sort of bouquet, but there was something rather attractive about it and the scent was delicious.

'We didn't think anybody would mind us picking them,' explained Daisy in her usual breathless way. 'They were all growing wild, you see, and nobody has been there for about a hundred years. I think they felt lonely and wanted to be picked. I do, really.'

'I'm sure they felt lonely,' agreed Alec quite gravely. He filled the baler with water from the loch and put in all the flowers.

'That will keep them nice and fresh till we get home,' he added.

2

Saturday was another day of sunshine and blue skies. It was Alec's last day at Loch Ron so he asked if we would like to have lunch with him at the inn and I accepted gladly. I was pleased, not only because it would be a pleasant change, but also because it would give Mrs. MacRam a break in her routine. I had asked when she liked to take her 'day off' and she had looked at me in astonishment.

Apparently the idea of having 'a day off' or even 'an afternoon off' had never crossed her mind. 'But who would be cooking the dinner!' she had exclaimed in horrified tones.

The children were delighted at the prospect of lunching at the inn, they made none of the usual objections when I called them from their morning's play at the loch-side and made them put on their best clothes for the occasion. Den looked neat and tidy in his grey flannel shorts and white shirt, and Daisy wore the summer frock I had made for her; it was yellow and sprigged with a pattern of daisies.

'It's my very own frock!' she cried as she danced gaily up the path. 'It makes me happy.'

I, too, felt happy. The little frock was a success; well worth the trouble it had given me. It was also very becoming. When we see people every day and all day long we cease to see them as they really are, but to-day it struck me that my daughter was very pretty indeed. Her skin, tanned by the sun, made her eyes look as blue as forget-me-nots and her hair was as golden as buttercups.

We walked through the wood and along the path which led across the moor and presently came to Loch Ron village. There was just one crooked street which sloped down to the little jetty. A few boats were lying there, fastened securely to bollards on the wide stone wall. The inn was half-way up the street, it had been newly painted and looked fresh and clean, with little net curtains in the windows. Opposite the inn was a large and very beautiful chestnut tree and beneath it stood Alec's car.

'Look, there's Clara!' cried Daisy, dashing forward in her usual impetuous manner.

'And there's Uncle Arly,' added Den. 'He's doing something to Clara's inside.'

Apparently whatever it was that Alec had been doing to Clara's inside had been done, for he looked up as we approached and waved a small spanner. 'Here you are!' he exclaimed, smiling cheerfully. 'I hope you're all frightfully hungry. I've ordered an enormous meal.'

'Meringues?' asked Daisy hopefully.

'Meringues, of course.'

'Is this where you keep Clara?' Den inquired.

'Yes, this is her garage. There's a dirty old stable behind the inn, but Clara doesn't like it so she stands here under the tree all the time.'

'Much nicer,' agreed Den approvingly.

Alec went off to wash his hands, which was necessary after his attentions to Clara's inside. Then we all went into the dining-room and sat down to eat the 'enormous meal.'

Zilla had said that the inn at Loch Ron was dreadful but it seemed a pleasant place to me; everything was spotlessly clean and the food was excellent. No doubt this was a 'special' meal, ordered by our kind host for our delectation, but at least it showed that there was a good cook in charge of the kitchen.

There were about half a dozen people there beside ourselves – mostly disgruntled fishermen. Alec knew them, of course, and I gathered from the conversation that there were rainbow trout in Loch Ron and salmon in the river. Fortunately I was now aware that none of these creatures would allow themselves to be caught in clear cloudless weather so I was able to disguise my ignorance and take a fairly intelligent part in the talk. Alec glanced at me once or twice and I could see he was amused. I remembered his remark that obviously I was not a fisherwoman.

Well, he would see that I could learn, I thought, as I listened with interest to an elderly gentleman at the next table who was allowing his delicious lamb cutlets to congeal upon his plate in order to tell me the story of a ten-pound salmon which he had caught some time ago in the Findhorn.

3

We had all eaten such a large meal that we felt disinclined for exercise, so we spent a lazy hour sitting on a wooden bench outside the inn. Then we walked slowly back through the woods to the cottage. Alec said good-bye to the children – but not to me.

'I'll look in after supper and tell you about my grasshopper,' he explained.

'Tell us about it now,' said Den.

'Is it a tame grasshopper, Uncle Arly?' asked Daisy eagerly.

'It depends what you mean by tame,' replied Alec, and so saying he turned and strode away.

The grasshopper had ceased to be a burden to Alec but

before tea was over it had become a burden to me. Neither Den nor Daisy had ever seen a grasshopper, so they wanted to know what it was like; did it make a nest and have baby grasshoppers? They wanted to know whether Uncle Arly's grasshopper was a boy or a girl, where he had found it and whether it had been difficult to catch. Daisy asked if he kept it in a box and what he gave it to eat.

Eventually I said quite firmly that I was tired of the subject, whereupon they betook themselves to the kitchen to consult Mrs. MacRam.

At first I had tried to keep Den and Daisy out of the kitchen, in case they should be a nuisance, but I soon discovered that Mrs. MacRam enjoyed their company – I could hear them all chatting away together quite happily – so I left them to do as they pleased. They would get nothing but good from Mrs. MacRam.

They were chatting now; I could hear their voices in the distance. I wondered if Mrs. MacRam knew whether or not grasshoppers made nests for their young.

Presently Mrs. MacRam came in to clear away the tea. 'We have been talking,' she informed me, quite unnecessarily. 'They were asking about grasshoppers. They are ferry interested in grasshoppers, it seems.'

'Yes, I know,' I agreed. 'Mr. Maclaren mentioned a grasshopper – it was just a joke, of course.'

'Chust a joke,' said Mrs. MacRam, nodding understandingly. 'It is nice to see Mister Maclaren so full of chokes. Mister MacRam was saying the same. We have never seen Mister Maclaren so happy. He is like a different gentleman altogether. When he is here with Miss Maclaren he has no life at all. She is a very difficult lady. No matter what you do there is no pleasing Miss Maclaren.'

I didn't like this much – but what could I say?

'And now there is trouble coming,' continued Mrs. MacRam. 'There is a letter from the lawyer to say that Miss Maclaren is going to sell Craig-an-Ron. It will be a sad day for me when it is sold because the money Miss Maclaren gives me for looking after it is ferry useful – ferry useful indeed,' said Mrs. MacRam sadly.

This was news to me, but not very surprising news. I was aware that Zilla had become bored with the cottage.

'I wonder when it will be sold,' I said.

'Och, Mistress Wentworth need not worry. There are

not many people who would be wanting Craig-an-Ron. It is a long way from the railway and there is no electric light. Mister MacRam says it will be a long, long time before it is sold.'

No doubt Mr. MacRam was right – and in any case Zilla's plans for selling the cottage did not concern me – but all the same I felt sorry. Craig-an-Ron was such a dear little house, such a happy little house, that already I had become fond of it and felt quite at home. I hoped that whoever bought it would love it too and would be kind and good to dear Mrs. MacRam.

CHAPTER 23

Alec had said he would come over and see me later, so when I had put the children to bed and had my supper I sat by the window waiting for him. I saw him come through the trees and down the slope. He had a large box under his arm, and when he came in he put it on the table.

'It's for Simon,' he said. 'A model yacht. I thought it would be fun for him to sail it on the loch.'

'How kind of you!'

'I just wish I could be here to help him, but I expect he'll manage all right. I could easily have taken my holiday in August – it's a slack time – but Zilla misled me. She said she had let the cottage to the Mitchells. She did it on purpose, of course.'

'Alec, I don't think —'

'Oh, yes, she did. I thought at first she had made a mistake but now I know better. She wanted me to be tied up in Edinburgh while you and the children were here.'

Although my first impulse had been to deny this, I felt that it might well be true (I knew that Zilla disliked my friendship with Alec) but it was a horrible idea so I banished it and changed the subject.

'Grasshoppers,' I said, looking at Alec and smiling. 'Why did you mention grasshoppers to the children? They've never ceased asking silly questions about the creatures – and the worst of it is I know nothing about them.'

'Neither do I,' he admitted. 'I only know mine was a burden.'

'Sit down and tell me about it, Alec.'

He sat down beside me near the open window. 'It's a long story,' he said. 'Not a very pleasant story, I'm afraid, but there's a special reason why I want to tell it to you – if you don't mind listening. You remember you suggested that I should go and have a talk with Zilla's doctor, don't you?'

'I didn't suggest it.'

'Well, not in so many words, but something you said put the idea into my head. You were quite right, Katherine. He never told Zilla that her attacks were dangerous. In fact he didn't believe in them at all. He said they were "put on." Those were his very words. When he saw that I was incredulous he said it was not uncommon nowadays; he had had several cases of the same kind. They were usually women – women who wanted more attention from their families. He asked if she ever had an attack when I wasn't there – she hadn't of course – so then he said it was my fault.'

'But, Alec, you've been so good to her!'

'I thought I was being good to her but in reality I was being bad for her. I was giving in and letting her trample on me – if you know what I mean.'

I knew exactly what he meant; I had seen her trample on him.

'The doctor said you shouldn't allow people to trample on you,' continued Alec thoughtfully. 'It isn't good for you and it isn't good for them. He said Zilla ought to be psychoanalysed – but I knew that was out of the question; she would never consent. So then he said that what she really needed was a firm husband and six children.'

I couldn't help smiling.

'Yes, I suppose it's funny,' agreed Alec. 'But I must confess I couldn't see the joke. Those attacks of Zilla's had frightened me out of my wits, so when the doctor assured me they were staged for my benefit – to make me do as she wanted – I was very angry.'

'No wonder!'

'But aren't you surprised?'

'Not really,' I admitted. 'I had a feeling that Zilla's attacks were a little too convenient to be genuine.'

'They were very convenient indeed,' said Alec bitterly. 'Of course my first idea was to tackle her and have it out with her then and there, but on second thoughts I decided to say nothing, but just take her to London as we had arranged and let her go off to France with the Carews. I decided that when she came home I would take a strong line and if she staged another attack I would deal with it firmly.'

'Much the best thing to do.'

'Yes, but wait,' said Alec. 'That isn't all the story. There's a whole lot more to come. When we got to London we went to stay with the Carews at their flat. I didn't want to, because I didn't like the Carews, but Zilla insisted and I thought I could stick it for a few days. The Carews seemed pleased to see us; they were in tremendous form. Jack Carew is one of those hearty types, he laughs loudly at everything you say whether it's funny or not. He's the sort of chap who drags you into a corner and tells you a dirty story and pokes you in the chest and roars with laughter. He calls me Sobersides . . . I really can't see any humour in his jokes. At dinner that night there were just the four of us. Carew began ragging me and giving out mysterious hints: "Old Sobersides isn't always so sober; put him beside a pretty girl and you'll see him come to life and laugh like a drain, ha, ha, ha!"' said Alec in gloomy accents.

'He sounds ghastly!'

'Yes, he's ghastly. Madeline joined in the fun; they were both chipping me. At last Zilla said, "What's it all about? What has Alec been up to? Why should I be left out of the joke?" So then they told her the joke.'

'What was the joke?'

'They had seen us at Moffat.'

'Alec!'

'Yes, they were lunching there, at that hotel.'

'Goodness, how awful! They must have been those people I told you about who kept on staring at us.'

'I expect so.'

'Is he bald, with a very red face?'

'Yes, and she's as pale as a ghost with enormous eyes and sticky black eyelashes.'

'The Londony people! Oh, Alec, if only we'd chosen some other hotel! What an unlucky chance!'

'Well, I don't know that it was unlucky, really,' said Alec in thoughtful tones. 'There was a frightful row, of course, which was extremely unpleasant, but it brought things to a head. Zilla stormed and raged and said the most dreadful things. She said . . . well, never mind what she said. The Carews were horrified, and it takes a good deal to horrify the Carews! Finally Zilla collapsed in a heap on the floor and had one of her attacks.'

'How dreadful!'

'Yes, Madeline was terrified – it really is terrifying when she does it. Madeline shrieked to Jack to ring up the doctor, but I said there was no need. I picked up Zilla and carried her to her room and laid her on the bed and I told Madeline to sponge her face with ice-cold water. The doctor had given me that tip.'

'Was the treatment successful?'

'It wasn't necessary,' said Alec grimly. 'When she heard me tell Madeline about it she came round at once. Zilla isn't very keen on cold water.'

'Oh dear,' I said sadly.

'I must say the Carews were very decent,' continued Alec. 'They apologised profusely to me for letting the cat out of the bag. Madeline kept on saying, "We aren't mischief-makers, Alec. We wouldn't have said a word if you'd been married . . . but you're just her brother!" They were both astonished that Zilla had been so upset. They thought she would be amused. In fact they thought she would be pleased.'

'Why did they think Zilla would be pleased?'

'It was natural, really. You see she had told them I was a dull dog and had no use for girls so she was afraid I would never get married. She had told them that I insisted on her living with me and doing the house-keeping – she had made herself out to be a martyr to duty. Isn't it amazing, Katherine?'

'Yes,' I said – but I was not amazed. Zilla had told me the same story.

'Oh well,' said Alec. 'I don't want to bother you by telling you about all the fuss and argument. I talked to the Carews and Madeline talked to Zilla and finally it was agreed that what Zilla really needs is a long holiday and a complete change of environment. When they come back from France Zilla will go off to New Zealand. We have cousins there and they've asked her several times to visit them and stay as long as she likes. Some friends of the Carews are going to New Zealand, so Zilla can travel with them. Madeline said that when Zilla comes back from New Zealand they'll find her a flat in London and Jack said he would find her a husband.'

'Alec!'

'That's how they talk,' explained Alec. 'It's wild sort of talk and I must say I don't like it, but they really were extremely kind. I was surprised at their kindness and at all the trouble they took. I think they were genuinely sorry that they had upset things.'

'Perhaps they're fond of Zilla in their own strange way.'

'Yes, I think they are,' agreed Alec. 'At any rate they're going to do what they can for her. They entertain and go about a lot when they're in London and that's what Zilla enjoys. I know it sounds queer but I believe if they could find a husband for her it would be the best thing possible.'

'Poor Zilla,' I said.

'Yes, poor Zilla,' Alec agreed. 'I told her I was sorry and apologised for everything, and eventually I got her to make it up.'

I looked at him and wondered at his magnanimity. He had apologised to Zilla! It seemed to me that Zilla should have apologised to him. Aloud I said, 'I'm glad you made it up.'

'Yes, so am I. She let me kiss her before I came away.' He hesitated for a few moments and then added, 'I'm sorry to have bored you with all this but I wanted to tell you because it means I'm free. I'm free, Katherine. Do you realise what that means?'

'Not really,' I said doubtfully.

'I'm free from Zilla,' he explained. 'I thought she was ill; I thought she needed my care. I thought it would be my duty to look after Zilla all her life. That's why I was so terribly depressed when I wrote you that stupid letter. I could see no hope – no future for me. I could never have a life of my own, never have friends of my own . . . never ask any woman to marry me.'

'No wonder you were depressed,' I said in a low voice.

'Katherine, do you think —'

'I think we've talked enough,' I said, smiling at him. 'It's ten o'clock, Alec. I like to go to bed early – and you've got a long drive to-morrow, haven't you?'

'Yes, I must go,' he agreed.

I went with him to the door. 'Good-bye,' I said. 'Thank you for everything and especially for being such a good friend. Take care of yourself and don't drive too fast. The roads are always terribly crowded on Sundays.'

'I shall start early,' he replied. Then he added impulsively, 'I wish I needn't go. I wish I could stay here with you, Katherine. I could easily have taken my holiday in August.'

'Perhaps you could come up for a week-end?'

'I'm afraid that's impossible,' he replied regretfully. 'One of my partners has gone to Brittany with his family, and the other, Andrew Forth, is having a well-earned rest. There's nothing much doing at the office but somebody has to be on the spot – I told you that, didn't I? As a matter of fact I wish I had lots of work to do, it's pretty sickening hanging about. Oh well, it can't be helped.'

I wanted to cheer him up so I said, 'Remember the grasshopper, Alec.'

'Yes, you're right,' he replied, smiling.

We said good-bye again – it was only afterwards that I remembered it was supposed to be unlucky.

Darkness comes late in these northern latitudes, so there was still enough pale grey light in the sky for me to watch Alec walk away. When he reached the trees he turned and saw me standing in the doorway – and waved.

I waved back to him.

Then he disappeared into the wood.

2

It was true that I liked to go to bed early, but that night I lay awake for a very long time. I was trying to tell myself to be careful. Once before I had given away my heart and had experienced the joy of loving and being loved, the happiness of feeling safe, comforted and cherished . . . and I had known the agony of losing it all. I had floundered for weeks in the Slough of Despond – miserable and rebellious – and then, for the sake of the children, I had struggled out. Gradually the pain had become bearable and my spine had stiffened; I found I could stand on my own feet. I was independent now and I intended to remain independent, barricaded in my stronghold. Alec was a dear; I wanted him as a friend – just a friend and nothing more.

Having settled this quite definitely I turned over and went to sleep.

CHAPTER 24

Sunday was a quiet day at Craig-an-Ron. There was no church within reasonable distance so I read some Bible Stories to the children and then sat on the shore of the loch and watched them playing. They had put on their bathing shorts so they sploshed about very happily making a harbour with stones. I decided to get them some little boats in the village but meanwhile they were quite contented with pieces of firewood, produced by Mrs. MacRam.

I thought of Alec and wondered where he was and hoped he was being careful. I thought about Zilla and decided that I must write to her and tell her how much we were enjoying our holiday in her charming little house.

On Monday morning at breakfast Daisy suddenly exclaimed, 'I'll tell you something. We better go to Inverquill and fetch the grand piano.'

This was Daisy's joke. 'Uncle Arly' had said he could take all our luggage in his car except the grand piano; and he had taken all our luggage except the bicycles. The joke seemed the height of humour to Daisy and Den, but it had palled upon me by this time.

'How can we fetch them?' I asked.

'Mrs. MacRam knows,' replied Den. 'She says Mr. Buchanan would take us to Inverquill and we can bicycle home. Mr. Buchanan often goes over to Inverquill to fetch things in his car for the people in the village.'

'You must come too,' said Daisy. 'Then you can ride home on Simon's bike. It's all quite easy.'

The idea did not attract me, but I realised that it would be much cheaper to go over and fetch the bicycles than to have them sent by road, so I put on my old tartan skirt, which was made like a kilt with pleats, and we set off at once upon the expedition.

We found Mr. Buchanan (who proved to be the owner

of a funny little tumbledown garage and an extremely ancient taxi) and he agreed to convey the three of us to Inverquill for a small consideration. It seemed to me a quite inadequate consideration for the hire of his car – but he explained this by saying, 'It would be more if you were wanting back.'

'Why?' asked Daisy with interest.

'It's chust because I'm always full,' replied Mr. Buchanan ambiguously.

The two children got in beside Mr. Buchanan and I sat behind. We started off at a good pace – a surprisingly good pace considering the age of the vehicle and the condition of the road – the noise of the engine and the jolting made me quite dizzy. I noticed that the children were talking to our driver in an animated manner and wondered what they were saying. Presently Daisy turned and shouted, 'Mums, Mr. Buchanan says it's twelve miles to Inverquill in his car but only seven if you walk. Isn't it funny?'

I nodded and smiled; there was too much noise in the car to attempt a reply.

Quite soon we arrived at Inverquill and were deposited at the station, where we found the three bicycles waiting for us. By this time I had hit upon a reasonable explanation of the elastic miles so I asked a porter if there were a short cut to Loch Ron.

'Yes, indeed, but it iss chust for walking,' he replied.

Another porter joined in, 'Och, I would take a bike. It iss not as rough as all that. There wass a boy went that way thiss morning early. I wass telling him the way.'

'But he wass walking,' objected porter number one.

The boy did not interest me so I left them arguing about it. I had heard quite enough to convince me that it would be better to return by the road.

Unfortunately I was a poor bicyclist at the best of times and I found the bar on Simon's machine extremely inconvenient. I was unable to mount unless there was something in the nature of a mounting block in the vicinity and the only way I could dismount was to fall off sideways. The road had seemed quite short in the car but now it seemed twice as long; it wound across the moor, uphill most of the way. On either side the moor stretched for miles, open and deserted, there was heather and bog; there was bog-cotton, blowing in the wind, and dark ridges where the crofters had cut their peat. Here and there we saw a lochan and scattered clumps of trees, gnarled and twisted by the winter storms.

It would have been an enjoyable walk for it was a fine breezy morning, but Simon's bicycle was so unruly that I began to be quite frightened and to wonder what would happen if I fell off and broke my leg. I was thankful when at last I arrived at Craig-an-Ron with no more damage than a grazed elbow. We put the bicycles into Alec's garage – Daisy remarking that it was a funny place to keep the grand piano – and went into the cottage by the back door.

Mrs. MacRam was in the kitchen and welcomed us as warmly as if we had been to the North Pole.

'The young gentleman is here,' she said. 'I have given him his dinner.'

'The young gentleman!' I exclaimed in surprise.

'Yes, it is Mister Simon; he walked over the hill from the station.'

'Simon! But I wasn't expecting him! He never let me know what day he was coming!'

'Och, the sooner the better. It will not take a minute to make up the bed. I have the sheets airing on the pulley,' said Mrs. MacRam cheerfully.

By this time the children had rushed into the sitting-room and were greeting Simon with their usual enthusiasm. I followed and greeted him no less warmly.

'But, darling! Why didn't you let me know?' I exclaimed. 'I could have arranged to meet you with a taxi.'

'Mr. Buchanan could have met you,' said Den.

'Then you wouldn't have had to walk,' said Daisy.

'I meant to ring you up but there's no telephone,' replied Simon.

This explanation was all right as far as it went but it did not account for Simon's sudden arrival so much earlier than I had expected.

'Didn't you play in the cricket match?' I asked.

'No, I just – came home. You don't mind, do you?'

'Mind? Of course not. It's lovely to have you.'

It was lovely to have him but I was worried by his look of exhaustion . . . and by a queer strained expression in his eyes. Simon's eyes were usually clear and bright and eager; they were not so now.

'You're tired,' I said. 'You were travelling all night – and then you had that long walk over the hills. I think you had better rest this afternoon. What about it?'

'Yes, I'll go to bed,' he replied. 'I didn't sleep much in the train.'

2

Simon spent the afternoon in bed. He did not come down till after five, by which time we had finished tea and the children had gone out for a walk with Mrs. MacRam.

'I'll make fresh tea for you,' I said.

'Don't bother. I'm not hungry,' he replied.

So far he had not told me anything nor explained why he had come without letting me know. He had intended to stay at Limbourne for another week and play in the cricket match, and to ride over to Hurlestone Manor. I wondered if I should ask him about it – or not. This was very strange because Simon and I had always been so close to each other that there had been no need to 'wonder' about him.

'Are you sure you wouldn't like some tea?' I asked.

'Quite sure. I found a hammock in the cupboard in my room. I expect it belongs to Alec but he wouldn't mind us using it, would he?'

'No, I'm sure he wouldn't.'

Simon took the hammock and spent some time slinging it between two trees. When I went out he was lying in it and he looked so pale and exhausted that I was alarmed. 'Are you feeling all right?' I asked.

'Yes, of course. Why shouldn't I be feeling all right?'

'You look – rather pale. I thought perhaps you had a headache.'

'I've told you I'm all right,' he said irritably.

There was a wooden bench beneath the tree. It was quite near the hammock, so I sat down. I looked at Simon lying in the hammock and again I wondered whether I should ask him what had happened at Limbourne. Usually Simon was only too eager to talk – information gushed out of him like water out of a fountain – but to-day there was a barrier between us. I couldn't ask questions, but I could talk. I began to talk rather feverishly about all that we had been doing, and I was in the middle of telling him about Alec bringing us to Craig-an-Ron in his car – and how it had rained all the way – when suddenly I realised that he was not listening.

'I think I'll go for a walk,' he said. He got up and walked off quickly and disappeared into the wood.

Perhaps it was silly to be surprised – and hurt. All this was new country to Simon so it was natural that he should want to explore. Perhaps he had decided to wait until after supper when the children were in bed and we could settle down comfortably. He would talk to me then and tell me all his news.

As usual the twins had their bath before supper and came downstairs in their dressing-gowns (I had found this much easier than giving them their supper in bed.) Simon returned from his walk just as we were sitting down to the meal and took the empty place between Den and Daisy.

'Simon, where have you been?' asked Daisy.

'I went for a walk.'

'You must come and see our harbour,' said Den. 'You'll come to-morrow morning, won't you?'

'It's a gorgeous harbour,' declared Daisy.

They went on talking about the harbour and about the boats they had got – and especially about a model steam-boat which had been carved for them out of a piece of wood by Mr. MacRam. Usually Simon was amused by the children's prattle and interested in all their doings, but to-night he seemed bored and listless.

'Simon, you're not listening,' said Daisy reproachfully.

'What? Oh, yes, I was,' said Simon.

'I expect you're thinking about Limbourne,' said Den. 'What did you do at Limbourne? Tell us about it.'

'I rode a good deal.'

'I'd like to ride,' said Den eagerly. 'Do you think we could go to Limbourne some day – and ride?'

'Are there ponies?' asked Daisy.

Simon did not reply.

'Perhaps, some day, when you're older,' I said.

'Everything nice is "when you're older,"' said Daisy in discontented tones.

When we had finished supper I took the children upstairs to bed; I heard them say their prayers and read them a story and tucked them up. As I bent down to kiss

Daisy good night she said sadly, 'Simon has got a pain. It's a pity, isn't it? Will it be better to-morrow?'

'Yes, I expect it will be better to-morrow,' I said.

Certainly there was something very far wrong with Simon, but I did not think it was a pain.

When I went downstairs Simon was sitting in a chair by the window reading a book.

'Well, they're safely in bed,' I said cheerfully. 'It's cold to-night, isn't it? Shall we light the fire and have a cosy chat?'

'I'm too tired,' said Simon. He rose and added, 'I think I'll go to bed.'

'Yes, of course you're tired,' I agreed. 'I'll come and say good night when you've had your bath.'

'Don't bother. I'll say good night now – perhaps I'll read for a bit.' He kissed me in a perfunctory manner and went away, shutting the door behind him.

For a few moments I stood and looked at the closed door. Simon had shut me out!

Never before had Simon treated me like this. I knew he was tired – but it wasn't that. Simon was – different. The happy friendly companionship, so precious to me, had gone. I felt that this boy was a stranger – not Simon at all. A stranger had looked at me unkindly out of Simon's eyes.

Alec had said, 'You won't lose the boy,' but it seemed that I had lost him.

I went and sat down by the window, thinking about it and wondering what to do. It would not have been quite so bad if I could have talked to somebody but I was alone and helpless. Two nights ago I had sat here waiting for Alec . . . I wished he were here now. I wished I could see him come out of the wood and down the slope to the cottage door. Perhaps Alec would have told me that I was making a mountain out of a molehill . . . but even that would have been a comfort.

I sat by the window until the blue sky faded into queer grey northern twilight and one pale star began to glimmer above the mountain top.

CHAPTER 25

The next morning at breakfast Simon still looked haggard and miserable but I could see that he was making an effort to behave more normally so I pretended that everything was just as usual.

The children were in very good spirits and full of chat. Now that 'the grand piano' was here they were determined to use it and announced that they were going to ride over to a ruined castle which Mr. MacRam had told them was 'ferry interesting.' They wanted Simon to go with them but he refused, saying that he intended to lie in the hammock and read. I was a little doubtful about letting the children go by themselves but Mrs. MacRam assured me that it would be quite safe. It was only four miles to the castle and the road was very quiet.

After they had gone I discovered that they had coaxed sandwiches out of Mrs. MacRam and intended to have a picnic lunch and come home in time for tea.

'Don't worry, Mums,' said Simon. 'Mrs. MacRam knows, so if she says it's all right it's all right.'

This was perfectly true, so I took my mending basket and the tartan plaid and settled down in my usual place beneath the rowan tree. It was not so warm this morning – the sky was overcast – but it was pleasant sitting there. Simon lay in the hammock reading his book – or pretending to read it – he did not seem to be getting on very fast. Presently he got up and wandered down to the loch; he stood there for a time and then picked up some stones and threw them into the water in an aimless manner.

Quite suddenly I decided that we could not go on like this; I should have to do something about it. I called to him and asked him to go and get two cups of coffee from Mrs. MacRam. 'We'll have it out here,' I said.

Simon went away and soon returned with coffee and biscuits on a tray. I made room for him on the plaid and he sat down beside me. He was tethered now. He could not get up and wander away until he had finished his coffee; I was glad to find that the coffee was extremely hot.

'Now tell me all your 'ventures,' I said, smiling at him

cheerfully. This was a joke between us. It was what Simon used to say long ago when he was a little boy and I had been to a party . . . but to-day there was no answering smile.

'There isn't much to tell you,' he said drearily.

'Did the D'Artingtons ask you over to Hurlestone Manor?'

'Yes, but I couldn't go.'

'Why not?' I asked in surprise.

'Grandfather said I was to wait until he could come with me.'

'What else happened? Did you enjoy the treasure hunt?'

'No.'

I looked at him and saw that his face had become as white as paper. 'Simon, what's the matter?' I exclaimed.

'The matter!' he echoed in alarm. 'There's nothing the matter. What makes you think —'

'There is,' I said firmly. 'You're frightfully worried. Tell me about it, Simon.'

For a few moments he was silent. Then he said, 'I owe Nitkin five pounds. I had to borrow it from him.'

'Goodness, is that all? I'll give it to you at once and you can send it to him by registered post.'

'Thank you, Mums. Perhaps you think it was funny to borrow it from Nitkin, but he's an awfully decent chap and I didn't want to ask anyone else. I'll – I'll earn it and pay you back. Mrs. MacRam says that when the shooting begins the village boys earn quite a lot by beating, so I could —'

'Simon, don't be idiotic! You know perfectly well that I'd give you all I've got . . . and anyhow it was my fault for not giving you enough.'

'You gave me enough,' said Simon in a droning voice. 'You gave me enough for tips and journey money and everything. I chucked it away. It would have been more sensible if I'd thrown it in the fire.'

'You put it on a horse,' I suggested.

'No,' said Simon.

He rolled over on the rug and hid his face. 'Why didn't I come home with you!' he said huskily. 'Oh, Mums, why didn't I? I very nearly did, you know. On Sunday night when you gave me the money I saw you were unhappy about it and I very nearly said I'd chuck the treasure hunt and come . . . just as nearly as – as nothing.'

'My dear lamb, don't worry. If it's only five pounds it doesn't matter a scrap. It isn't worth worrying about.'

'It isn't only the money.'

'What is it, Simon?'

'I can't tell you,' he said.

For a few minutes there was silence. I didn't know how to tackle it. At last I said, 'You've always told me things, haven't you?'

'Yes, and I want to tell you – but I can't.'

'Is it a secret?'

'Yes. At least I suppose it's a secret. I didn't promise not to tell – they never asked me to promise – but all the same . . .'

'Why not tell me? We could talk it over. It's a good plan to talk things over.'

'You might feel you had to do something about it. That's the trouble.'

'Do something about it? What do you mean?' I asked in bewilderment.

He was silent – except for a muffled sob.

I was terrified now. 'Listen, Simon. If I promise to keep it a secret you can tell me, can't you?'

'No, I can't.'

'Yes, you can,' I said earnestly. 'You can tell me if I promise faithfully —'

He turned and looked at me. 'But could you?' he asked. 'Could you promise without knowing what it was?'

I hesitated. Could I tie my hands like that?

'You see?' said Simon. 'You see what I mean? You couldn't promise without knowing.'

'Yes, I can,' I declared in desperation. 'I promise not to say a word about it to anybody.'

'It's a frightful thing; you'll be horrified. Are you sure you want me to tell you?'

I was quite sure. I didn't care what it was. I wanted to share it with Simon. 'Go on,' I said encouragingly. 'I've promised, haven't I? Tell me what's worrying you, Simon.'

For a moment or two he hesitated and then, pulling himself together, he blurted out the whole extraordinary story.

2

It was the 'treasure hunt.' Simon had been told to go upstairs to bed as usual and to change into his oldest clothes. While he was changing he heard several cars arrive in the stable-yard beneath his window . . . and he heard the sound of subdued voices. He heard Oliver Wade say, 'Are you sure Simon is all right? Don't you think it would be safer to leave him at home?' Lance replied, 'He's all right. Don't worry.'

'Well, it's your responsibility,' said Oliver. 'I'm not in favour of taking a kid like Simon; he'll just be a damn' nuisance – if not worse.'

'He's all right, I tell you,' repeated Lance.

Simon was ready now so he ran down and joined them. He felt pleased and excited, determined to keep his end up and to show them he was not such a 'kid' as they thought.

Oliver was collecting the money and making a joke of it: 'Come on, walk up and put your pennies in the kitty. It's a good pool to-night. Who's going to win?'

'We are, of course!'

'You haven't a dog's hope.'

They were all talking and laughing; they were all tensed up with excitement.

Simon noticed that they were all giving Oliver five pounds for the pool, so when it came to his turn he produced one of the five-pound notes which I had given him and handed it over ('in a moment of madness,' said Simon miserably).

When that was settled the competitors divided up into couples; Anthea went with Oliver in his sports car and Simon with Lance on his motor-bike. Each 'observer' had been given a card with a pencil attached.

Simon looked at his card and saw it was blank. He showed it to Lance.

'Yes, that's all right,' said Lance. 'You have to fill it up as we go along. You'll soon get the hang of it.'

When Simon got thus far in his story he stopped – and there was silence. Then he said, 'Are you sure you want to hear what happened?'

'Yes, of course I want to hear. There was a treasure hunt when we were at Oxford and I went with Antony Finch, so I know what happens. You go to a place and find a clue. Then you —'

'There were no clues. It wasn't really a treasure hunt at all.'

'What was it, then?'

'It was – just – destroying things.'

'Simon, I don't know what you mean!'

'They destroyed things – that was the game. The people who did the most destruction got the prize.'

For a moment or two I was dumb with amazement and consternation. Then I managed to find my voice. 'They destroyed things? What sort of things, Simon?'

'Various things,' he replied in a voice that was scarcely more than a whisper. 'I didn't know what was going to happen until suddenly Lance stopped at a telephone-box and told me to hold the bike. He went in and smashed the instrument with a sort of small pick-axe – he had it hanging on his belt – "There, that's number one. Write it down on the card," he said. I was absolutely flabbergasted; I told him he was crazy but he just laughed and said I wasn't to be a spoil-sport. He said, "You wanted to join in the fun, didn't you? Go on, make a note of it on the card." I said I wouldn't, so he snatched the card and wrote on it himself and put it in his pocket.

'Then he went on. We went for miles – all over the country – I don't know where we went. It was a very dark night, cloudy and cold. The wind was like a knife. There was a house standing by itself in a lane, with three cars at the gate. Lance stopped and bashed the paintwork of the cars and broke the windows. It made a frightful noise and several people came running out of the house to see what was happening – they had been having a party or something. They shouted at us but Lance jumped on to the bike and we were off at full speed. He was laughing in a crazy sort of way – like a lunatic.'

'Oh, Simon, couldn't you do anything?'

'I know,' agreed Simon in a shaky voice. 'That's the worst of it. That's what's making me miserable. I ought to have done something – but what could I do? What could I have done? Even now I don't see what I could have done. I think and think. Of course I tried to argue with him – but it was no use. I asked him to take me home; but he wouldn't listen. He kept on saying that it was fun

– it was just a game. He said it was good for people to be shaken up and startled; it bounced them out of their rut. Then he got angry with me and said, "You persuaded me to bring you and now you won't play the game." That was true, of course; I had persuaded him to bring me. He said, "I told Oliver I'd be responsible for you." That was true too. I had heard him say it to Oliver.

'Well, I've told you enough,' added Simon. 'It isn't a nice story, is it?'

It wasn't a nice story but I knew that somehow or other I must make him tell me more. I must dig into his mind and pull out every detail. When he had told me he would feel better. (I don't know how I knew this; I just knew it – quite definitely.) 'Go on,' I said. 'You can't stop in the middle.'

'Do you really want me to go on?'

'Yes, tell me everything.'

'I can't remember everything he did – it was like a nightmare. I was frightfully cold and that made me stupid. You see I didn't expect it would be cold so I hadn't put on nearly enough clothes. I hadn't put on my coat – just a jersey. I was numb all over and my teeth were chattering. Perhaps it was partly because I was frightened – I've never been so frightened in all my life. Lance seemed to have gone mad. He smashed some traffic lights – I remember that – and he stopped at a cottage with a little garden and went in and pulled up some bushes and a whole row of sweet-peas and strewed them about all over the place and trampled on them. I suppose that wasn't as bad as some of the other things, but I kept on thinking about the people coming down in the morning and finding their nice little garden spoilt and ruined. . . .

Simon was leaning forward, picking at the turf with his hands. He looked so young and defenceless that I could have wept. I felt that I should have been able to protect him. I felt as if I were to blame. I wanted to take him in my arms and soothe him – as I had done when he was a little boy and he had fallen down and grazed his knees – but that was not the way to deal with Simon's troubles.

'There's more, isn't there?' I asked, trying to keep my voice steady.

'Yes, there's more. We came to a place where the road had been dug up – for drains or something. There was a deep trench with little lamps along the edge. The moment I saw it I knew what he meant to do. I said "No, Lance! No, you can't! It's dangerous." "Shut up, you little sap!" he said furiously. We both got off the bike and he started swearing at me and saying that what I needed was a thrashing. I said he could thrash me if he liked but I wasn't going to let him move the lamps. The trench was quite deep so there might have been a frightful accident. I told you it was a very dark night, didn't I?'

'Yes, you told me.'

'He was in a steaming rage. He said I was a prig and a smug little rotter and – and a lot of other things. At one moment I thought he was going for me. Perhaps he would have beaten me if the watchman hadn't wakened. There was a watchman in a little hut close by. He came out and shouted at us – called us a pair of drunken hooligans. Lance told him to keep his hair on. He said, "My cousin and I are having a little argument, that's all." The man said, "Well, you can go and have it somewhere else." Lance laughed and kicked one of the lamps into the trench. Then we got on the bike and were off. The man called out that he had taken our number and we'd hear about it – but that didn't worry Lance. He had a false number-plate, you see. I forgot to tell you that. It was raining by that time – horrid drizzly rain – so we went home.'

'What happened when you got home?'

'Two cars had arrived before us; they were in the yard. I didn't wait. I got off the bike and went up to my room and undressed. I was wet through. I heard them all talking under my window, they were waiting for the others to come. Then Oliver came, with Anthea, and they compared notes of what they had done, making jokes about it. Lance kept on telling them to be quiet or they'd waken everyone in the house. Oliver collected the cards and said he would take them home and decide who had won. The others wanted him to do it then and there, but he said it was too late to do it to-night. He had bottles in his car, so they all had drinks and after a bit they said good night and went away. I had gone to bed but I couldn't sleep. I kept on thinking about it and wondering what I ought to have done. I ought to have done something. It was frightfully cowardly of me not to do anything, wasn't it?'

'I don't see what you could have done.'

'Really and truly?'

I nodded. 'Yes, really and truly.'

'Well, that's a comfort,' said Simon with a sigh. 'I thought you'd say I ought to have told Grandfather . . . but I simply couldn't. He isn't the sort of person you can tell things to. You won't do anything about it, will you?'

I reminded him of my promise. As a matter of fact, even if I hadn't given my promise, I didn't see what I could do.

'What will happen if they get caught?' asked Simon.

I couldn't answer that. I remembered what the Heaths had told me about vandalism in the neighbourhood; there had been quite a lot about vandalism in the papers as well. Now, incredible though it was, the problem had come very near. It was no longer a theoretical problem – and the vandals were not hooligans from the city slums, but young men and girls who ought to know better.

'Would they be put in prison?' Simon asked.

'They ought to be put in prison,' I declared emphatically. 'It would do them good . . . but I suppose it would depend upon how serious the damage was.'

'Some of it was pretty bad. Some of the things that the others did were worse than I've told you. Lance didn't win the prize. At least he never spoke to me about it – never mentioned the subject.

'It was funny, really,' said Simon thoughtfully. 'When I went down to breakfast next morning they were just the same as usual – Lance and Anthea, I mean. It was all so much as usual that I could scarcely believe it had happened. It was just like a bad dream.'

'But it wasn't a dream.'

'No, it was real and horrible. I had made up my mind in the night that I would go home. I just felt I had to get home as soon as ever I could. When I told Lance and Anthea that I found I had to go home to-morrow they looked at each other and smiled.

'Anthea came into my room while I was packing and asked why I hadn't enjoyed the treasure hunt. She said, "Of course it's wrong but it's so exciting." She said she hadn't liked it at first, but now she enjoyed it more than anything . . . it was half the fun to be frightened. I told her that some day she would be caught and she said, "Not with Oliver, he can twist his way out of anything. He thinks of terribly thrilling things to do." She told me that one night they set fire to an empty house and then rang up the fire-station . . . and when the fire-engine came they joined in the crowd and Oliver helped the firemen with their hose. She laughed and said, "That was tremendous fun. Oliver is marvellous".'

CHAPTER 26

When Simon had finished speaking we sat for some time in silence.

At last I said, 'They must be mad to do things like that.'

'I thought so at first . . . and then I remembered that dog in the house next door when we were at Oxford. Its master was a horrible man and always kept it on a chain. When he let it off the chain it ran wild and attacked any dog that happened to be passing. There was something fierce inside it that just had to come out. Dad said it was "bottled-up violence." Do you remember?'

Of course I remembered.

'Well, Lance and Anthea are chained up; they've always been chained up since they were children – never been allowed to do what they wanted. That's why they run wild.'

'You don't feel like that, do you?' I asked anxiously.

He smiled and shook his head. 'I've never been chained up.'

'You will be – when you go to Limbourne.'

'I know – and I couldn't stand it – so I'm not going.'

'Not going to Limbourne!' I exclaimed incredulously. I couldn't believe my ears. It was too good to be true.

'I couldn't bear it,' declared Simon. 'I just – couldn't. It's very comfortable and I enjoyed bits of it – riding with Nitkin and all that – but you can't do a thing you want. There were several things I wanted to do and he just said I couldn't. For instance, Wilfrid D'Artington rang up and asked me to go over to tea and I accepted. I told Nitkin and he was all for it. He brought the horses round at three o'clock, and we were just starting when Grandfather came out and said I wasn't to go. He said I must wait until another day when he could come with me. I couldn't understand it. I reminded him that he had said I could ride whenever I liked, but he didn't listen. He told Nitkin to take the horses back to the stable – and of course Nitkin had to. I was fed up, I can tell you! I'd been looking forward to riding over and meeting Wilfrid and seeing the place – it would have been fun – and of course I felt a perfect fool having to ring up and say I couldn't come after all. There were other things too – silly things – but you can't talk to him and explain. He just gives orders as if he were Hitler or somebody. The fact is you can't call your soul your own. That's why I've decided to go to Butterfields with Mark.'

'I thought you liked your grandfather.'

'I do – in a way,' said Simon thoughtfully. 'He was kind to me, especially at first. He's quite all right if you do exactly as he says, but you've got to be careful not to put his back up. You've got to do everything you're told – without question. After a bit I began to feel – to feel —'

'Chained up?' I suggested.

'Yes, that's right. It's a horrible feeling. I wouldn't mind going to Limbourne for a week or so in the holidays, but I couldn't go and live there.'

'Perhaps Sir Mortimer would agree to that.'

'Not a hope! If you don't do exactly as you're told you're finished. I haven't told him yet. I didn't dare tell him; I was afraid he might try to – persuade me. It's very difficult to stand up to him . . . if you know what I mean.'

I nodded. There was tremendous force in Sir Mortimer; I had felt it myself.

'I'll have to write to him,' continued Simon. 'He'll be furious, of course, but I can't help it.'

Simon rose and stretched his arms above his head. 'I must be free to breathe,' he said.

'You're giving up a lot, Simon.'

'I know, but it's better than giving up my freedom.'

'You're giving up a lot,' I repeated. I wanted him to count the cost.

'You mean going to Austria – and hunting – and having a car of my own? Yes, I've thought of that . . . and I'm afraid it means he won't pay for Den's education. All that goes west.'

'Let it go west!'

'You're pleased,' said Simon, looking at me in surprise.

'Yes, I'm pleased. There's a queer unhappy atmosphere about Limbourne. I found it terribly depressing.'

'I know what you mean, but I thought at first I could bear it. Then suddenly I knew I couldn't.'

'Like Dad. He felt he had to escape from Limbourne because he valued his freedom so highly.'

'Like Dad,' said Simon and nodded thoughtfully.

2

We talked for some time; we talked until I felt fairly certain that Simon had told me all there was to tell. Then for a while we were silent.

'Well, that's all,' said Simon at last. 'I'm glad I've told you, it seems to have cleared the air. Perhaps I shan't have that horrible dream again.'

'What was it?'

'Oh, well . . . dreams are rather silly when you tell them to people, aren't they?'

I made him tell me. Like all dreams it was very vivid to the dreamer but difficult to narrate. Simon had dreamt 'over and over again' that he had rushed out in the middle of the night to ring up the doctor and had found the telephone smashed to pieces. 'It was in that village I told you about,' he explained. 'It was that red telephone-box. I know it sounds silly, but it's a ghastly dream; I always wake up dripping with perspiration. You see it's Daisy that's ill – frightfully ill – and I know she'll die if I don't get the doctor.'

'It's over now, Simon.'

'Over? How do you mean?'

'They've mended it,' I said firmly.

He looked at me – and laughed. 'You *are* funny,' he said.

'They've mended it,' I repeated with conviction. 'Telephones are always mended at once; the people in that village can go and ring up the doctor whenever they want.'

Simon nodded thoughtfully.

'Come on,' I said, leaping to my feet. 'We'll get Mr. MacRam's boat and go for a row on the loch.'

'Oh, I didn't know there was a boat!' exclaimed Simon in delight.

We got the key of the boat-house, and took out the boat and Simon rowed me across the loch. He was not an accomplished oarsman and at first he rowed like a maniac: the boat went scudding through the water, spray flew in all directions and I was almost drenched, but I remembered what Alec had said about letting off steam so I bore it in silence.

When we reached the opposite shore he stopped and, taking out a somewhat grubby handkerchief, wiped his face. 'Gosh, I'm hot!' he said.

'Hot!' I echoed, raising my eyebrows. 'I wonder why you're hot. I'm perfectly cool and comfortable.'

He chuckled. 'It's fun being with you, Mums. There was no fun at Limbourne. As a matter of fact I believe that's what's wrong with the place,' he added in thoughtful tones.

'Let's row round the island,' I suggested. (I didn't want him to talk about Limbourne.)

Simon took up the oars and rowed slowly and steadily across to the island. I told him what Alec had said about the vitrified wall; he was interested but there was no time to go and look at it to-day, and although we found a huddle of stones, which had once been a landing-place, we could see no path leading from it. The whole island was completely covered with thorn trees and brambles and nettles right down to the edge of the water.

'Difficult to explore,' said Simon.

'Impossible,' I declared firmly; I was thinking of the rents and tears I should have to mend if such an expedition were to take place.

'Not impossible,' objected Simon. 'You could do it in gum boots.'

'You might do it in a suit of armour,' I said.

The day had been cloudy at first, but now the clouds had vanished and the sun was shining with the clear brilliance which is typical of the Scottish Highlands, the brilliance that makes one forget clouds and mist and rain. It was really hot, so we rowed home slowly and were late in getting back for lunch.

Fortunately Mrs. MacRam was unperturbed. 'Och, it does not matter,' she said in answer to my apologies. 'I saw you on the loch. The young gentleman was enjoying himself – and the sun is shining.'

'Yes, the sun is shining,' I agreed.

Simon ate a hearty meal and then went out and lay

in the hammock; later, when I went to look at him I found him asleep, so I covered him with a light rug. I tucked it round him – and he never stirred.

It was nearly eight o'clock when Simon woke; he strolled into the sitting-room with the rug over his arm.

'Hallo,' he said cheerfully. 'I must have gone to sleep. Have the children come home yet?'

I laughed. 'The children came home hours ago and have gone to bed.'

He looked at the clock and grinned; it was his same old wide grin that stretched nearly from ear to ear and crinkled the corners of his eyes. 'Well, what d'you know!' he exclaimed. 'I thought I'd been asleep for about twenty minutes.'

CHAPTER 27

At Craig-an-Ron the days passed quickly; Simon spent hours sailing his model yacht. Quite often I went with him in Mr. MacRam's boat and manœuvred it for him while he set the sails and sent the yacht gliding gracefully through the clear water, bending to the breeze . . . it was a charming sight. At first Simon had found it difficult to adjust the sails correctly but he learnt by trial and error. Sometimes the children came with us, but more often they preferred to play with their own little boats at the water's edge.

One day we had a picnic, walking along the shore of the loch to a sheltered cove, where we bathed; another day Simon took the children for a bicycle expedition. In a week we were as brown as West Indians; even Den was brown, his eyes were brighter and he was putting on weight. The good plain fare provided by Mrs. MacRam suited us all.

Zilla had warned me that it would be dull at the cottage, but I did not find it dull. Rest was what I needed. It was only now when I was relaxed and peaceful that I discovered how tired I had been. I realised that I was worn out in body and spirit with the strain of struggling along by myself, coping with the children and trying to make ends meet on an inadequate income. I had prided myself upon my independence and somehow or other I had managed . . . but now

I began to wonder whether independence was so important. Perhaps one could pay too highly for it.

Here, in this peaceful spot, with Mrs. MacRam to provide a firm cushion to lean upon, I gradually began to feel like a different creature. I felt years younger, with a returning zest for life – as one sometimes does when convalescent after a long illness. Colours looked brighter, food tasted delicious and every day was a pleasure.

Never before had I enjoyed a holiday so much . . . there was only one fly in the ointment.

After the first day when Simon had told me about his experiences we did not speak of them again. I knew that Simon would have to write to his grandfather but there was no hurry about it and I decided to ask Alec to help us. It would be Simon's letter, couched in his own words, but Alec's advice would be valuable. Meantime I watched Simon, sailing his yacht, swimming in the loch and playing happily with the children.

Simon's unhappy experiences at Limbourne were fading rapidly from his mind – which was what I had hoped would happen – but he had unloaded his troubles on to me and I could not get rid of them so easily. Every now and then I had ' an attack of the worries (as Aunt Liz would have said) and lay awake at night – and wondered what mischief Oliver and Lance and the other members of the 'club' were up to. I was so angry that I should have liked to sit down and write to Sir Mortimer and tell him what I thought of him and his family. Failing that I should have liked to write to Mr. Heath; he was a good, kind, sensible man and would know how to tackle the matter . . . but I had promised faithfully not to do anything about it. My hands were tied and my lips were sealed. I couldn't even write to Alec and tell him what had happened. How I wished I could!

Her Majesty's Mail was delivered at the cottage by a young woman on a bicycle; she was the daughter of the postmistress in the village and, incidentally, a cousin of Mrs. MacRam (I had discovered that nearly everybody was related in cousinship to nearly everybody in this part of the world). As there are no other houses in the direction of Craig-an-Ron our 'postie' had to make a special trip to deliver our letters and did so when it was convenient to her – sometimes in the early morning and sometimes late in the evening – but no matter what time she arrived she was always regaled with cakes and tea in the kitchen.

Daisy was enchanted by this young woman – who, I must admit was a delightful creature with dark curls and a ravishing complexion – they had long conversations which were retailed to us faithfully at meal-times.

'I'll tell you something,' Daisy said. 'Last February the snow was so deep that Morag had to wear snow-shoes. She says they're like great big tennis rackets and she fixes them on to her boots. Another day she got lost in the mist and suddenly she found herself right in the middle of a bog – sinking fast. She had to fling herself flat on her face and crawl out.'

'What a hard life for a girl!' I exclaimed.

'But awfully exciting,' said Daisy. 'I'd like to be a postie when I grow up. Do you think I could, Mums? I told Morag and she said it was a good healthy life.'

'Yes, it must be,' I agreed. 'Morag looks the picture of health.'

I was quite used to my daughter's sudden ideas about what she wanted to be when she grew up. When she was in hospital having her appendix removed she had decided quite definitely to be a nurse, but had abandoned this noble ambition after a visit to the Zoo, where we had seen a girl-assistant. Daisy had made up her mind that this was the life for her. 'Perhaps, when I had been there for a bit, they would let me feed the lions,' she had said hopefully. This phase had lasted until Christmas, when she had been taken to see *Peter Pan* and had been so thrilled with the idea of flying that she had decided to go on the stage.

Now she was going to be a 'postie' – like Morag!

'You keep on changing your mind,' said Den with scorn.

'I know,' agreed Daisy. 'There are so many nice things to do. That's why. But being a postie, like Morag, would be the nicest of all because you'd be out of doors all the time . . . and it would be such fun to take letters to people. Morag says people are always so pleased to see her and get their letters from her. It's so *interesting*, Morag says.'

Our post-bag was not heavy. One day we all received large brightly-coloured picture post-cards from Copenhagen, which caused a great deal of excitement; another day I received some bills, which was not nearly so pleasant; I had one or two letters from friends and, one evening, Morag brought me a letter from Alec.

It was a nice long letter telling me what he had been doing: he had played golf several times; he had been to Jedburgh to see an old client about a right-of-way and had enjoyed the run; he had attended a very dull dinner, had eaten too much rich food and been bored stiff by a lot of speeches. The letter continued:

> To-morrow I am going to dinner with the Forths. I think I told you about my partner, Andrew Forth. He and his wife have a charming house at Murrayfield. They have a cook who is a friend of Ellen's so they have asked me to take Ellen to have supper in the kitchen. It is very kind of them – but that is what they are like; very kind and thoughtful. Ellen is delighted and you can imagine the two of us going out to dinner together in the car! Zilla would be horrified if she knew – but Zilla will never know.
>
> I had a long letter from Zilla, she is enjoying herself immensely; she tells me about some of the lovely old castles they have visited, especially about one ancient château where she saw the apparition of a lady who lived in the time of Le Roi Soleil and was locked up in a dungeon by her jealous husband. Being 'solid and sensible' I do not believe in ghosts – I wonder if you do! – but I am not surprised that Zilla imagines she saw the grey lady. Zilla had steeped herself in the history of the place and therefore was open to suggestion. On the strength of this experience Zilla believes herself to be psychic and has decided to join some sort of club – or circle – in London which meets regularly to communicate with the spirits of the departed. I am not at all sure that this will be good for Zilla but I can do nothing about it. Madeline and Jack seem to be encouraging her in this new plan. Zilla has decided to go to New Zealand for six months, meanwhile Madeline will find her a suitable flat in London. Zilla says she would like to have some furniture from The Cedars – including all the furniture in her bedroom – and naturally I shall be only too pleased for her to

have anything she wants. It will be quite easy to re-furnish the bedroom, when necessary. Zilla's letter is very friendly and it has taken a weight off my mind; obviously she is quite happy – and willing to let bygones be bygones.

I wish I could see some prospect of a free week-end so that I could run up to Loch Ron and see you, but there is no hope of that. Some unexpected work has turned up and I am fairly busy. I hope all goes well with you and that you are enjoying a peaceful holiday. You certainly deserve it.

Ellen, who is going to post this for me on her way to church, wishes to send her 'best respects.'

Please accept the same from your affectionate
friend,
Alec

2

When it rained – as it sometimes did at Craig-an-Ron – it rained very softly in a deceitful sort of way and gave you the impression that it was hardly raining at all, so it was not until you had gone some distance that you discovered that it was very wet indeed – by which time you were wet through to the skin. A shower-proof coat was useless, it had to be oilskins and rubber boots.

Simon and Den were perfectly happy on rainy days; they had discovered a bookshelf in Simon's room (it was really Alec's room, of course). Obviously Alec's taste was catholic; Dorothy Sayers rubbed shoulders with Sir Walter Scott, Edgar Wallace, John Buchan and Zane Grey. There were also some paperback editions of authors whose names I did not know. I told the boys they could read these books if they were very careful with them.

Den had pounced upon *Memory Hold the Door* and was working through it slowly but steadily; Simon's tastes were different, he was racing through *The Green Archer* at break-neck speed.

On this particular morning it was raining, so the boys had settled down with their books . . . but Daisy was made of different stuff.

'It isn't raining very badly,' she declared as she flattened her nose against the window-pane.

'Go out,' muttered Simon.

'It's dull going out by yourself,' said Daisy sadly. 'I want somebody to come. It's such a *waste* to stay indoors – it is, really. Boys oughtn't to mind a few drops of rain.'

The boys made no reply.

'I want Mums to come,' said Daisy, looking at me hopefully.

'I'm writing to Aunt Liz.'

'Well, finish quickly and we can walk to the village and post it.'

'We'll see . . . presently.'

'Now, this minute,' urged Daisy. 'It's such fun walking through the woods in the rain and I ought to have exercise, you know. I'm getting fatter and fatter. You said I ought to have lots of exercise, Mums.'

'Shut up,' growled Den.

I had to go. To tell the truth is was no great hardship for I shared my daughter's predilection for walking in the rain – not in town, of course, where the rain splashed on the pavements and the houses dripped, black and gloomy, but here in the woods where the trees welcomed the crystal drops and the birds twittered happily and everything smelt fresh and sweet.

I finished my letter hurriedly and we sallied forth to post it.

Zilla had said the village was 'no great shakes' but I had been there several times and had found it surprisingly pleasant. There were half a dozen shops: butcher, baker, grocer and ironmonger, besides quite a well-stocked shoe-shop and a tiny store for 'fancy goods' where you could buy plaids and nylons and reels of cotton and toys. In fact Mrs. Mackay had such an amazing variety of goods, all stowed away in cardboard boxes, that she could produce almost anything you wanted – provided you were not impatient.

When we had posted the letter we visited Mrs. Mackay and I asked if she had any socks to fit Daisy.

She smiled happily. 'Yes, indeed,' she said, 'I'm sure I have them. I just can't remember where I put them,' and forthwith she began her search, taking out one cardboard box after another and rummaging through them slowly as if she had all the time in the world at her disposal.

'I'm sure I have them,' she repeated. 'Are they here? Och, these are pullovers! You would not be wanting a pullover, Mistress Wentworth? Lambswool, they are – and such pretty colours! I have some lengths of Harris tweed – would you care to see them? Och, this box is full of shooting stockings – hand-knitted, Mistress Wentworth. There are gentlemen that come to me every year for shooting stockings. I am wondering if you would mention it to Mister Maclaren?'

'He isn't here, Mrs. Mackay.'

'But he will be coming soon. I would let you take the box on approval and —'

'He isn't coming,' I said.

She sighed and climbed on to a chair to reach a higher shelf. 'It was gloves for the wee girl you were wanting.'

'Socks,' I said. By this time I had fallen in love with a lambswool pullover; it was deep blue with an open neck and was softer than silk. 'Is this my size?' I asked.

'Och, that is beautiful!' exclaimed Mrs. Mackay ecstatically. 'Would you slip it on, Mistress Wentworth? There is such a softness in lambswool – there is nothing so kind.'

'Is it very expensive?' I asked apprehensively.

'Not at all,' she declared. 'Besides it is more thrifty to buy a good garment that will be a friend to you for years.'

'Mums, look at this dear little doll!' exclaimed Daisy. 'Can I have it, please?'

'But, Daisy, you never play with dolls!'

'I would play with this one – I would, really. I'd rather have it than socks.'

'You need socks,' I said firmly.

'I need this doll, Mums. I *need* it. I would take it to bed with me.'

Mrs. Mackay climbed down from the chair. She said, 'If you are wanting a dolly to cuddle in bed you are wanting a nice soft one. Now, where did I put the soft dollies?'

'We want socks, Mrs. Mackay,' I told her.

She was still searching, but whether she was searching for socks or soft dollies nobody will ever know for before she had found either the door opened and a man came in – a tall, thin, soldierly-looking man in a tweed suit. He was wet through. Water was dripping from him on to the floor.

Mrs. Mackay abandoned us and smiled sweetly at the newcomer. 'It is shooting stockings the gentleman will be wanting!' she suggested.

'I don't,' he replied crossly. 'All I want is a garage – but there doesn't seem to be such a thing in the place. My car has broken down about two miles out of the village. It's these ghastly roads. Can you direct me to the nearest garage, please?'

'There is not a proper garage —' began Mrs. Mackay in flustered tones.

'There is!' exclaimed Daisy. 'I mean of course it isn't a proper garage, but there's Mr. Buchanan. He's awfully nice and very good with cars – Uncle Arly said so – and he has a petrol pump.'

'Where is this improper garage?' inquired the stranger.

'I'll show you,' said Daisy.

This offer did not surprise me in the least for my daughter is a friendly soul – shyness is unknown to her. I was about to tell her to come straight back (for I was aware that if anything interesting was going on she might be away for hours) but it was too late. Daisy and her new friend had vanished.

'What a kind wee lassie!' exclaimed Mrs. Mackay admiringly.

It was true of course, Daisy was very kind-hearted, but she was also somewhat inquisitive and eager for adventures. There was nothing that she enjoyed more than going to new places and meeting new people. She is still the same and always will be – Life is one big adventure to Daisy.

Now that Daisy had gone I was able to pin down Mrs. Mackay and finish my business with her. I bought two pairs of socks and the lambswool pullover (this was an extravagance, and I felt somewhat guilty, but it was so entrancing that I could not resist it). I emerged from the shop to find it was still raining gently but the sky had lightened, so perhaps the afternoon would be fine. Daisy was not in sight but there was no need to wait for her; she could come home by herself quite easily.

3

Having decided not to wait for Daisy I set off across the moor and had almost reached the woods when I heard a piercing yell and turned to see her running after me at full speed.

'He's nice!' cried Daisy breathlessly. 'I showed him the way. Mr. Buchanan is going to mend his car but it won't be ready till to-morrow. He said he was wet through to the skin and he hoped he wouldn't get newmonia. He said the rain here was wetter than other places. Do you think it is – really?'

'It's certainly very wet sort of rain and he hadn't a waterproof, had he?'

'He had left it in the car because he didn't think it was raining very hard – and then he found it was. He said, "It's very kind of you to show me the way. What's your name?" and I said, "Miss Marguerite Wentworth" and he said, "The devil you are!" I'm not saying devil,' explained Daisy virtuously. 'I'm just telling you what he said, that's all.'

I took the point.

'So then he said, "Well, if you're Miss Marguerite Wentworth I'm your uncle," and I said, "You can't be, because I haven't got an uncle except Uncle Arly and he isn't a proper uncle," and he said, "I'm a very proper uncle." Then he asked Mr. Buchanan where he could stay the night and Mr. Buchanan said he could stay at the hotel. So I said, "It isn't a proper hotel – just an inn – and the aunt is at the bottom of the garden in a wooden shed."' Daisy paused in her recital to giggle. Then she continued, 'He didn't know what the aunt was – but Mr. Buchanan knew. Mr. Buchanan said, "It is an earth-closet, sir, but ferry clean and wholesome. There is nothing nasty about it," and I said, "There's spiders." I know there are, because Uncle Arly told me. Uncle Arly likes spiders because they remind him of Robert the Bruce. Do you know about Robert the Bruce and the spider?'

'Yes.'

'It tried over and over again to climb up the thread and at last it managed to do it. Uncle Arly said *he* was like Robert the Bruce because there was something he wanted very badly and it wouldn't be easy to get, but he would go on trying till he got it – no matter how long it took. Robert the Bruce wanted a kingdom,' said Daisy thoughtfully. 'What does Uncle Arly want?'

'What else did that gentleman say? Did you find out who he was?'

'But, Mums, I've told you! He's my uncle.'

'He can't be your uncle. He just said it for fun.'

'Oh, I see,' said Daisy in a disappointed voice. 'I thought it was true. It's a pity, because I liked him.'

'You like most people, don't you?'

'Most people,' she agreed. 'But I don't like Miss Sims – who teaches us sums – and I don't like Zilla.'

'Zilla?' I asked in surprise.

'Yes, Uncle Arly's sister. She isn't nice to Uncle Arly so I don't like her. I love Uncle Arly,' declared Daisy ecstatically. 'I adore Uncle Arly – don't you, Mums?'

'Look, Daisy, there's a chaffinch!' I said. 'Hush, don't make a noise. Let's watch him.'

We stood and watched the chaffinch for a few moments. He was sitting on a wooden rail, preening himself and chirping sweetly.

'Isn't he a darling?' whispered Daisy.

CHAPTER 28

After lunch the weather cleared, as I had hoped, so the three went off together on their bicycles, taking sandwiches and a Thermos flask and a bottle of milk for their tea.

'It's a pity you can't come,' said Simon. 'Couldn't you hire a bike in the village? Or perhaps Mrs. MacRam would lend you hers.'

'Don't worry, I'm perfectly happy,' I told him. Bicycling had no charms for me; I much preferred a lazy afternoon in peace and solitude.

When I had seen them off I settled myself comfortably in Simon's hammock with a cushion behind my head. The sun was golden, the sky blue and cloudless; it was difficult to believe it had rained this morning. Above me were green leaves, moving gently in the almost imperceptible breeze.

I had lain there for some time when I was disturbed

by the sound of the front-door bell jangling in the distance. It was an unusual sound at Craig-an-Ron; nobody ever called, and any message that came was delivered at the back door. However, Mrs. MacRam was there and would answer the summons. I turned my head to watch, and a few moments later I saw the tall, soldierly-looking stranger – Daisy's new friend – approaching down the slope.

'Don't move,' he said as he took off his cap. 'It's difficult to get out of a hammock unless you've acquired the knack. The woman said you were here and I wanted to see you. I'm sorry to disturb you, but I haven't much time.'

'It's all right,' I told him. 'I was just being lazy. I hope Mr. Buchanan is able to deal with your car. Won't you sit down?'

He sat down on the wooden bench and said, 'Peter Wentworth is my name.'

'Peter Wentworth!' I exclaimed in astonishment.

'Didn't your daughter tell you who I was?'

'Not really. She said you were her uncle, but – but I thought it was a joke. I never imagined —'

'Perhaps you'd like me to produce my credentials?'

'There's no need,' I said – nor was there. Now that he had taken off his cap and I could see him clearly the resemblance to his family was obvious. In some ways he was like Gerald; his nose and the shape of his head and the manner in which he was leaning against the tree with one leg crossed sideways over the other were all exactly like Gerald . . . but his mouth and eyes and expression were entirely different. It was a queer experience to look at this stranger and to see bits of Gerald in him.

'Well, are you satisfied?' he asked.

'I'm sorry I was staring, but family likenesses are so – so very strange.'

'Well, if you're satisfied that I'm Peter Wentworth it's unnecessary to explain why I've come.'

I looked at him in surprise. He had spoken in rather an unpleasant tone – or so it seemed to me. I said doubtfully, 'I suppose you happened to be in this part of Scotland for shooting or something. If so it was natural that you should look in and see us. I'm very pleased —'

'What's the use of beating about the bush!' he exclaimed. 'I've come to speak to you about Simon's letter.'

'Simon's letter?'

'His letter to my father,' said Major Wentworth irritably. 'When my father received it he sent for me at once and after some consideration we decided that I had better come and see you. You dictated the letter, of course.'

'I didn't even know that Simon had written.'

'Are you asking me to believe that the boy changed his plans without any reference to you?'

'No, I'm not,' I said. 'Simon told me that he had changed his mind and intended to write to his grandfather, but I had no idea he had written so soon. As a matter of fact I meant to consult somebody before —'

'A lawyer, I suppose?'

'A friend. He happens to be a lawyer but it wasn't as a lawyer that I meant to consult him. He's very sensible and he's fond of Simon, so —'

'In that case he would tell you that what you're doing is the height of folly. Don't you realise what it means? My father likes the boy and was willing to accept him and give him all he wanted and have him trained to look after the estate. In addition to that he intended to make himself responsible for the education of your children – which was what you wanted, I believe.'

'I never asked him to do that. I never asked him for anything.'

'Don't you think you're behaving rather foolishly?'

'Some people might think so,' I admitted.

'Most people would think so.'

'Yes, perhaps; but it isn't for me to decide. It's Simon's life; he must do as he thinks best.'

'But that's nonsense!' exclaimed Major Wentworth. 'Do you mean to tell me that a boy of his age is fit to decide his own future? Does he know what he wants?'

'He knows what he doesn't want.'

'Oh!' said Major Wentworth. 'Yes, I admit there's a difference. Why doesn't he want to come to Limbourne?'

I tried to remember Simon's exact words. 'He doesn't want to be chained up.'

'Chained up? What an absurd expression!'

There was silence for a few moments. Then he said, 'It's no good talking like this – we aren't getting any further. I came here to explain my father's point of view. He liked the boy and the whole thing was arranged. Now, suddenly for no reason at all, the boy seems to have changed his mind. You say it's Simon's choice – but it's really your doing. My father is convinced that you've influenced him.'

I shook my head. 'Sir Mortimer is wrong, I didn't influence Simon. I was astonished when he told me he had changed his mind.'

'Well, anyhow, I can tell you this – it's only fair to warn you – my father is very angry indeed and unless Simon behaves himself and does as he's told my father will have nothing more to do with you or your family.'

'Yes, that's what I thought Sir Mortimer would say.'

'You expected that?' asked Major Wentworth in surprise.

'It was the way he treated Gerald,' I explained. 'I'm sorry about it because I don't like family quarrels, but I can't help it.'

'You can't help it? Haven't you any control over the boy? Can't you talk to him seriously and explain the advantages of accepting his grandfather's offer – tell him it's the sensible thing to do?'

'No, I couldn't. You see I don't think it would be a good plan for Simon to go and live at Limbourne. Simon is like Gerald.'

'I don't know what you mean.'

'Gerald valued his freedom above everything.'

'That was different,' declared Major Wentworth. 'Gerald had no expectation of inheriting the property. Simon has every expectation of inheriting the property so he ought to learn how to look after it. Surely you can see that?'

I was silent. Of course I saw it – I had seen it from the beginning – but to me Simon's happiness and well-being were more important than all the property in the world.

'Look here,' said Major Wentworth persuasively. 'I can see you're doubtful about it. I'm sure if you consider the matter seriously you'll realise that my father's plan is best – for everyone. Best for Simon, best for you and best for your children. Won't you change your mind and persuade Simon to do what his grandfather wants? Simon says in his letter that he intends to take a post in a firm of export merchants in the City. Do you think that would be good training for a boy who is going to inherit a place like Limbourne?'

'No, not really,' I admitted.

'What's your idea, then? I suppose you have some plan for the boy's future?'

'There's plenty of time to decide Simon's future. He'll be at school for another eighteen months – or more. I should like him to go to Cambridge, but I'm afraid —'

'Cambridge! You needn't think my father would consent to that. He would be furious at the mere idea of Simon going to Cambridge. If I were to mention the word he'd go straight off the deep end,' declared Major Wentworth emphatically.

'I didn't intend you to mention it to Sir Mortimer. As I told you before, I've never asked him for anything. I'm not asking for anything now. I've managed to look after my family without help from Sir Mortimer and I shall just – go on – managing.'

He looked at me with a straight piercing gaze. 'You're proud,' he said.

'Not really – proud,' I said thoughtfully. 'I just try to bring up Gerald's children as he would have liked. That's all.'

2

There was quite a long silence. Major Wentworth turned his head and looked out over the loch. At last he rose and said in a much more amiable tone, 'Well, I've done my best. I can see it's no use discussing the matter further.' He added under his breath, 'Heaven knows what Father will say. . . .'

It was the first sign he had shown of human feeling and for the first time I felt sorry for him. I realised that he would have to return to Sir Mortimer and admit defeat. I thought of Sir Mortimer and became even more sorry for his unsuccessful emissary! However there was nothing I could do for Major Wentworth – except offer him tea. Whisky would probably have been more acceptable but I had none to offer.

'Tea?' he said with a rueful smile. 'Oh, well – why not. But isn't it a bit early in the afternoon for tea?'

'It's never too early – nor too late,' I told him. 'Mrs. MacRam drinks tea morning, noon and night. I expect she has got it all ready for us,' and so saying I struggled out of the hammock – never a very graceful performance – and led the way into the cottage.

Mrs. MacRam met us at the door with a beaming smile. 'I was just thinking Mistress Wentworth and the gentleman would be wanting a cup of tea,' she declared. 'I have it all arranged – and the kettle is boiling.'

We sat down at the table in the window. It was all arranged (as Mrs. MacRam had said). There was a large plate of hot scones, butter and jam and honey, a bowl of strawberries and a jug of cream.

'Strawberries!' exclaimed my guest in surprise.

'They're later here,' I told him. 'We've been having them nearly every day. The children love them – with cream.'

'So do I,' he said. He hesitated and then added, 'I'm not going to say any more about it – I can see it would be useless – but I should like your permission to speak to Simon. It would be better if I could tell my father I had spoken to him. You see that, don't you?'

'Yes, of course. You don't need my permission to speak to Simon. He's perfectly free – that's what I've been trying to tell you. The children are out on their bicycles this afternoon but they'll be back in time for supper. Would you like Simon to come and see you at the inn? He could come about eight o'clock if that would suit you.'

'It will suit me admirably,' he said. Then he smiled and added, 'I suppose I call you Katherine – is that right? I've been wondering all afternoon what I should call you.'

'I've had the same trouble,' I confessed.

We were laughing when Mrs. MacRam came in with the large brown teapot and hot-water jug.

3

It had been a difficult and somewhat disagreeable half-hour but now that it was over I was glad that the interview had taken place. Obviously Peter had resigned himself to the failure of his mission.

'It will be better, really,' I said as I poured out the tea. 'Florence would have been very disappointed if Simon had come to Limbourne. She was looking forward to having Lance at home. It was all arranged that Lance was to be assistant to Mr. Marsh, wasn't it?'

'Lance is going to South Africa next week.'

'What!' I exclaimed in surprise. 'But I thought he had got another year at Cambridge! Do you mean he has been sent down?'

'No, just removed,' said Peter. 'I suppose I shouldn't tell you about it, but – well – the fact is Lance has been incredibly silly – to say the least of it.'

'Silly?'

'Crazy,' declared Peter. 'On Monday night the young ass went out on his motor-bike and started to smash up a small car which was standing, unattended, in a country lane. Unfortunately for Lance, its owner was lurking in the bushes. When he saw – and heard – what was happening he sprang out and went for Lance with his fists. He was young Heath, the vicar's son; a hefty sort of type,' added Peter with the ghost of a smile.

I was speechless.

'He's a naval officer,' continued Peter. 'Sailors are often pretty hefty and useful with their fists. There are no half-measures with sailors. Poor Lance was properly beaten up; he was considerably the worse for wear when Heath had finished with him.'

'Was he – seriously – injured?' I asked in a trembling voice.

'No bones broken – just bruised and shaken.'

'When – did it happen?'

'It happened the night I arrived at Limbourne. I was with my father in his study, discussing Simon's letter, when the front-door bell rang. It was long after midnight – we had been talking for hours – and as Bassett had gone to bed I answered the bell myself. I found young Heath standing on the doorstep with Lance clinging to his arm. I thought there had been an accident so I helped to get Lance into the study and we lowered him onto the sofa. Naturally my father wanted to know what had happened . . . so Adam Heath told him.'

After a short silence Peter continued, 'There was a frightful scene: my father raging and storming and Lance spread out on the sofa, half dazed, with blood dripping from his nose. Adam Heath said nothing. He just stood there, looking on. It seemed to me that we ought to decide upon a plan of action so I tried to get my father to calm down and discuss the matter sensibly – but it was hopeless. He stamped up and down the room and declared that Lance was a scoundrel, a blackguard – and other things, unfit to repeat. He declared that Lance had been at Cambridge for years and had learned nothing but hooliganism (quite illogical, of course, but logic isn't my father's strong point). Lance must leave Cambridge forthwith, meantime what he deserved was a sound thrashing.

'"He's had one," said Heath, smiling and lighting a cigarette.

'By this time Lance seemed to have recovered a bit, so I helped him upstairs to bed. When I came down I found Adam Heath in the hall – he was just going – so I went out with him and had a look at his car. It wasn't badly damaged; he had brought Lance home in it, but I told him to have it repaired and send us the bill. I was glad to have a private word with him; there had been no chance of any sensible talk in the study. I asked if he intended to go to the police and make a charge against Lance. He laughed and said perhaps Lance would like to bring an action against *him* for assault and battery. That was ridiculous, of course, so I asked him again, seriously, if he intended to inform the police. He replied that he couldn't – even if he wanted to – because he had taken the law into his own hands and given Lance a hiding which he wouldn't forget in a hurry. He said that in his opinion it was the best way of dealing with a young fool like Lance. I told him I couldn't agree more.

'Then, just as he was starting, he said perhaps I had been wondering what he was doing out in his car at that time of night. As a matter of fact I had thought it a bit queer, but I had decided in my own mind that he had been out with a girl. He's a good-looking chap and girls are usually keen on sailors. I told him I wouldn't dream of asking what he had been doing. "Oh, it wasn't what you think," he said. "I was big-game hunting and Lance happened to fall into my trap." What do you suppose he meant by that, Katherine?'

I knew exactly what he meant. 'Have some more strawberries, Peter,' I suggested.

He took another large helping of strawberries and coverd them thickly with cream. 'It was very decent of Heath,' he said. 'I was grateful to him – I can tell you! It might have been extremely unpleasant if the police had got wind of the affair. You see there has been quite a lot of vandalism in the neighbourhood and the police are searching diligently for the culprits. Traffic lights have been broken, tombstones daubed with paint and every window in an empty house smashed to pieces . . . other things, too; I can't remember them all. It's senseless, isn't it? What on earth makes people do things like that?'

'Did you ask Lance about it?'

'Of course I did! I went up to his bedroom next morning; he was a lot better, but he wouldn't talk – wouldn't answer any questions – wouldn't open his mouth. I couldn't get a word out of him. None of us could get a word out of him. He remained absolutely dumb. We can't do anything with him; we don't even know if this was his first offence – just a sudden mad impulse – or whether he has done anything of the kind before. I'm told that the police are of the opinion that the damage had been done by a gang, but somehow I can't believe Lance is mixed up with a gang of toughs – he hasn't enough guts for one thing. All the same the police would have been only too glad to get hold of someone to charge. It might have been very nasty indeed,' added Peter in a thoughtful voice.

I moistened my lips and said, 'So he's going to South Africa.'

'Yes, I managed to fix it up. I know a chap who grows oranges (he was in the gunners but had to retire owing to ill-health) so I cabled to him and he has agreed to give Lance a job on his farm. Florence is furious with me – if words could kill I'd be stone dead. The idea of her precious son being sent out to Africa amongst all those black people!'

'She ought to be grateful to you.'

'You think I was right?'

'Absolutely right. It's the best thing possible for Lance.'

'I'm glad you think so,' said Peter. He sighed and added, 'I don't know why I've told you all this, Katherine.'

'I'm quite a safe repository for secrets.'

'Yes,' he said, looking at me thoughtfully. 'I expect quite a lot of people confide in you.'

CHAPTER 29

After tea I walked back with Peter through the woods; we had been talking about birds. Suddenly he laughed and said, 'Well, I never thought it would end like this!'

'You mean your visit to Craig-an-Ron?'

'Yes, I envisaged various different endings, but never tea and strawberries – and birds. I still don't understand your point of view, but I'm willing to admit you have one.'

'That's something,' I said, smiling.

'I'm afraid I started by being rather disagreeable but you were very patient with me.'

'I wasn't angry,' I told him. 'You say you don't understand my point of view, but I understand yours. Sir Mortimer has every right to be annoyed – and you too, of course. If people have a right to be annoyed you can't blame them for being disagreeable.'

'My father will blame me for my failure and he'll be very disagreeable indeed.'

'You can tell him I'm sorry – if that will be any help.'

'It won't be the slightest help. I'm in for a very unpleasant interview when I get home to Limbourne. My father must have exactly what he wants – exactly when he wants it – otherwise there's a most unholy row.'

'Peter,' I said earnestly. 'Do you think it good for a boy to be brought up under the rule of a dictator? Has it been good for Lance? Do you think Gerald would have broken away if he hadn't found it unbearable?'

We had stopped in the middle of the wood and were standing facing each other on the path.

'Oh!' exclaimed Peter in surprise. 'I never thought of that.'

'It was different for you,' I pointed out. 'You were always your father's favourite, so —'

'It wasn't different. I had to toe the line like everyone else.'

'But you escaped and made your own career. How would you like to live at Limbourne and be dependent upon your father?'

'I couldn't stand it!' declared Peter emphatically. Then

suddenly he saw the point and his face changed. 'Yes, I see,' he said slowly. 'I suppose that's what you meant when you said Simon didn't want to be chained up?'

'You said it was an "absurd expression,"' I reminded him. 'Perhaps it is absurd . . . but can you think of a better description of the conditions at Limbourne? Everyone in the place is terrified of Sir Mortimer. It isn't good, Peter. Fear leads to deceit. You know that, don't you?'

'Yes,' he said in a low voice. 'When we were children we were frightened and – and deceitful.'

'It isn't only children, it's everyone,' I declared. 'The whole atmosphere is unhealthy. I found it so oppressive that I was thankful to get away.'

'You felt like that? But surely —' he began in horrified tones.

I was wound up now, so I interrupted him and rushed on breathlessly. 'It's like a prison, Peter. None of them has any freedom at all. Lance, Anthea – even Florence —'

'Florence!' he exclaimed. 'Florence is so foolish that she wouldn't know what to do with freedom if she were given it.'

'Because she has been ruled with a rod of iron all her life. She has ceased to mind – if she ever minded – but that's why she's silly. Lance has to go out at night and smash up cars to let of steam.'

'Katherine! Do you really mean —'

'Yes, I do. Think about it, Peter. You must have had a great deal of experience in your profession – experience of men.'

'It's true. There's always trouble if you keep them on too tight a rein. Why on earth didn't I see it before?'

'Perhaps it was because you know them all so well. I went to Limbourne a complete stranger – an onlooker – so I was able to see them in a different way.'

For a moment or two he was silent, considering the matter, then he said, 'I've never had any say in those children's upbringing. As a matter of fact I've had very little to do with Lance and Anthea, yet here I am burdened with Lance's troubles. Now that Henry has gone there's nobody in the family with any sense at all – nobody to talk to about family matters. I feel absolutely helpless.'

'You aren't helpless,' I declared. 'You've let Lance off

the chain and given him a chance to make good. Try to do the same for Anthea.'

'Anthea!' he exclaimed in alarm. 'What do you mean, Katherine?'

I hesitated. Then I said, 'Anthea is very unhappy – she's desperate. Get her away from Limbourne . . . otherwise there may be serious trouble.'

'Serious trouble?'

I nodded. 'It wouldn't be fair to betray Anthea's confidence; I can only urge you to get her away as quickly as you can.'

'This is frightful!' he exclaimed, looking at me in dismay.

'It's true, Peter. Every word I've said is true.'

'Of course I believe you – but what am I to do? Good heavens, this is an awful problem!'

'Talk to her. She has nobody to talk to.'

'I've told you I scarcely know the girl.'

'If you talked to her kindly I believe she might confide in you. She's miserable – and you're the only person who can help her. You'll try, won't you?'

'Yes, I'll try. I'd better get a week's leave and see what I can do.'

He looked so distressed that I felt sorry. 'Peter,' I said, I didn't mean to burden you with all this. It just – came out.'

'I could see that,' he replied with a rueful smile. 'I could see it pouring out. Obviously you've been worrying about it.'

'Yes, but now I've worried you.'

'I'm glad you told me; we don't want "serious trouble." Leave it to me, I'll do what I can for the wretched girl. Perhaps I could find her a job in London – or something.'

'Good,' I said, smiling at him. 'I must go home now, Peter. I'm glad I've met you. We've had a troublesome sort of talk but I've enjoyed bits of it.'

'So have I. When shall I see you again?'

'You won't see me at Limbourne.'

'No, I suppose not . . . but I should like to write to you, if I may.'

'Write and tell me how you get on,' I suggested.

We shook hands and said good-bye.

2

Simon was startled when I told him about my visitor and the arrangement I had made.

'But I don't want to see him!' declared Simon. 'There's no object in me going to see him. When I wrote I made it quite clear —'

'You didn't tell me you had written.'

'I know. I didn't mean to write so soon, but you see I had to write a bread-and-butter letter and, when I was in the middle of writing it, I just thought – well, I mean it seemed a bit deceitful to write and thank Grandfather for having me without telling him what I'd decided. So I told him. It's easier to do difficult things if you do them suddenly without thinking about them too much.'

'Yes, I think it is.'

'And I wanted to get it off my chest,' added Simon frankly.

I understood that too. 'Yes, of course. But all the same I'm afraid you'll have to go and see your Uncle Peter. He has come all the way from Limbourne, so you can't possibly refuse. As a matter of fact I think you'll like him.'

'I'm sure I shan't,' declared Simon emphatically.

No more was said, but it was unnecessary to remind Simon of the appointment. After supper he got up from the table and stood, looking at me for a few moments.

'Well, I suppose I'd better go and get it over,' he said reluctantly.

He went away and I heard him getting his bicycle out of the garage.

I expected him back quite soon, so I took a book and sat down by the window. I read for about an hour – and then I began to watch for him to come. Time passed slowly. I wondered what they were talking about. I thought I had convinced Peter that his mission had failed, but perhaps I was wrong. Perhaps he was trying to persuade Simon to change his mind and accept his grandfather's offer.

Peter Wentworth was clever and persuasive and forceful – I knew that – so perhaps he would succeed. The idea that he might succeed filled me with dismay. I had said that Simon was free to choose for himself, but now I wished

I had taken the responsibility of refusing Sir Mortimer's offer. I wished I had refused to allow Simon to go and see his uncle at the inn. I told myself that I had been a fool.

The evening was cloudy and mild; the light began to fade; Mrs. MacRam brought in the lamp and stayed to chat. Then she went away and I heard her shutting up the windows and doors in the kitchen premises as she always did before she went home.

By this time it was dark . . . and I had become so worried that I was nearly crazy. Simon must have started home long ago – what could have happened? The path through the wood was rutty and uneven, not too bad if you could see where you were going but quite unfit for bicycling in the dark. There was a lamp on Simon's bicycle, but I had no idea whether or not it was in proper order.

At last I could bear it no longer. I took a small torch and went out to look for Simon, convinced that he had fallen off his bicycle and was lying, injured, somewhere in the wood. Unfortunately the battery in the torch had run down, so all the light it produced was a dim flickering glow which made the darkness darker. The wood was pitch dark and somewhat eerie – but I pressed on, picking my way as carefully as I could. When I had gone about half-way along the path I saw a light wavering about through the trees, then I heard someone whistling 'Bye Bye Black-bird' – so I knew it was Simon. A moment or two later I saw him approaching, wheeling his bicycle.

'I thought you were lost!' I exclaimed.

'Sorry, Mums. I didn't mean to stay so long but we got talking and I forgot the time.'

'I was awfully worried; I couldn't think what could have happened.'

'Sorry, Mums,' he repeated.

I turned and we started to walk home together. Simon's bicycle lamp was very bright so it was easier to see the way.

'It was funny, really,' said Simon. 'You see I thought he would try to persuade me to change my mind and promise to go to Limbourne when I leave school; I was all keyed up to say no – no – no, but he never mentioned the subject.'

'What on earth did you talk about – all that time?'

'He talked a lot about you,' replied Simon with a little

chuckle. 'You seem to have made a favourable impression upon my Uncle Peter. Perhaps you didn't know that you've got a logical brain – an unusual thing in a woman – that's in addition to your charm of manner and your sympathetic personality, of course.'

'What nonsense! I'm sure he said nothing of the sort.'

'He did – really. Then we talked about cricket. He saw Alec play for Cambridge at Lord's, so he was frightfully impressed when I said Alec had been coaching me; he said I ought to keep it up after I leave school but I told him there wasn't a hope. When I go to Butterfields I shall have to work like a horse. It's a pity, but it can't be helped. We talked about lots of other things too. He's at the War Office at present and he said the next time I was in town I must come to lunch at his club. That would be fun, wouldn't it?'

'Yes. You could let him know when you're on your way back to school. Did he seem quite cheerful, Simon?'

'Cheerful? I should jolly well think so! He was laughing and joking like anything. Why shouldn't he be cheerful?'

'I just wondered – that's all.'

'He's awfully decent,' declared Simon. 'I liked him a lot. Lance said Uncle Peter was stuffy. It's absolute bilge; there's nothing stuffy about him. He's clever and amusing; that's what he is. Then, when I was coming away – hurrying, because I'd just discovered the time and I knew you'd be getting in a flap – he gave me this.' Simon put his hand in his pocket and took out a five-pound note. 'Five quid!' said Simon. 'Super tip, isn't it?'

'How kind of him!'

'Here you are. It's for you.'

'What do you mean?'

'It's for you,' repeated Simon, trying to thrust it into my hand. 'I want to pay you back for the money you gave me to send to Nitkin.'

'Nonsense! You must keep it and —'

'Please take it,' said Simon earnestly. 'Honestly, Mums, I'll feel better if you take it. I was a fool to give the money to Oliver – worse than a fool because it wasn't my money to give – I don't know what made me do it. Something queer got into me. If you take this I can put it out of my head. I shall feel the whole thing is over and done with.'

'Very well. If that's how you feel —'

'Yes, that's how I feel.' He put his arm through mine and added, 'There's something else. He told me about Lance. You know what happened, don't you?'

'Yes.'

'It's awful, isn't it? When Uncle Peter told me I was absolutely staggered. I suppose I must have looked a bit queer because he leant forward and said, "Look here, Simon. You know something about this matter, don't you?" and then, when I didn't answer, he said, "Did you swear you wouldn't tell?"'

We walked on for a few yards in silence. Then I said, 'I think you were wise to tell him all about it.'

'I didn't,' said Simon hastily. 'I just said, "Why don't you ask Oliver Wade?" You see, I thought it was a bit hard on Lance to get all the blame when it was Oliver who managed the whole thing. Uncle Peter said, "Is that all you can tell me?" and I said, "It's quite enough for anyone as clever as you are, Uncle Peter." That was all. It wasn't telling, was it?'

I tried not to laugh. 'Simon,' I said, 'if you had thought for a week you couldn't have found a better answer.'

3

There was no need to worry any more. Between us, Simon and I had unloaded our secrets and placed them upon the shoulders of Peter Wentworth. His shoulders were best fitted to bear them – I had no doubt of that. Peter's personality was forceful and he would tackle the problems we had given him without delay. First, he would do what he could for Anthea and, second, he would get into touch with Adam Heath. Peter and Adam Heath would put their heads together and plan a campaign. Yes, that was what they would do – and when the Navy and the Army join forces the success of the operation is assured! Mr. Wade's treasure-hunting would come to an abrupt conclusion.

I felt vindictive towards Oliver Wade, not only on account of the vandalism but also because of the way he had treated Anthea. I hoped he would be caught red-handed, setting fire to a house or something equally wicked, so that he would be sent to prison. It would be a thousand pities if he were caught in the act of perpetrating some minor offence.

That he would be caught, somehow, somewhere, was a foregone conclusion with those two redoubtable warriors on his track.

For the next few days I thought about it a great deal and wondered what would happen – and hoped Peter would remember to write and tell me how he got on.

Simon did not mention the subject, and did not seem to be brooding over it, so I kept my thoughts and wonderings to myself.

CHAPTER 30

Now that I was rested and refreshed it had become a habit to waken early. I enjoyed those early hours, lying in Zilla's comfortable bed. I had the windows wide open; I could hear the dawn chorus of birds in the rowan trees; I could see the sun rise from behind the mountains. The sun still rose very early (though a few minutes later every day). More often than not he rose in splendour from behind Ben Ron so that suddenly my room was filled with golden light and his effulgence ran down the waiting slopes like golden water.

I watched for him every morning and was absurdly disappointed if he were hidden by a bank of cloud.

When His Majesty had risen and was shining brightly I turned over and went to sleep again or sometimes rose and went out to enjoy the tranquillity of the early morning hours, to wander down to the loch and listen to the birds.

One morning I wakened earlier than usual in the grey light of dawn. I lay and listened. An owl screeched as he flew quickly to his retreat, a lamb called to its mother on the hill, far off in the distance I heard the sound of a car. It was so faint – the soft purr of an engine – that I thought I must have been mistaken; then I heard it again, slightly louder. Suddenly the noise ceased.

Craig-an-Ron was so far from everywhere – at the back of beyond – that no cars nor any other traffic came near it unless they were coming to the cottage . . . and who could be coming at this hour?

I went to the window and looked out from behind the curtain. There was nobody to be seen – not a creature –

even the little birds were not yet awake. The loch was silver-grey, still and peaceful; the leaves of the rowan trees hung limp in the morning air. I looked up the path to the woods – and saw a tall figure standing at the edge of the trees.

He stood there quite still, looking up at my window.

At first I couldn't believe my eyes – it must be a trick of light or a shadow that had deceived me – but the light from the eastern sky was growing stronger every moment and soon I could see him distinctly; tall and broad-shouldered in Lovat tweeds with his thick dark hair brushed back from his forehead.

Why had he come at this hour of the morning? How had he come? What was he going to do? I was so bewildered that I couldn't move; I was rooted to the spot with astonishment.

He stood there. quite still, for some time – I don't know how long – and then turned and went back into the wood.

In a few moments I heard the sound of the car starting and driving away. Then there was silence.

2

Alec to do that! Sensible, solid Alec! It was a revelation!

I had told myself that we were friends . . . but a man does not come at dawn and stand and gaze at a woman's window unless drawn there by an irresistible force. Friendship is not that sort of force.

I had known before that Alec was fond of me, but I certainly had not realised that he loved me – like that. I had told him he was 'solid and sensible' – he had seemed so to me – but there was nothing solid and sensible about his action this morning. It was the action of a man deeply in love, a man whose heart was full of romance.

I began to wonder how Alec had managed to get away from the office (he had told me it would be impossible for him to come to Loch Ron). I began to wonder how long he would be able to stay. Supposing he had just come in the night to stand and look up at my window and was now already on his way home!

But that was absurd – even for a knight of romance. Alec would have gone to the inn. Even if he could not stay for long, he would have gone there to rest and have breakfast before starting home. He was there now, of course, and if I hurried I could see him and talk to him and find out what he intended to do . . . if I hurried.

I dressed – it did not take long – and went softly down the stairs. I was half-way up the path to the wood when I saw Mr. MacRam coming down the hill from his own little cottage with his dog at his heels.

To anyone else it might have seemed strange that I should be setting out for a walk at such an hour, but to Mr. MacRam it seemed the most natural thing in the world. He greeted me in his usual dignified manner.

'It iss a grand morning for a walk,' he declared.

'Yes. I woke early. I'll be back in time for breakfast.'

'Och, it would be a pity to hurry,' he said. 'Mistress MacRam can see to the chiltren.'

This was kind and thoughtful, but quite unnecessary – I intended to be back long before eight – however I thanked him and agreed that it was a grand morning and hurried on through the wood.

All this time there was only one idea in my head: I must see Alec. It had become a vital necessity to see him. I never thought of what I was going to say to him or how I should explain my visit at this early hour. I must see him – that was all.

When I came out of the wood the sun had risen from behind the mountains and the dewdrops on the heather were sparkling like diamonds in his rays. I took the path which led to the village. It was not far now. When I got there Alec's car would be standing in its usual place – and Alec would be having an early breakfast at the inn.

At this hour the village was deserted, all the little houses had their windows tightly shut and curtained. I turned the corner and saw that the inn was shut – the outer door firmly closed, the windows fastened securely with green shutters – and there was no car standing beneath the chestnut tree.

The inn was shut – and there was no car – so Alec was not here!

The disappointment was so bitter that I felt quite stunned. I stood for a moment or two gazing at the empty place beneath the tree – and wondered what to do next.

Gradually I began to recover from the shock and to

realise what a fool I had been. Alec had been here – he had come to the cottage – I had seen him standing on the path. Why hadn't I called to him?

Looking back and thinking about it, I couldn't understand myself at all. Why hadn't I called and waved and welcomed him? It had been crazy to watch him from my window and make no sign. It had been unkind. Now it was too late; he had come – and gone.

Friendship was what I had wanted – or thought I wanted – and Alec had given it to me generously; he had served me and helped me in every way he could. He had said he could read my thoughts – but I had never tried to understand him. I had been utterly selfish and blind. I had taken all he offered and given nothing in return. By this time my 'solid and sensible' knight of romance was on his way back to Edinburgh. He was tired – yes, of course he was tired – and probably he was unhappy. He was in no mood to be careful. I could see him speeding along those narrow twisting Highland roads in his powerful car. . . .

The sound of footsteps roused me from my miserable thoughts and I turned to see Alec striding towards me down the empty street.

'Alec!' I cried – and ran to him and put my arms round his neck.

3

Time seemed to have gone adrift that morning so I can't tell how long it was before Alec and I came to our senses. We had sat on the bench beneath the tree for a bit and then we had started to walk back to the cottage. When we were half-way through the wood we had seen a fallen tree and had sat down upon the trunk. It was warm and pleasant sitting there with Alec's arm round my waist.

So far we had had no sensible conversation at all and I was still feeling slightly dazed by the suddenness of everything.

'You haven't told me why you were wandering about the village at that unseemly hour,' said Alec.

'I was looking for Clara.'

'Clara?' asked Alec in bewilderment. 'Do you mean the barmaid at the inn?'

I laughed. 'Not that Clara. It was your car I was looking for. When I didn't see her standing there I thought you had gone.'

'I left her with Mr. Buchanan. He's giving her a check-up and changing the oil.'

How simple it was – when you knew.

'He's very good,' explained Alec. 'He does it all himself, of course, and he's careful and conscientious, so I always . . . but, Katherine, how did you know I was here?'

'A little bird told me. Look, Alec, there he is! Isn't he a pet?'

There he was. It was the same chaffinch that Daisy and I had seen – or else his twin brother. He sat on the top rail of the fence preening his feathers and chirping to himself in a contented sort of way.

'Yes, he's very sweet,' agreed Alec. 'But you haven't told me —'

'And you haven't told me how you managed to come. You said you wouldn't be able to get away.'

'Oh, this was just a flying visit. I meant to look in at the cottage when you were all having breakfast, and give you a surprise, and then go straight back to Edinburgh.'

'You can't!' I cried. 'Alec, you can't leave me like that!'

'No, I don't think I can,' he admitted. 'I had better phone to Andrew directly after breakfast and explain what has happened.'

'Your partner?'

'Yes, Andrew Forth. I'm sure he'll agree to stand in for me. He's the kindest fellow in the world. As a matter of fact he can't very well object because he and Anna have been telling me that I ought to get married. They were married, themselves, about three years ago and they're blissfully happy, so they think everybody —'

'Alec! Are you sure you want to marry me? I mean, we had better be sure before we go any further.'

Apparently Alec was quite sure.

When that was settled I suggested that Alec should come and have breakfast at Craig-an-Ron. I knew there would be plenty of food; there was always more than enough for everybody.

'Yes, later,' he agreed. 'It's only just after seven so we can sit here a bit longer and get things settled. There are all sorts of things to arrange. I must phone to Ellen – after breakfast.'

'Why Ellen?'

'To tell her about it. Ellen thought those two small rooms at the end of the passage would be nice for the twins, but they'll have to be done up, of course.'

'Ellen thought? What do you mean?' I asked in bewilderment.

'Oh, well,' said Alec apologetically. 'Ellen has been with us for years and years. She chats to me a lot, especially when Zilla isn't there. She thought it would be nice if I married you – that's all.'

I laughed. 'Well, that's one person who will be pleased.'

'She'll be delighted . . . and of course she loves the children.'

'She only saw them for a few moments – in the hall.'

'Well, anyway, she thought they were "little dears." That's why she decided that they must have those two rooms. What a good thing The Cedars is so large! There will be plenty of room for us all.'

The Cedars! It was an amazing idea to me. 'Alec, are you sure —' I began.

'Sure about what?'

'About having us all to live at The Cedars.'

'Don't you like the house?' he asked in surprise. 'I thought you liked it. Would you rather live somewhere else?'

'No, of course not. The Cedars is a perfectly lovely house. I was just – just feeling a bit bewildered. Have you thought about it seriously? Do you really want to – to take on the whole family?'

'I've thought about it seriously ever since the first moment when I saw you in the garden having tea with Zilla.'

'Not really?'

'Yes, really and truly. Do you remember you left your scarf? Well, I pushed it down behind the cushion in the swing-seat, hoping that you'd forget about it and leave it behind. I wanted an excuse to go and see you. It worked out splendidly,' added Alec with a little chuckle.

'It was very wicked of you,' I told him.

'Yes, frightfully wicked. But it was the only way to get your address. If I had asked Zilla for your address she wouldn't have given it to me. However, don't let's bother about that now. We were talking about The Cedars. You must have Zilla's room, of course; it's a lovely big room looking out on to the garden and there's a dressing-room next door. Simon can have my room, and —'

'Your room? But what about you?'

Alec looked at me in alarm.

'Oh, I see,' I said. 'Yes, of course. It's all right, Alec, I'm – I'm – sort of dazed this morning.'

'You aren't feeling ill, are you?' asked Alec anxiously.

'No, just dazed, that's all. Tell me more about your plans. Zilla showed me over The Cedars but I don't remember it very well.'

'There are several other rooms – besides the ones I've mentioned – they aren't furnished of course, because Zilla and I didn't need them, but it would be quite easy to furnish them if necessary.'

'I love babies,' I said thoughtfully. 'The twins were terribly soft and cuddly.'

There was a short silence. Then Alec said, 'You can do exactly as you like – always.'

'That's a bit reckless, isn't it? Perhaps I shall remind you of your promise some day when you least expect it.'

He took my hand and put it gently against his cheek. 'We must be married soon,' he said.

'We can't be married all in a hurry.'

'We can and we will. We shall be married as soon as possible – at Inverquill. It's a dear little church and I know the rector. I shall ring him up this morning and ask him how soon —'

'Alec, we can't!'

'We can,' declared Alec. 'We'll be married at Inverquill and all go back to Edinburgh together.'

'Alec, you're going too fast! I must have time to – to think. Really, Alec, we can't —'

'Listen, darling,' said Alec earnestly. 'My plan is best. You don't want an Edinburgh wedding with hundreds of guests and a lot of fuss, do you?'

'No, of course not. It would be frightful.'

'Frightful,' agreed Alec. 'Much nicer to be married quietly at Inverquill. Besides, there's Zilla.'

'Zilla? She isn't coming back to live at The Cedars?'

'No, definitely not. I told you that before. But she'll

have to come back to pack up all her belongings. If we're safely married she can't do anything to – to upset things.'

'You're frightened of Zilla?'

'A little bit frightened,' he admitted. 'Ever since I found out . . . I mean, you can't tell what she's going to do next.'

I, too, was afraid of what Zilla might do – and say. She would be furiously angry, of course. I was afraid, not so much for myself as for Alec. He had been under her thumb for years – and she was unscrupulous. A woman like that can be very dangerous indeed.

'If we're safely married she can't do anything,' repeated Alec.

'Yes, I see what you mean. Let's be married before we go back to Edinburgh – only I shall have to tell Aunt Liz. She will want to come.'

'Of course she must come,' said Alec joyfully. He tightened his arm round my waist and I leant my head against his shoulder.

For a little while we were silent.

There was something I wanted to tell Alec – something important – but for a moment or two I couldn't think what it was. Then I remembered. 'Did you know that Zilla is trying to sell Craig-an-Ron?'

'No! How did you hear that?'

'Mrs. MacRam told me. She's very sad about it, poor thing. It's a dear little house – I've been very happy there – so I hope somebody very nice will buy it.'

'I shall buy it and give it to you as a wedding present – unless you'd rather have something else.'

I laughed hysterically. 'Yes, I'd rather have a diamond tiara, please. I've often thought it would be nice to have one to wear when I was cooking dinner.'

'Have that as well,' suggested Alec, smiling. 'As a matter of fact a small car would be more useful. Don't you agree?'

'Oh dear, I'd forgotten you were so rich! Everyone will say I'm marrying you for your money. All your friends will be sorry for you – have you thought of that, Alec? – they'll say you've been caught by a designing widow with three —'

'Let them say! I don't care a tinker's curse what anybody says – besides we'll be married before "they" know anything at all about it. You don't mind what people say, do you?'

'I think I do – a little.'

'Silly,' said Alec, giving me a gentle squeeze.

'Not silly,' I told him. 'I wish I had a little more money of my own. You're marrying a beggar-woman, Alec.'

'When we're married I shall endow you "with all my worldly goods," so you'll be reasonably well off.'

'I wish I had money of my own – now. For one thing I should like to be able to give you a really nice wedding present.'

'You can,' said Alec. 'I want a half share in the children.'

There were tears in my eyes and a lump in my throat. I couldn't speak.

'I hope they'll be pleased,' continued Alec in doubtful tones. 'It's bound to be a bit of a shock to them – we must be prepared for that. You'll have to watch them carefully; don't let them brood about it and get all sorts of wrong ideas into their heads. Daisy and Denis will get used to it, if we give them plenty of time, but I'm worried about Simon.'

'Simon thinks you're marvellous.'

'Yes, perhaps, as a friend and a cricket coach, but I have a feeling he may be a bit jealous. He has had you all to himself, for so long. We shall have to go warily, Katherine. We mustn't spring it on him suddenly.'

Perhaps Alec was right. 'Very well,' I said. 'I'll get him alone and – and try to explain.'

'Good. That's settled then. We won't say anything about it this morning. To tell you the truth, I've been dreading it – feeling a bit shy,' said Alec with an apologetic smile. 'You must choose the right time to tell them. By the way, it's twenty to eight. Is it too early to stir up Mrs. MacRam and ask for breakfast?'

'Not a bit. We always have breakfast at eight.'

'I'm hungry,' he explained. 'Perhaps it isn't the right thing to feel hungry, on an occasion like this, but I'm an ordinary sort of bloke. I'm "solid and sensible" – not romantic.'

'Are you sure you aren't just a little bit romantic?'

'"Solid and sensible,"' said Alec. 'Let's go and eat porridge and bacon and eggs at Craig-an-Ron.'

Alec took out his handkerchief and made a knot in the corner. 'That's to remind me to tell Andrew to buy your wedding present,' he explained. 'I shall ask him to do it at once in case somebody else takes a fancy to Craig-an-Ron. You'd like it, wouldn't you?'

'I should love it. We could use it for holidays – and for your fishing. Mrs. MacRam will be delighted. Oh, Alec, what a lovely present!'

We rose and walked on.

I slipped my arm through Alec's. 'You said you wanted a half share in the children,' I reminded him. 'Which do you want? Simon, I suppose. You know him best, don't you?'

'Half of all three. They're all good value. If I had to choose between them it would be Denis.'

I was surprised – and pleased. Den was a quiet little boy and often was overlooked and put in the shade by the others, so it was good to find that Alec appreciated him. I had noticed that Alec always called him Denis; perhaps I should try to give him his proper name.

'There's a lot of *you* in Denis,' continued Alec thoughtfully. 'He's a whole person and made of the right stuff. Some day we're both going to be very proud of Denis.'

'What's his line?' I asked, half smiling.

'Medicine. We must find out all about it and make sure that he has the best possible training. You knew he wanted to be a doctor, didn't you?'

I had known it, vaguely, but I hadn't paid much attention to Den's aspirations; to me he seemed little more than a baby.

'Isn't it fun!' exclaimed Alec.

'Fun?'

'Yes, to have a ready-made family, all so different from each other and so interesting. We mustn't let Simon go to Limbourne. We shall have to —'

'It's off. He decided not to go.'

'Good!' exclaimed Alec. 'That saves a lot of trouble. Has he quarrelled with his grandfather – irrevocably?'

'I'm afraid so.'

'Good,' repeated Alec. 'Nothing could be better – you must tell me all about it some time. Let's hope the old man will live to a ripe old age.'

'Why?' I asked in surprise.

'Because if he dies before Simon can cope with it himself we shall have the property on our hands. It would be a bit difficult.'

'It would be frightful! I never thought of that.'

'Don't worry,' said Alec cheerfully. 'It's a mistake to worry about future problems. The baronet will probably live to be ninety. When Simon leaves school he must go to Cambridge; that's the place for him. I shall go and see him and watch him make a century for his college.'

'Alec, you're dreaming!'

'Nice dreams, Katherine. Don't grudge them to me.'

'Of course not!' I cried. 'I feel so grateful to you for – for everything. I can't begin to tell you —'

'Listen!' he exclaimed, stopping and looking at me seriously. 'Let's get this straight. My father built up a very fine business and left me shares in it, which bring in a considerable amount of money. I'm making quite a good income myself – so I've got much more than I need. (I give away a good deal but that's not the point.) Sometimes I've felt the money to be a burden; it's doing no good – if you see what I mean. Now, it's going to be useful. I'm going to be able to use it in the best possible way.'

'Yes, but I still feel —'

'That's why I'm happy, Katherine; that's why I'm dreaming dreams; that's why you must never feel grateful. You understand, don't you?'

'Yes,' I said. There was nothing more I could say. It would be difficult not to feel grateful, but at least I could refrain from expressing my gratitude – if that was what he wanted.

'Not gratitude – from you,' said Alec in a low voice.

'Love,' I said, and slipped my hand into his.

'Yes,' said Alec, holding it in a warm, firm clasp.

We walked on in silence, hand in hand, until we came to the edge of the wood, and there we stopped of one accord looking down at Craig-an-Ron. The dear little cottage lay peacefully in its hollow with the cliff behind; around it was the sward of emerald-green grass.

It was going to be mine – my very own. I felt so pleased and happy that it was difficult not to feel grateful.

'Alec,' I said. 'You've made all sorts of wonderful plans for me – and the boys. Have you forgotten Daisy?'

'Daisy!' exclaimed Alec, laughing. 'Goodness, we needn't make plans for Daisy! She can look after herself all right.

In another ten years she'll have a string of young men – all ready to die for her, if need be!' He paused and then added thoughtfully, 'We shall have to see that she chooses the best.'

CHAPTER 31

The children were about to start breakfast when we went in; they jumped up when they saw Alec and greeted him with cries of delight. They wanted to know when he had arrived and how long he was going to stay and they all wanted to tell him what they had been doing.

The noise was astounding. Anyone might have thought there were half a dozen children all talking at once.

Mrs. MacRam peeped in to see what on earth was happening; she welcomed Alec cordially and rushed away to the kitchen to prepare more food.

'Hush!' I exclaimed loudly. 'You're making too much noise. Alec has been driving all night and he's tired and hungry.'

'But I want to show him my yacht,' objected Simon. 'It won't take a minute. I just want to ask him —'

'How exciting to drive all night!' exclaimed Daisy. 'Did darling Clara go like lightning?'

'Where is Clara?' asked Den. 'Is she standing in her usual place underneath the —'

'I just want to ask him —' repeated Simon, raising his voice to be heard above the din.

'Presently,' said Alec. 'Let's have breakfast first. Here's Mrs. MacRam with the porridge.'

'Come and sit next to me, Uncle Arly,' cried Daisy, seizing him by the hand.

The advent of Mrs. MacRam with her large tray made a welcome diversion; we all sat down round the table and began our meal. For a time there was silence (except for the usual requests to pass the cream and other necessities). It was broken by Den.

'Uncle Arly,' he said, 'you're going to stay, aren't you? I want to show you our harbour. Mums got us some little boats and we've made a harbour for them.'

'And I want to show you a water-mouse's hole,' put in

Daisy. 'We found it under the bank. We haven't seen the mouse yet and we wondered whether it only comes out at night.'

'I was wondering about the island,' said Simon. 'Mums said you told her there was a bit of an old wall. I want to —'

'I know you'd like to see the harbour,' said Den earnestly. 'You'll come and see it, won't you?'

'Yes, of course,' said Alec. 'I want to see everything. I shall stay as long as I possibly can.'

Daisy had begun to bounce up and down in her chair with excitement. 'I'll tell you something!' she cried. 'Mums ought to marry Uncle Arly and then he could stay with us all the time.'

There was a momentary silence. I couldn't think how to deal with the situation.

'Not a bad idea,' said Alec reflectively.

'It's a good idea,' declared Den. 'It's a splendid idea. Don't you think so, Mums?'

Simon said nothing.

We had not intended this to happen – but it was happening and it had gone too far. It was impossible to retreat. I had to say something because they had all stopped talking and were waiting for me to reply to Den's question.

'We might – think about it,' I said feebly.

'It would be much cheaper,' urged Daisy. 'Uncle Arly could come and live with us at the flat.'

'There wouldn't be much room, would there?' objected 'Uncle Arly.' 'It would be rather a crowd. Don't you think it would be better if you all came and lived at The Cedars? Plenty of room there for everybody.'

'Mums!' exclaimed Simon. 'Is it a joke?'

'No, not a joke, Simon. Alec and I have been – thinking about it. You see, I'm rather lonely when you're all away at school, so Alec suggested . . . I mean we both think —'

'We're both lonely,' said Alec, coming to my rescue. 'Mums is lonely in the flat and I'm very lonely all by myself in that great big house. It's silly for two people to be lonely when they could be together, isn't it, Simon?'

'Gosh, what an extraordinary idea! I never thought . . .'

'It isn't extraordinary,' Alec said. 'People often —'

'It's a gorgeous idea!' cried Daisy.

'It won't make any difference,' I said earnestly. 'It will be just the same, Simon. We'll still be a complete family – all of us together – with Alec.'

Simon drew a long breath. 'It will be absolutely smashing,' he declared.

Alec began to laugh and I joined in, somewhat hysterically. We laughed and laughed. Every time we stopped, and Alec and I looked at each other, we started off again.

At last we managed to control ourselves and went on with our interrupted meal.

When we had finished Alec glanced at his watch and said he must go.

'But you haven't seen the harbour!' cried Den.

'I'm coming back,' Alec explained. 'I'm going to the inn to make some telephone calls and I shall have to look in and see Mr. Buchanan for a minute.'

'Can I come with you?' asked Simon.

Alec looked at me – and I nodded. It was a good idea for Simon to have a quiet sensible conversation with Alec about our plans.

They went off together. I watched from the window and saw them walk up the slope and disappear into the wood.

Den and Daisy had gone to put on their bathing shorts; a moment or two later they came out from the house and stood on the path talking earnestly. Alec had said I must not let them brood. Were they brooding and getting all sorts of wrong ideas into their heads? I leant out of the window to hear what they were saying; their voices came to me quite clearly in the still air.

'It's a pity,' said Daisy. 'I mean it's so nice just as it is.'

'I know,' agreed Den. 'But it can't be helped.'

'We must make it bigger.'

'Yes, bigger. There isn't enough room for *all* the boats . . . and there might be a storm.'

'All right – let's hurry – we'll have to get a lot more stones out of the burn.'

'Big ones,' said Den.

They took to their heels and ran.

2

I was alone now. It was the first moment of peace since dawn. I thought of Gerald and spoke to him silently in my heart, as I had done before, so often: You don't mind, do you? It isn't disloyalty. I still love you, and I shall never forget you as long as I live, but it has been so lonely all these years without you, so terribly lonely and difficult. I love Alec – and we need each other. You understand, don't you, Gerald?